PRINCESS PAPAYA

PRINCESS PAPAYA

A NOVEL BY

HIMILCE NOVAS

Arte Público Press
Houston, Texas

This volume is made possible through grants from the City of Houston through The Cultural Arts Council of Houston, Harris County.

Recovering the past, creating the future

Arte Público Press
University of Houston
452 Cullen Performance Hall
Houston, Texas 77204-2004

Cover design by Giovanni Mora
Cover Art "Madonna Saurie, 2004" by
Antonio Broccoli Porto

Himilce Novas.
    Princess Papaya / by Himilce Novas.
       p.   cm.
    ISBN 1-55885-436-3 (trade pbk. : alk. paper)
    1. Cuban American families—Fiction. 2. Jews—United
States—Fiction. 3. Jewish families—Fiction. 4. Cuban
Americans—Fiction. 5. Cuba—Fiction. I. Title.
PS3564.O9147P75   2004
813'.54—dc22   2004048532
                                                          CIP

∞ The paper used in this publication meets the requirements of the American National Standard for Information Sciences—Permanence of Paper for Printed Library Materials, ANSI Z39.48-1984.

4 5 6 7 8 9 0 1 2   10 9 8 7 6 5 4 3 2 1

For my father, Lino Novas Calvo, in celebration of his brave and infinite art.

With many thanks to Nicolás Kanellos,
prophet, pioneer, leader.

PRINCESS PAPAYA

"There are more things in heaven and earth, Horatio, than are dreamt in your philosophy."

—*Hamlet* (I, V, 166–167)

One

+2 THE WHITE MAN OF THE SHINY EGGHEAD, with aquamarine eyes and thin hairy wrists, sat in an unlit corner of the *botánica* store, waiting his turn with Princess Papaya. Priestess of El Barrio and spiritual counselor, she was sorceress of the night, witch of his desire.

He stared blankly at the crimson image of Santa Barbara, Changó, god of thunder, lightning, and earthquakes. The spiked scent of votive candles and Florida Water aroused and nauseated him. To the right of Changó, behind a beaded glass curtain in all the colors of the *orisha* gods, Bembé observed the visitor. A miniature, milk-chocolate boy of nine, he transfixed his identical aquas on the man's hispid hands, holding his breath in the pit of his stomach whenever he suspected exposure and auscultating the caller's purple aura with the uncanny skill of a deaf-mute who has transcended the five human senses.

At last, Princess Papaya emerged girthed in the beadwork of the Seven African Powers, *Las Siete Potencias*, the graven images who spirited her incantations. Her six-foot frame, smooth like buffed ebony, filled the width and height of the door. Ideliza Mercado was larger than life; she was the white man's Princess Papaya of the pendulous breasts—gravid, defiant, unslit papayas. Eyes like blazing mine shafts, her plum-plump mouth whispered so sweet on the air, soughing his name between its calla folds.

"Roberto!" She motioned him in.

Bembé ducked behind the glass beads, hoping his mother would not catch him spying again. Then, as soon as Roberto and Ideliza were locked inside her room, he climbed on his ready stool, placed his right aqua over the mouse hole on the door, cupped his left eye in the palm of his hand, and zoomed in on his mother and the man with his same color eyes.

Roberto Lobo peeled off his red silk tie and pinstriped jacket, slipped out of his soft weave loafers, and sat across from Ideliza, pressing his knees against her. His thin, aristocratic torso was erect and his white-starched arms outstretched. Behind her, in a shrine, stood a four-foot plaster-blue statue of Yemayá, Virgin of Mercy and goddess of the waters, seashells, pearls, oysters, ships, sirens, and all sea creatures. Ideliza's divination cowries lay on the altar, as did baskets of fruits and foods for her orishas—papayas, bananas, Spanish pastries laced with coconut, guava, sweet potatoes, condensed milk, eggs, honey.

Roberto inhaled the inebriating mulch of rotting fruit, thick sugar, and Ideliza's jasmine candles in the railroad room. He glanced quickly at the single, narrow bed on the other side. The bed where Ideliza's spirits had beckoned him to lie with her so many times, where her infinite, liquid body had sucked him in like quicksand, swallowed up his manhood in one excruciating, mesmerizing trance. It left him awash for days, the scent of her *coño,* her creamy sweet *papaya,* lodged in his nostrils long after he had returned to his daily life, paid a visit to his parents, and dutifully mounted his Mayflower Brahmin wife. The bed where they had made a child. His only offspring at age forty-five; the child was a deaf-mute, balloon-headed colored boy whose singular aquamarine eyes claimed his paternity. His mother had named him *Bembé,* the Yoruba term for a *religious hoedown.* Roberto had despised him in infancy but now regarded him as an amulet, a rabbit's foot, a set of red and black Eleggua beads to shield him from the hissing serpent coiling and spitting at his heels.

"What happened, Roberto? I didn't expect to see you again until the first of the month. . . ." Ideliza's voice was thunderous, like that of a great Wagnerian diva, yet soothing like the great Earth Mother. Here, in the womb of her divination room, in the place where she counseled him and fed him the only passion fruit that satisfied him, Roberto felt safe. The intonation in her voice alone could distract, at least momentarily, that seven-headed hydra stalking him since before the morning stars sang together.

"They have started calling me again, Princess. They keep saying the same thing and then hanging up."

He swallowed dry. Sweat beads on his soft, bald head. He had sharp, handsome features—sharp eyes; sharp nose; sharp chin with a prominent cleft; high cheekbones like his Ashkenazi mother, Sara Margolis; and rich eyebrows like his Sephardim father, Don Abram Lobo. The fact that he had started balding at thirty and that by now only a fringe of brown hair extended from his sideburns around to the back of his head had not taken away from his looks. Women still found him engaging. His marriage to Kitty Cabot, his dark, brusque temperament, and his detached, brooding blue eyes had helped create a compelling mystique that beckoned the blond-streaked, trust-fund patients to The Lobo-Meyer Clinic on Tenth Avenue and Fifty-Ninth Street, not far from St. Clare's Hospital, where he was an affiliated obstetrician. Kitty often joked that Roberto could sell Guantanamo base to the Japanese. For him alone, these erstwhile debutantes of railroad baron provenance were willing to chance an ambulance rush to St. Clare's, an inner-city hospital Roberto referred to as Placenta Place, because his black Mercedes had once run over a detached placenta at the curb by the emergency entry.

"What are they saying to you, angel?"

Ideliza called him *ángel*. He was a rare orchid who thrived in thin air; a brittle-boned, pearly skinned doctor who'd been to school; an *exiliado*, who ten years ago had shown up at her *botánica*, handpicked by Changó and Yemayá to sow a sweet man-child in her belly—Bembé, blue-eyed baby of the *orishas*, apple of her eye.

Roberto and Ideliza never met outside her store and only saw each other four or five times a month, depending on his and the *orishas'* temporal needs. And yet, theirs was a special bond, *un amor* that suited each lover for special reasons. It was a blessed union as long as their trysts were held before the altar, in plain view of her jealous gods. Ideliza had turned forty in August. She had had many suitors over the years, but that was moons ago. Now she was happy with her *vida libre*, as she called it, a free life, with her conjuring and her sacred potions.

Her *botánica* store earned her more fried *yuca* and plantains than she and her boy could ever desire. From time to time, she even got to dress up like an African princess and taxi up to the Palladium to hear Tito Puente's band and Celia Cruz shout *bongo, bongo, bongo, bongocero!* She bought Bembé some fine jumpsuits at Macy's on Herald Square and paid a private tutor to come by twice a week—no more public school or public humiliations about his head, his looks, his handicaps. Bembé would show them some day who he really was, that he had a royal lineage all the way back to the eyes that rule the universe.

Roberto was generous. He felt awkward about handing her money outright, so he would slip a few hundred-dollar bills under the statue of Yemayá each time he came. Yemayá, they both knew, was both Roberto's and Bembé's *santa*, the *orisha* who claimed them and watched over them. Her color was blue, as mystifyingly blue as both their sets of eyes.

Ideliza had big dreams for Bembé, a conviction that some day he would become a fine professional like his natural father, that the *santos* would see fit to unplug his ears and breathe speech into his mouth, and that they would be merciful enough to also shrink his head to a normal size. In her morning prayers, she visualized the gods Changó—ruler of fire, lightning, and earthquakes—and Oshún—ruler over love and gold—picking Bembé up by his feet and emptying his straw-basket head of all the things they had crammed inside it and forgotten to take out before they dropped him on planet Earth.

Ideliza prayed for her Bembé to grow up to be a *man of respect*, and not the bastard son of a *curandera* witch, or worse, the son of a *criada*, a maid, as they called her in Cuba. The label had been hers in the days when she was a girl in Regla, and later, when she came to New York with her mother Caridad Bayombe, *sirvienta* to the Alfonso family for half a century.

Roberto continued: "They said . . . this last time, this morning . . . they said my days are numbered."

There had been other threats against Roberto in recent months, and each time Ideliza had done her *amarre*, her binding of the evil tongues and spirits, and then for a while the threats would stop. But now, *chingen sus madres*, they were even calling him at home, at his unlisted number, in the middle of dinner, in front of Kitty.

Ideliza pulled him close and spread her legs over both sides of her chair. Her fuchsia caftan rolled out like an accordion across her knees. Roberto rose slightly and then sat on her lap, as he had done many times before, enfolded by her arms and by her soft, undulating middle, pressing his nose against her neck, and feeling her sweetsop mouth on his cheeks and five o'clock shadow, firmly cradled, rocking from side to side.

"Don't worry, angel. We are going to fix those mean, jealous people this time, this time for good. The *santos* want it, I know they do . . . but it would be better for the *amarre* if you knew their names. Did you find out their names for me yet?"

"No, they just say I'm going to pay for what I've done. They yell *murderer* and then hang up. At least three different guys in the past few days. No Latinos, though, just regular scumbags from Queens or Staten Island, I guess."

"You told the police?"

"Yeah. A bunch of imbeciles. Key Stone Cops with high tech wires up their asses. They bug my phone, then tell me they could only trace one call. Phone booth in Astoria somewhere."

"Well," said Ideliza, still rocking him in her arms, absorbed and staring into space, "then we are going to start by asking Santa Clara to help us. . . ."

She lifted him after a few seconds of silence, then rose like a crystal obelisk, facing her altar, scatting prayers in *sotto voce*—the plucking of a bass chasing Ella Fitzgerald down *How High the Moon*.

Roberto watched half-dazed, standing behind her in the middle of the room, eyes fixed, arms folded across his chest. Ideliza filled a glass halfway with water and carefully slid an egg into it. She lit white candles, knelt her heroic figure down, and implored her gods to break this evil spell against Roberto Lobo.

"You must do this on your own for nine days. Buy a brand-new glass and fill it with water and put the egg inside. Then pray to Santa Clara to send those people far from your life," Ideliza commanded him.

"I don't know how to do these things, Princess. You do them!"

"But this time you have to cooperate with the *santos* a little, angel. At the end of the nine days, you throw the water from the glass into the street. . . ."

"In the street?"

"Yes, and you take the egg to Central Park and smash it on the ground. . . . Then, at that moment, ask Santa Clara sincerely that, in the same way the egg was broken, she will break this *mal de ojo*, this evil spell, against you."

Roberto sat on the single bed across from the altar. He cupped the erection that had sprung up against his pinstriped trousers while watching her blazon her incantations before the plaster statue.

Ideliza sat down by him quietly, reclined against the headboard. She held him to her papaya breasts and massaged his buttocks like Amapola, his nanny, had done to him long ago when he was just a child of nine, buck naked in the shower with his little *petseleh* stick in the air. Amapola was the sweet, burnished color of molasses, full of music and laughter, happy to satisfy his little boy needs in her warm, soft, slippery hand covered with Castile suds.

Silently, Roberto straddled Ideliza. She reached for him and guided him inside her, rubbing and stroking him in her folds, squeezing his seed hard into her, cooing softly because they both knew Bembé must be somewhere in the house and that, although he could not hear, he could detect their throats' vibrations.

It took Roberto some time to come back from Ideliza's spell. She always seemed to leave him supine by the lush shores of the Congo Basin, or slumped over on the side of a grassy savanna. She held his head against her breasts and stroked the halo hair around his ear.

When he opened his eyes, he lit on the mouse hole under the door frame. The white candles were still flickering in the middle of the room. Night had fallen and now their radiance filled the air. In an instant, he caught Bembé's large turquoise eye in the cranny, a speechless witness to their libidinous liturgy. Roberto smiled, but the eye remained silent. He smiled again, this time broadly, hoping to elicit a glint of recognition, but the boy's eye was fixed, still and hard as a glass marble.

"What are you smiling at, angel?"

"I was thinking I'd like to have Bembé with me for a little while."

"Why . . . I thought you were not sure . . . who would you tell your people he is?"

"My physical therapist's son."

"Is *that* what I am? A physical therapist? A skinny, *raquítica,* prissy American nurse in white stockings and a little white cap! Me, Princess Papaya, *señor, por favor!*" Ideliza had music in her voice. Sometimes it was red Latin jazz, and sometimes it was cool, and it laughed like a stream over rocks.

"That's what I'll tell them. Still have a bum knee from jogging."

"Okay, *señor doctor.*" She was amused at his sudden insistence on having their son at his side.

"But why?"

"Maybe your *santos* will protect me more if I have the kid by my side."

Ideliza straightened the bed while Roberto washed up quickly, soaking a towel in a small wooden bucket with her *agua sagrada.* She popped a Celia Cruz CD into her portable yellow Sony. Instantly, her hips and buttocks began quaking to the conga rhythm. The tinkling of the *claves,* the hollow call of the *timbales,* the cry of the trumpet and the bongo drums—Ideliza knew how to let the music bathe her. *Amalia Batista / Amalia Bayombe / Qué tiene esa negra / Que amarra a los hombres. . . .*

"Besides," Roberto continued, attempting to make his point above the electric percussion, "I think Kitty has grown fond of Bembé. . . ."

"She's only seen him once!" Ideliza stopped singing along with the words.

"I know . . . but I think it will do her and me and my parents and my sister, Victoria, and everybody good to have him around for a little while."

Ideliza shook her breasts and shoulders, smiling at him, then danced her way behind Roberto and whispered in his ear, "You feel the child has *aché,* don't you, angel? You feel my sweet Bembé has special powers?"

"I do."

"I know you do."

"So . . . can I take him with me tonight?"

"Not tonight. Too late."

"Sometime this week?"

"Okay. On three conditions: that you treat him like a prince and that you let him play with your computer . . ."

"You're Princess Papaya, so the child would be a prince, right?"

"And that you do your *novena* to Santa Clara with the egg and the glass of water."

"That, I can't. No way."

Roberto went back to his chair. He was looking up at Ideliza surrounded by the lights and metallic drums, planted on the floor like an African Walkure, her pomade-straightened, blue-black hair shining and spread open in a fandango fan.

She waited for him to make his point.

"You're the one who can do those things, Princess, not me! I can't go to Central Park and just hurl an egg against the ground, and I can't put an egg in the water for nine days straight without being seen by Kitty or someone at the clinic."

"But you believe, Roberto, don't you? You believe in God, you believe in the *orishas*?"

Roberto sighed, sank in his chair, stretched his legs as far as he could. He still felt chloroformed by her sweet papaya smell. His back ached from arching. His testicles felt numb and as small as roasted chestnuts.

"I believe in your believing, Princess. . . . Oh, okay, I believe, yes, yes, of course, I do, but I believe you can do it, not me."

"Okay, angel, don't get fussed. *No te sofoques*, *negro*. I'm going to work the *amarre* for you. But if those people, whoever they are, keep calling and threatening, we may have to do other things. . . . "

"Like what?"

"Like find out a name, at least one name, so I can do a bigger *trabajo* spell: take a piece of parchment paper and write the person's name and dip it in snake oil, you know, *aceite de arrastrada* . . . and sew it to a snakeskin that Bembé can go and get for me somewhere up in the Bronx, by the zoo."

"What does that do?"

"It makes enemies crawl at your feet, just like a snake crawls, worthless and humiliated."

"Whatever you say, Princess." Roberto understood that Ideliza was in touch with omnipotent forces he knew nothing about. The gods talked to her at the drop of a hat, yet had ignored him for almost half a century. In Roberto's book, G-d had embarked on a long *siesta* and left Ideliza's *santos* in charge. Naturally, they favored sassy mulatto Cuban women—*mulatas cubanas zandungueras*—over Jewish Cuban-American obstetricians any day.

"Here," Ideliza whispered at the door, "take this sprig of *anamú* tied with a red ribbon, and put it behind your door at your office. It wards off *las cosas malas.*"

Roberto looked for Bembé on his way out, but the boy had vanished. Once in the street, on Ninth Avenue and Forty-Eighth, he turned back and saw Ideliza's newly repainted sign: *Botánica Yemayá—Consultas Espirituales.* The window was a subway jam of earthen saints, candles, dried culinary herbs, amber potions, Florida Water, coconuts, and sacred pictures. He noticed her latest feature: a life-size poster of Celia Cruz along with bongos, maracas and CDs for sale.

It was late autumn in Manhattan and there was already a prickly chill in the air, but Roberto felt the full weight, moil, and sweat of the worsted suit against his skin. He had lived in it for twelve hours, and his clean lemon and lavender Guerlain Imperial had long ago faded. He could not be seen or smelled like this. He would head straight for the shower before greeting Kitty. He remembered he had walked to Ideliza's and that his car was parked in the garage by the clinic. It would keep until tomorrow. He stepped onto the curb and waited for a cab to find him—a Spanish grandee poised for his coachman's arrival. Hailing taxis was for others, for tip-hustling doormen and private nurses escorting incontinent old men.

"Trump," he ordered to the driver behind the plastic divider, "Forty-Ninth Street side."

TWO

"SHE LONGED FOR THE OTHER ONE TO BE WITH her tonight, he who was part of her, with his dark hair and dark eyes so like her own. He who had not come yet, but who stared at her out of the future, and walked with her in her dreams."

Victoria Lobo Córdova finished typing the words of Daphne du Murier's *The Loving Spirit*. She wore the paisley silk robe her husband, Francisco Córdova, had given her on September 9th. It was the last time she had felt the rush of him inside her before the crash that two days later turned him into a human bomb.

What last thing could she have said to him, had she known? Would she have wished for a child then, a memento that reassured her that she had once loved and been loved by someone whose existence she could no longer prove? What do you say to someone just before he keeps a rendezvous with the dark demons that lie in wait for constellations to go retrograde and the Serpent of Sorrow to strike? What word, what final sentence could she have breathed into her husband's ear before he was blown up? One moment he was discussing his itinerary from the gate—he said "love you"; a quarter dropped; the phone went dead. Moments later, he was spun sugar in the clouds, his body carved and readied for the fire in the emblazoned towers, charred flesh for the craving sharks in the indigo mirror underside, hard and silvery like the planes overhead, south of Logan Airport.

Francisco would have loved finding her in this light, under the mauve of the Tiffany lamp—outspread fingers tapping impatiently on his Toshiba, upright rosettes pushing against silk, her copious copper hair electrified midair. Victoria would never age, or so he used to say. At thirty-five, she challenged gravity. Her skin was as luminous, olive-washed, and tight as it had been at twenty, when they wed at Tavern on the Green. If anything had seasoned, it was her eyes, now touched by an autumn melancholy that made her all the more desirable for their solemnity and grace. Tragedy, her mother Sara had said, is a great equalizer. *It humbles the proud and grows poppies of remembrance in sullen backyards where only sumac spread.*

At times, it seemed that only seconds had passed since she had clicked on Tom Brokaw for company and, instead, had been cleft asunder by the instant replay of Francisco's out-of-body voyage in the void and flames.

A year later, she watched herself erect before the Parsons table, night after night, surrounded by the mustard walls and Andalusian landscape canvasses of what used to be their home. Here she composed e-mails to a stranger whose disembodied words appeared in front of her like clockwork at midnight, a total stranger whose virtual existence had become her life and lifeline.

They had never exchanged pictures and, as far as she knew, he was a younger man—he would not say how old, not yet—who shared with her the sudden and devastating loss of a loved one. He called himself Cooper and said his grandmother had named him after Gary Cooper. Victoria signed on as Penelope. *Penelope, as in Ulysses' steadfast wife.* But who was *he*, really? And she, who was *she*, now that there was no longer a *we*, an *us*, a currency converter, a calibrating system, a hairy Spaniard with the legs and chest of a soccer player who tumbled to sleep on her breasts when the sun fell and rose?

Her brother, Dr. Roberto Lobo, had insisted she liquidate her possessions in SoHo at once, move into his guest apartment at Trump Tower, take a rich bimbo for a lover—*a fucking machine with a cock like an eggplant and a stipend to pay for his own silk suits, so you can forget the Spaniard and burn the past like enemy bridges.* This, from a man who had a Brit Milah on his eighth day, attended Hebrew school, then joined the Quakers at sixteen as life insurance, in case the Pentagon got the strange notion of staging a war and preempting his prime time. This from a man who now decapitates the partially born for a living.

She bristled at the thought of moving into his building or having to check in at a certain time of day, as a virgin would with a chaperone in the old days. Even if his intentions were sincere, Victoria suspected some ulterior motive. Roberto never did anything spontaneous or for its own sake. There was always an angle, a hidden agenda, a strange payoff for his *schadenfreude*, even when it pertained to his own flesh and blood. It had been that way between them from the beginning, back in Newark, under the billboard of the Galletas Lobo Factory their father had founded in 1960, the same year the family had fled Cuba. David, their older brother, was always rescuing her from Roberto's antics. Not that he pounced on her or threw mud on her school uniform the way boys his age did. His tactics were swifter, smoother, invisible, below the belt.

The first time she was old enough to buy herself a dress, he questioned her spendthrift ways at the *seder* table. When he caught her kissing a boy under the boardwalk on the Jersey shore, he complained to their parents about her wanton ways, implied she was doing more than just kissing, and scared Abram with stories about the rise in teenage pregnancy in America.

David had it out with him about once a month. The last time, he punched a front tooth out with his powerful right hook and warned Roberto he would personally cut off his balls if he ever bad-mouthed Victoria again. By then David was twenty and Roberto eighteen and half his size. He never went after her again. Not that she knew, anyway. Now David was no longer there to protect, counsel, or lend his strength. Now Francisco too had vanished into space.

David was somewhere in Cuba, rotting in jail for the past eighteen years, or else dead and forgotten—another *desaparecido*. She wondered if it were possible in this century for her to be one of those fabled women who bring bad luck to the men they love, since the two men she loved most had been taken from her so soon, so violently, and so senselessly. That notion alone was sufficient reason to lock up her heart and throw away the key for all eternity. She pictured Francisco laughing at her thoughts. *If you're going to go that far, mujer, don't forget the chastity belt también, ¿no?*

Her parents, Abram and Sara Lobo, at least tried. They could not reach in far enough to medicate the wound, but they were there for support. They didn't push or come up with Roberto's glib, quick-fix solutions. Sara consoled her, cried with her, and even did some of the crying for her. She hugged her until she squeezed her lungs flat, cooked enough white bean soup—*habichuelas judías*—to last forty years in the desert, and kept tabs on her like a Cuban chaperone.

Sometimes she'd call twenty times in a single day—*Just wondering how you're doing,* she'd say when faced with Victoria's wall, when she knew her daughter was home staring silently at the answering machine and not picking up.

In desperation, Abram begged Victoria to see a therapist. "Do it at least for your mother's sake. At least check out the Twelve-Step bereavement group that meets at the Ninety-Second Street Y, the one on *20/20.*"

And she had, for almost three months, until it struck her how Francisco's absence overtook her each time she found herself in that Gothic limestone basement, surrounded by men and women with hollow eyes and tears in their throats who went by *Hi, I'm Nancy* and *Hi, I'm Joe,* and called themselves *survivors.* Their collective acceptance of the loved ones' departure kindled the unbearable understanding that Francisco would never again be waiting on the other side of the door, or spooning his thick, strong body against hers, or lying in the dark singing Spanish songs—*my bull baying at the moon.*

She had to bail. There wasn't world enough and time enough to build sufficient antibodies to endure the pain and get to what they called the other side of mourning—if ever there was a there, there. She was certain the people with the hollow eyes and tears in their throats would not miss her—her *confrères* who knew the most intimate minutiae of her life by now, and with whom she had nothing in common except the loss of someone whose life meant everything. *Grief exiles the soul to a penal colony, grinds at the self like tide shells, crumbles the cliffs at the edge of the world. You can no longer think of others, or care for others, without mourning in advance, without fearing even the most casual attachment and what its absence would do.*

The slightest indication of human suffering—the withering, tearful face of another, a homeless woman crouched on Prince Street with a dog in her arms, news of a tornado in Kansas, famine in Africa, or an earthquake in Japan—would spin her into that free-fall dark hole where she tore at herself like a rag doll, ripping her cuticles, skinning her lips, plucking out strands of her long, curly hair like Penelope's yarn.

Of all the well-meaning mourners at the casket, only Cooper had supplied the necessary morphine to stop her from bleeding her nails to the quick. He provided enough opiate for her to sit still with both hands around a cup of tea, sufficient ether to hold out one lonely night, as she sat clutching a long-stemmed cocktail of Nembutal, Demerol, and Rioja wine.

Victoria had shadowed Cooper's path—*or was it the other way around?*—while clicking her way from link to link on the Internet, a sleepwalker trailing the satyrs, insomniacs, and lonely hunters who prowl the corridors of Hotbot, Excite, and MSN to open and close the doors of empty chat rooms.

Cooper was the first solid food she'd had in months. She'd never known anyone like him—if it was true she knew him at all and that his name was Cooper. He was arrow-straight, simple, complex, foolish, wise. *No-guile*, as Francisco would say. *A no-guile Galahad with grit and gusto.* Not that she'd ever write him that. She wouldn't push the envelope intentionally, pull class or rank on the one person she could hear without being deafened by the vortex and frenzied whir of flames eating their way up the twin buildings that had become a mass grave and mausoleum, the one voice she could take in without feeling the sharp rip of a metal hook to the heart. She hadn't told Cooper about her poems, her languages, her Oxford, her Fords and Guggenheims, her travels, her Kabala, her Cuba, her lapsed religion . . . What can those things matter in the end if a man or a woman loses their soul?

Dear Penelope:

I was thinking a lot on the road about what you said regarding our first meeting. You seemed to be putting yourself down, blaming yourself for having stooped to talk to strangers on the Net, like it was a grungy strip joint on Bourbon Street or something. I felt pretty bad. I wanted to make you stop beating yourself up for having feelings. Then I remembered some old saying. A proverb, I guess, about pride going before a fall. Did you ever

*think we survivors are too proud, that we think we have to be
better than other people and not need anybody else? I mean, it's
okay if other people are needy. Just not us. Pride. I felt that way,
too, when MJ left. But one day it came crashing down on me like
a ton of bricks that maybe my suffering could actually help
someone else feel better. That maybe we all need each other.
Sounds kind of goody-goody the way I just put it, right? Corny?
I'm no writer, like you. All left brain or something. Is it right
brain? Good with my hands.*

*Did I mention I built our house myself, here in Lompoc? Took
me five straight months, which was a good thing because I was
out of work back then. Laid up, sort of. Union strike. Anyway,
that's how I happened to go into the survivor's chat room that
night. Thought I could actually do something for somebody else
for the first time since MJ. Anyway, I'm glad I was yellow-
streaked and mealymouthed enough to go in that chat room and
say whatever it was I said that made you write back. What did I
say, anyway? And here's something else for you, Penelope. Here's
something else: Someday we're going to have to move on, you
know. Move on or die, I guess. But it's better not to move on 'til
it's our real time to go, when the Man upstairs says so. I have to
stick around, anyway, for my kid, Michael, even though he lives
with his grandparents down in Mobile and I hardly get to see him
these days. He's getting to be a big man. Just turned eleven and
looks like he could join the army tomorrow. Big guy like MJ's dad.
Good Welsh bones, his grandma tells me.*

*Anyhow, I know MJ would want it that way. Would want me
to move on with my life—just for me, even if the kid wasn't
around, or even if we had no kids, like you. How come you never
had kids? Didn't like them? I bet your husband would feel the
same way MJ does. About getting on with your life, I mean. How
come you don't use his name, or at least his initials? It's always
"my husband." Someday, you'll have a new husband, and then
you'll have to call "my husband" something else. Don't call him
'ex', though, whatever you do. Ex sounds like somebody was x-
ed out. MJ will never be x-ed out for me, no matter what. She's
always with me. Do you feel your husband with you? I mean, do
you feel his presence, like he's breathing next to you? I do some-*

times. And when I do I know it's real. Like dry concrete. Like those presidents' faces on Mount Rushmore. Not that I'm drinking or anything when that happens. Most of the time I'm stone sober (in my line of work, I have to be, anyway).

Say, Penelope, I wanted to say that knowing you has made me feel a whole lot better about things. About life. You say a lot of weird things and a lot of deep things, too. I don't know exactly how you can tell a poet, but I figure you're a poet. You could write songs or something. Some of the things you say remind me of Willy Nelson. I caught him on the road a while back. In person, I mean. Houston. The Astrodome. Great guy. You like him? Ever listen to his stuff?

Okay. Here it comes. Ready? I was thinking maybe it's okay if we see what we look like. Got a Polaroid? I mean, if we hate what we look like, we already got a friendship, right? And maybe we're ready for surprises. . . . Cooper

Dear Cooper:

Yes, yes, and no. I'll start with this: I promise not to call my husband "ex" if you don't use that word—"survivor". It means other things to me. And, anyway, having been left behind on this earth because he died (his initial: F.) doesn't make me a survivor. I didn't survive his death. I just didn't happen to die. Sorry if I'm a stick in the mud about this. Don't know if you know what I mean. And here's my take on "we survivors are proud and it's okay if other people are needy." To me, it's not pride. It's fear. Fear that if I let my guard down and feel whatever it is that I'm supposed to be actually feeling but don't know it, that I'm going to get totally unhinged and cry me a river and a whole delta.

Anyway, Cooper, it's all sort of academic because I still haven't been able to really DO it, anyway, whether I want to or not—I mean go way down there to the gorge where tears gather and just let fly. My poor mother has done most of the crying for me. As far as the Polaroids . . . I don't know. Can I think about it? I've toyed with the idea, but I'm afraid something could get destabilized. Right now it's pure—I mean, it's just soul-to-soul communication. Pure is not the right word. Sounds holy. There's a better word: single. Not as in unmarried, but as in whole. If

*your heart is single, your whole body is full of light—it's in the
Christian Bible.*

*You say you hear MJ? It's concrete? Last night I felt something
like that. It's strange that you brought it up tonight. I didn't actually hear F, but I heard a tap-tap behind the bed—like someone
calling behind the wall. It didn't scare me. Went on for about an
hour. I could see F's face in my mind's eye, as I always do, but it
was different. Larger. Concrete really tells it. I like how you
mention the Mount Rushmore presidents. It was just like that,
larger than life, carved in stone. Weird, no? Penelope.*

*PS: I finally listened to Willy Nelson. Had to download it
from the MP3 site you mentioned. Can't stand going into stores.
Yet.*

Dear Penelope:

*It's not weird. It's MJ's and F's (thanks) way of comforting us.
They're around, right as rain, as my grandma used to say. Don't
know where or how they are—but they're around. Never leave
us. Love never leaves us; I know that. Cooper.*

Dear Cooper:

*I believe you, I don't believe, mind you, but I believe you. After
a life of—I guess, for lack of a better term—spiritual quest, the
locusts that ate this year put me back at square one—back at the
starting gate, with more doubts than legitimate questions. The
overriding one being WHY. Why life, why ticks, why flies? Why
dogs or cats or people or planets? Why death, why love, why
anything?*

*Trying to taper down the sleeping pills. Leave an awful taste
in my mouth and then I feel so groggy the rest of the day. Do you
still take something? I was thinking I'd like to start working
again but feel so tired. Like I need to curl up for ten years in
some out-of-the-way cabin in a completely strange town where
maybe I don't even speak the language, with no television, computers, phones, or even mirrors, so I can stop dissecting my face,
looking for answers in the glass. Maybe that way I'll feel rested.
You know what I mean?*

Have to go to my brother and sister-in-law's for Sunday brunch tomorrow. They've adopted a child. Going to need an extra boost of energy for that. At least I won't be the center of attention for the first time in seven months—let's hope this time they won't be riveted on me, staring at me like the traveling freak show. There's usually such terrible pity and wonder and fear in their eyes. I think I finally understand what the person in the wheelchair feels like, the way strangers pass them and look at them askance, bypassing their gaze, in pity and sheer terror—terror that having seen their condition, they might invite it in. Good night. Bed bugs bite. Penelope.

Three

ROBERTO'S SHINY EGGHEAD was the first thing Victoria registered. Looking back on it, it resembled more a distant silver moon edged on a Tiffany than the semicircle of her brother's head—except there was no window, because Kitty had brocaded the glass panes in Scalamandre fabric to match the soft moiré walls and mute-pink Berber carpet.

The death rattle of a callow creature at the altar, heaving for life. You could hear it in the hall, clear out to the elevator. Long, wounded, moribund cries. A sorrowful jazz trumpet in sostenuto. Only a sound this ominous could have caused her to trespass Roberto's private domain, burst in with her family key, forego the doorbell with the Mozart clarinet concerto.

Her sister-in-law, Kitty M. Cabot, homecoming queen, cheerleader, erstwhile Maharishi cult follower, beautiful alabaster statue of thirty-five, lay naked four-square across the satin bed, thighs and knees pressed tightly against washboard stomach and budding cuneiform breasts while Roberto's silver moon was a chronometer, keeping time to the syncopated rhythm with his pounding pelvic thrusts.

Victoria had a sudden flash of her brother at fourteen, on the white tile floor—reclining against the toilet, spread-eagle, with peach fuzz still on his face, his large, erect manhood in full bloom, spanking Jesse Norman's picture on the cover of *Ebony* magazine with brimming hand. She could not see his robust member now, only its urgent shadow, plunging fiercely into Kitty against a cobalt light.

Neither uttered a sound. Victoria could have guessed her

19

brother demanded utter silence in bed. He was never there when he was there. Only his fantasies would keep him hard inside his statue wife. She scanned the room, looking for the source of the afflicting, terrifying moans, careful not to close her gaze in on Roberto or Kitty and rouse them from their mating daze.

Above the carved mahogany bed, on a deep hollow niche in the wall, Bembé, the deaf-mute boy of nine, was cooing faintly now, spending the last of a single vocal chord, looking down on Roberto and Kitty's seesaw dance, clutching the soles of his Nikes, tugging at his shoelaces.

It was clear that Roberto and Kitty could see the child from their vantage points if they but looked beyond the veil of their impending orgasm. Victoria was seized by a sudden revulsion; a bitter gulp sprang in her mouth. She understood they *knew* the child was there and that Roberto had most likely staged it. And all at once, she realized this chocolate boy of nine, small for his age, was the reason for her visit, the very reason for the family gathering due to start in a few minutes—as soon as her parents made it through the Midtown Tunnel from New Jersey in their pre-owned Cadillac Seville.

Victoria decided this was no time for confrontations or fruitless condemnations. Her disapproval or revulsion would not make a dent. *People will do what they do. It never happened*—she whispered it as confirmation, releasing this nauseating image like a dove in captivity, never to be sought again. *I have not seen this. I am party to none. Three monkeys. See no evil.* She repeated the mantra and edited it for her own understanding. *Hear, O Israel.* God knew the rest of the words.

She closed the door gently, turned on her rubber heels and suddenly, just as she had managed to elude direct contact with anything animate or inanimate in that lurid, pink, padded womb, was seized by the laser-cool splash of Bembé's aquamarine eyes on the back of her head. She made a split decision not to look back for the source of this extraordinary sensation—although she knew instinctively, as though Bembé and his eyes were both one and the same, facing her iris and pupil, looking head-on into her.

The new computer Roberto had recently mentioned on the phone was on, like a new millennium R2D2 monitoring the study and entrance hall, playing *Desafinado*, scanning dust particles for light and sound and human isotopes. A new fixture had been added since her last visit—a narrow, polished steel daybed, equidistant from all four corners of the Bloomingdale's room, sheathed in white Pratesi linens. The child's new bedroom, with nothing of the child in it—no toy trucks or trains or teddy bears or pictures of rock stars. A single bed and a computer *cum* butler and ubiquitous eye.

Had Victoria known of Bembé's uncanny knack for high tech and of his *aché* gifts from the *orishas*, she might have realized the MAC 4000 had been procured at his behest. As it was, she supposed that Kitty and her brother had neglected to provide toys for their newly adopted son and that Roberto had furnished him with his very own computer as a substitute. She also concluded that Roberto had neglected to warn Sara and Abram that his newly adopted son was clearly a child of color and, in all probability, not Jewish, unless Roberto had managed to smuggle in an Ethiopian child from the Left Bank, which she doubted.

Kitty had obviously not counted on being late to her own party—much less on being exposed by the baying child. She had planned well for her in-laws, despite the fact that Felicita, their mulatto maid of seven years, had suddenly vanished and, as Kitty put it, left her *up the creek without a paddle*. Kitty had even lit the Shabbat candles, although she did not know what Shabbat meant.

She had ordered baskets of narcissus, freesia, and tiger lilies from Fellan Florists and placed them strategically at corresponding angles. She had carefully orchestrated Paul Revere silver platters rife with Dean & Deluca's Thai Chicken, artichoke pasta, and baby vegetables—*below the age of consent*, as Roberto insisted vegetables be served. As a centerpiece, Kitty had cradled new harvest bottles inside a Chinese-red African *ceiba* basket. Lobo Vineyards: an antique yellow label with the Lobo family crest—a wolf atop the Pyrenees baying under a crown of stars.

What family crest? The one King Fernando personally designed for the Marranos before he handed them their heads?

Victoria could hear Francisco's postmortem admonitions. *Your brother can't constantly offend you! Just laugh at it! What will it all matter in ten years?* Did she ever tell him about the times Roberto had pulled his cat ambush on her, trapped her in an army net, locked her in the storage basement of the Lobo warehouse for hours, till David rescued her, brought her back in his arms, trembling and awash in tears, blinking under the neon billboard against the night? She had it on her list of tell-alls, which she updated now and then. Perhaps she would have gained the strength to tell him this year. Or next. Now, who would know for sure?

Victoria sat down by the window overlooking the damp, gray buttresses of St. Patrick's Cathedral, the polished steel Chrysler Building, the transparent, bloody burial site where the Twin Towers had stood before sky fire, clawed steel, and mortar had crushed her life, rent her heart. She glanced at the obstetrics and gynecology journals on the Carrara marble table, interspersed with issues of *ArtNews* and home decorating magazines—*shelter magazines, they call them. Why?*

Francisco would have welcomed this evening and the anticipation of what he'd dubbed her family's *mishegash fandango.* But he would surely have silently condemned Roberto's behavior—fucking his wife a few minutes before his elderly parents and widowed sister were due to arrive, with his newly adopted son propped on a niche, a brown spectator in the peanut gallery. *Or would he?* Francisco wasn't easily scandalized. From the start, they had shared a doctrinal disappointment in the nonlinear pattern of human evolution—*expect the unthinkable.* A preemptive strike, he used to call it. Except, like Abraham and Lot, they parted ways when it came to visceral reactions.

Francisco turned disillusionment into a cosmic joke, brushed off invading thoughts like lint, while Victoria took them to heart, gnawed at her cuticles and hangnails until they bled. She could never depersonalize. Like Lot's wife, she looked back, and back, and back and turned to salt and tears of salt.

Sara and Abram were exactly on time, standing side by side at the door, two bewildered orphans sheathed in gabardine, ranch mink, suede hats. She still admired them. Abram for his tenacity, for the way he had made it in the world in spite of—or because of—an eighth-grade education and a farcical accent from an alien tongue. He had made his way in a world booby-trapped with people who called him Jesus Killer, hurled epithets in mock Ladino, and pillaged his father's grave looking for Dutch diamonds and gold teeth. Sara, she admired for a hundred other reasons. For resisting the Castro militia with her bare hands when they came for their house in El Vedado. For surviving another exodus of bitter herbs. For keeping her faith, her Yom Kippur and seder, her mezuzah on the door frame when those around her had defected, denied their names, or scattered like snowflakes. For starting life over again at forty with the cookie factory in Newark. For raising three peculiar children in peculiar times. For living through the pain of David's sudden disappearance, Francisco's death, Roberto's oblique and alienating ways, and her daughter's moods and enduring mourning.

"You're alone?" Sara's way of breaking the ice. Roberto, Kitty, and the child were still in the bedroom. Victoria had eaten her way through a plate of chicken since her arrival and had listened to Pepe Romero play the full Concierto de Aranjuez. It had helped drown the haunting one-chord moans, the image of her brother and Kitty and the little hydrocephalic boy in the pink bedroom. Francisco used to play Romero for hours while he painted. She wondered if Cooper had ever heard of Aranjuez or Pepe Romero or, for that matter, classical guitar. The Willy Nelson song she'd downloaded twanged in her head like a distant sitar. *Just one love. Just one love. Just one love.*

"¡No, vieja, no digas! She's not alone! I can see there is a little afikomen left over from Pessah, hiding there, see, behind Victoria. . . . Say, say, how are you? . . . Peek-a-boo, peek-a-boo, peek-a-boo! . . . how are you? Peek-a-boo!!"

Victoria and Sara exchanged arched eyebrows. Abram was seventy-five and although his heart had twice warned him of the Iceman's rattle, he was still in full command of his mental faculties, with the exception of an ever-increasing penchant for Borscht Belt buffoonery. But he was not yet in the habit of shouting goo-goo and peek-a-boo at the air.

To Victoria's astonishment, Bembé had silently transubstantiated to her side, dressed in the khaki jeans, Tiger Woods T-shirt, and satin-white Nikes she had found him in earlier—perched like a fallen angel over the rocking cradle of his new white-satin parents.

"Bembé! Bembé? How are you! Great to meet you!"

Victoria was determined to make this their first official greeting. She held his shoulders, kissed his enormous forehead, and lifted him in her arms, face to face. He came up in the air like a feather and met her gaze head-on, with a lead-glass, mesmerizing stare. At first contact, his aquamarine eyes shot a singular, quick-blinding, liquid laser light into her. Seconds later, when she could see again, she found herself fixed on the boy's broad grin, pulpier than a ripe papaya, creamier than a Milky Way.

For a few moments—how long?—she had gone dark on her surroundings. Her parents' voices had vanished. She never heard Roberto and Kitty come into the living room. She wondered how she came to be sitting on the settee with Bembé at her feet and the rest of the family gathered around her like doctors around the operating table.

"You feel better now, *chiquita*?" Sara had sandwiched Victoria's hands in hers.

Victoria nodded. Well, physically better than she'd felt since Francisco had dematerialized midair over Battery Park. Sharper, as when the cobweb mist begins to lift at sea. The weight of Bembé's balloon head and his razor-short, nappy hair scratching her legs brought her comfort. His body anchored in her space, a reassuring propinquity, a tree planted by the rivers of water. The light that had pierced her eyes still glowed inside her.

"Your mother keeps telling me my jokes are no good . . .but she didn't say anything about making pretty girls faint! Am I that bad, tell me!"

Victoria smiled at Abram—full-mouthed and grinning like the child he had fixed in his mind forever, the little girl of nine with the gap in her mouth, all dressed up in a pique dress.

"What? I missed one of your famous jokes, Abba?" Only she called him that.

"Nothing we need a full dress rehearsal of, right?"

Roberto was suddenly in focus. He looked freshly scrubbed, dowsed in Guerlain Imperial, starched and ironed in his dark worsted suit and neon-white bespoke shirt. Kitty was faithfully at his side, reclining against a pillow embossed with the Lobo crest, sheathed in a Palm Beach-green hostess caftan—a tight tulip, cool and self-contained. Only a faint, intermittent flicker on her collagen-enhanced upper lip gave her away. Victoria had written a poem about it ages ago, when Roberto first introduced her as his favorite patient. She called it *the blinking light of quiet desperation.*

"You're right, Robertico," Sara agreed, "there's no need for a dress rehearsal! Abram, your children Roberto and Kitty have adopted a beautiful child. It's no good to tell even innocent jokes about him because he can't speak back. I told you that before we came, Abram, remember?"

"Speak is one thing . . . but can he hear, that would be my question! If he can't, what's the harm! So we laugh a little and he's none the wiser!"

Is this how it starts? Will he end up staring at the moon, misplacing people's faces for tree trunks? Francisco had made Victoria promise that she would call the Hemlock Society if he ever got that way. But he didn't. Instead, he died in his prime. His paintings had just begun to live.

"He can't hear. Bembé is a deaf-mute. But he's not stupid. He knows exactly what goes on around him," said Kitty, smiling with hard hazel eyes, looking straight at Abram, conveying in no uncertain terms that her child was off-limits.

The mother lion had not taken long to surface. Bembé might just as well have spilled from her womb an hour ago. Then again, she had been pregnant for years, waiting for Roberto's son to arrive. She would have given up almost anything—her charity work, her PBS fund-raising, her painting classes by the Metropolitan, even her long-stemmed figure and Boston pedigree—if only she could bear Roberto's child in the hidden equator where all his seeds had died.

How long since the child moved to Trump Plaza? A week? Victoria would check later. She had written Cooper about it. *And how can she let Roberto bring the child into their bedroom, prop him on the wall, force him to watch him thrust his wanton sword in her?*

"He's got Roberto's eyes, which are really his grandfather's eyes, so the child has my father's eyes," declared Sara proudly.

There was no doubt. She could spot those eyes anywhere.

Pogrom Eyes, her grandmother called them. It came from a family story about little Sara, ten years old, asking her Sephardim/Ashkenazi parents of Spanish, Portuguese, and Dutch descent, why, if they were really Jews, were her father's eyes so blue. Her mother had shrugged her shoulders and sighed, "Darling, a pogrom is a pogrom!" and Pogrom Eyes was born into the family lexicon.

Roberto flashed Victoria a familiar Mayday look. Victoria telegrammed back: *What's wrong?* He rolled his eyes, pointed at their mother with his chin. *Get her off the blue-eye shtick!*

She cocked her head. *Oh?* It clicked. It *is* his child, really *his*. And if his child, then her nephew and if her nephew, then her flesh and blood. Again it surfaced, that flash of Roberto at fourteen, letting fly on the cover of *Ebony* spread across the bathroom floor.

"We both thought this was really an omen," explained Kitty, "to find a boy in need of a good home with eyes just like Roberto's. . . . Well, you might say it was God's way of letting us know He had earmarked this little brown one for us!"

Her debutante instruction was in full gear. She would make Episcopalian talk around the fact that she had agreed—perhaps begged—to adopt the strange fruit of a voodoo witch pollinated by Roberto. A strange fruit she had taken to be morally hers.

"Too bad David can't be here with us today," said Abram, then caught himself, remembering he'd promised Victoria he would refrain from mentioning him in front of Sara.

Roberto stood up, impatient, urging them to taste his new wine, pouring, pointing to the catered hors d'oeuvres that filled the coffee table and were meant to stand in for the Sabbath dinners Sara used to prepare when all three children lived at home.

"David didn't care for children," said Roberto, avoiding eye contact with his sister, "and I don't think he would have exactly approved that I adopted a black child, either . . ."

"And one with a . . . disability," piped in Kitty.

"Yes, that's right," agreed Roberto, "David didn't like shortcomings. He was perfect. Maybe too perfect."

Sara sprung the cataract film in her eyes that usually accompanied any mention of David.

"He was a good boy and a good son, Robertico," she said in a monotone, "why don't you like him even now, when he's probably dead? When he's probably dead and piled in a common gentile grave . . ."

"We don't know that, mami!" Victoria rushed to parry the self-inflicted blow.

"Vic is right, mami! With his brawn, he's probably alive! And sorry, mami, I wasn't *not* liking David when I said that. I just meant that given his purist ideologies, he might have disapproved of Bembé. . . . Remember how he used to say he could never marry out of his race? And remember how he used to work out in his bedroom, hulking up like he was runner-up to Arnold Schwarzenegger?"

"No, he wouldn't, he wouldn't disapprove. He'd love this child," said Abram somberly. He reached for a plastic bag of Galletas Lobo crackers he kept in his shirt pocket, leaving the Thai chicken and glass of Reserve Lobo Wine untouched.

"Yeah, Roberto. If anything, just the opposite," said Victoria, "David loved children. He loved people in general. He had a big heart. Why else would he have gone down there and put his life on the line?"

"What happened to David?" asked Kitty. "Roberto is so mum. Just like a doctor, you know, he never wants to tell me about things. . . . Did he just go to Cuba and get arrested? Was he working for our government?"

"He went down to help get an old rabbi out of Havana in a boat," answered Victoria, who also preferred not to discuss it, "but apparently the militia found them just off the coast of Caibarién and threw them in jail . . . him and the rabbi. . . . At least that's what Roberto told us he heard from his friend at the consulate. Right, Roberto?"

"Yeah," he nodded, looking down, dropping his head on his china-thin cupped hands.

"So long ago now . . . and not a word from our boy since then," murmured Sara, loud enough to make Abram rock to and fro in silence like the bearded men in black Victoria had seen in Jerusalem, divining before the Wailing Wall.

"But isn't there any way to find out what happened to him,

though?" Kitty excelled at social pragmatism. As if the Lobo family would not have tried every possible means. As if Victoria and Francisco would not have pulled every string, visible and invisible. As if Sara would not have called the White House directly, rattled the female governor out of bed, gotten the *New York Times*, the UJA, and the *Newark Star Ledger* on the case.

"Oh yes, my dear Kitty," sighed Abram, "we tried. And continue to try. Right, Roberto?"

"Right, Papá. Things are definitely getting worse and worse for Castro, the creep. Maybe we'll get some answers soon." He called Fidel 'the creep'. It would please Abram.

Bembé had receded into the chiaroscuro of his shadow world. Only Victoria seemed to feel his articulate presence rubbing against her knees, watching and listening—although it was not clear how much he could actually hear. With his human ears, that is. His other secret senses lay in wait at all times, and now that his laser had captured her iris with cabbalistic light, Victoria envisioned him like a twinkling watchman in a high tower, casting wide his beam on the horizon to the ships leaving port on the other side of the Middle Passage.

"Good wine, isn't it? I think it's Roberto's finest harvest since he bought the winery . . . gosh, when? Almost five years ago?" said Kitty.

"Yeah, it's good Riesling," said Victoria, "sweet as hell but better than Manechewitz. . . ."

"The way it's supposed to be," Roberto rushed in, "eighteen percent sugar and the cream of the cream . . ."

"The cream of coconuts!" blurted Abram.

"Coconuts? What do you mean, coconuts?" asked Roberto. "These are the best of the best Central California grapes we're talking about, Papá!"

"He doesn't mean anything by it," explained Sara. "Your father is just repeating a commercial Hermione Gingold used to do for Goya Foods before she died, years and years ago. Pay him no mind. He's in his own world a lot these days."

"*It's the cream, it's the cream of coconuts . . . you'll adopt them!*" intoned Victoria in a high pitch. "Don't you remember that commercial, Roberto? I think we must have watched it together!"

"No. I missed it. We rarely watch television. And now with Bembé playing with the computer and the Internet and the joy-stick all the time, I don't even know what television is. . . ."

"We hardly have time for television," added Kitty. "This is the first time in a long time we actually get to sit down and just relax. . . . Roberto is always so busy. . . . But we wanted you to come and meet Bembé as soon as possible."

"Bem-bé . . . Bem-bé . . . What kind of name is that?" asked Abram. "It's not a prophet and it's not any dead relative's that I know of. . . ."

"It's probably the name his own mother gave him," interject-ed Victoria.

"Right," agreed Roberto.

"She's colored?" asked Abram.

"Abram, you need new glasses?" said Sara.

"Bembé is some sort of African name. It means fiesta or big party or something. . . . We thought we should not complicate things for him. Somehow he seems to recognize his name," said Kitty.

"Probably just as well to let him keep his own name. God knows, he must feel strange enough living up here on the twenty-fifth floor, with an elevator they spray with French perfume till you sneeze and wheeze. Does that black singer, you know, the boy that looks like Diana Ross, does he have an apartment in the building? Didn't we read that somewhere?" said Sara.

"So, Robertico, I got a question for you. Who's this mother who gave up her child? Someone you know?" asked Abram.

"Why, yes, she's Roberto's physical therapist, you know, the one who's been helping him off and on with his jogger's knee. She's a single mother . . ." started Kitty.

"Mazel tov! A physical therapist?" Sara winked at Victoria with a familiar glint in her eye. "Is she any good, Roberto? I bet she's good, don't you agree, Victoria?"

"She's quite good, very highly trained." Roberto answered firmly, stemming her tide.

"So how's business, big bro'? Saw your clinic in the *Times* the other day. You're glad you got into the wine business?" Victoria was used to getting his irons out of the fire.

"Good. I think the winery is actually on the brink of turning a profit. Trouble is, I need to be there more. . . . *El ojo del amo engorda el caballo*. . . . and my patients won't let me. Maybe you could go for me one of these days, Vic, as soon as you feel a little stronger maybe, and help me out for a while? I need your great head for dealing with people . . . need the locals to put together a face with the winery and schmooze with you, invite you to parties, write you up in the papers, that sort of thing, so we start building a presence in the Santa Barbara community. On the West Coast. Right now, I think I'm seen more like an absentee landlord or something. What do you say, Vic? You could write your poetry out there. Weren't you writing another poetry book? It's a beautiful place. You could even get back into teaching. They have a couple of good liberal arts colleges right in the area. Up in San Luis Obispo, and even down in Santa Barbara. UCSB. You know, you heard of them, no?"

"That would be an excellent idea! Wouldn't you want to take a little trip to California and do some work for your brother . . . and finish the book you were writing before . . . and maybe even teach a little again? I think it would do you good, Victoria!" Sara had been after her for months. *Do something! Do something! Work! Write! Teach! Get out of the house! Go make some new friends your age! Maybe even a special friend?*

"What does that mean, *caballo*?" Kitty had been pondering Roberto's unusual introduction of Spanish in his conversation. He hardly spoke it, not even to Felicita, the maid, who was no longer their maid since Bembé's arrival.

"It's an old Spanish saying," explained Abram, who had been tickled by his son's impromptu Spanish, "the eye of the owner fattens the horse. Get it?"

"It translates something like 'you have to mind the store if you expect it to do well'," Roberto stepped in. He had grown accustomed to simplifying Byzantine concepts for his Pilgrim wife.

"Oh? I see. Well, I like the fat horse thing." She didn't see. Kitty couldn't make the leap. No one in her family had been a merchant for generations. Still, she liked the image, the horse thing.

"So, Vic," Roberto came back, "you think you might want to give me a hand in Santa Ynez? There's a house right in the vineyard you could use. Looks like a cowboy outhouse, if you ask me, but with your taste you could probably make it look like a million dollars in no time."

"But I thought the vineyard was just a tax write-off for you, Roberto. So how come you want me to go out there now to do your PR and help you turn a profit? Isn't that going to cost you, with all the *dinero* you rake in at the clinic?"

"But wine is good business, Vic, and it so happens that I got lucky with the grapes my broker got from Chile a few years back. So, *a caballo regalado no se le mira el colmillo*, right?" Again, the horse thing.

Abram hastened to translate. "It means don't look a horse gift in the mouth!" He looked straight at Kitty for recognition.

"Oh? That's cute," she whooped, "a horse gift!"

"Right," said Roberto, turning his back on his wife, looking at Victoria for an answer.

"Tell your brother, yes, *sí, sí, sí*, Victoria! It'll be good for you and good for everybody. Maybe your father and I will come visit in December or January. That would be nice! Get away from the cold . . . going west instead of going to Florida . . . it's getting so dangerous there. . . . Did I tell you our friend Betty Gertz was held up in her own home? She opened the door to a man saying he needed milk for his child, and he pulled a gun on her . . . even took her china. . . ."

"Not me, Sara, you can't take me," Abram protested. "I don't want earthquakes. I don't want floods. I don't want to drive a million miles just to go to a deli and then come to find out they're closed on Sundays and their bagels are boiled in pig stew! She's better off if she doesn't go. What can she possibly do to help Roberto there? Victoria's no businessman, for Pete's sake, she's . . . she's, you know what she is! A po-et, a po-et, a *poeta*, one of those people with their heads in the clouds! What does she know from grapes and profit and cowboys."

"Abram, didn't you hear Roberto? Victoria would make a great, you know, spokeswoman for Lobo Vineyards! And she can also do what her brother asks her to do over the telephone. She can be the hands, and he, the brain, since you say he's the one with the business brain. Everyone will like her! Remember what a

number she did on that Spanish ambassador? He bought five of
Francisco's paintings right on the spot! Does that say it all?" Sara
had sat up, toy soldier-straight, in her size-sixteen, red-and-black
knit dress. She was clutching her Ferragamo purse, as she was
wont to do even while visiting her children, narrowing her olive
eyes, shaking her head like a Gypsy dancer and talking with her
chin pointed straight at her husband—a familiar warning that he
had crossed the line.

"Yeah, yeah," Abram shrugged, "that ambassador, he probably
felt guilty for being Spanish. And he should have. Also, it doesn't
hurt that Victoria is a girl with such tremendous looks, my mother's looks. . . . My mother could have sold anybody the Brooklyn
Bridge, too! . . . At least, if you're going to do it, make sure your
brother pays you for this, Victoria. Don't let him be a cheapskate!"

"Oh, do go, Victoria!" said Kitty. "It's heavenly gorgeous out
there! Wait till you see those mountains and the surfers flying on
that wild sea and that incredible weather that won't quit!"

"Okay, okay, stop everybody! You're ganging up on me! Tell
you what, I'll think about it! Okay?"

"Sold!" agreed Roberto. "We can talk about it some other
time." He seemed satisfied he'd won the first round.

Whatever he had up his sleeve had made it worth the effort.
Victoria couldn't tell for sure. *Perhaps Bembé knows, the child that
is privy to all and tells nothing . . . an exceptionally suitable son for
him, a son whose words can never betray his trust.*

Victoria stood up for the first time since she blacked out under
Bembé's gaze. She leaned on him, stretched her back, patted his
inflamed head. *A meteor on my hand, incandescent coal, hot like the
axis and spin of Earth, luminescent of fire and wind, peaceful like
waters in a vestal stream.*

It dawned on her that Cooper had mentioned Santa Ynez in
his e-mails, probably lived there, although he'd never said exactly
where he lived for sure, only that he traveled a lot, was always on
the road but home was, she thought, California, somewhere
between San Francisco and L.A. The same small town where he
had built his bride a house with his own hands, overlooking
mountains that changed colors like moonstones, perhaps somewhere in the shadow of Roberto's newfound Riesling grapes. If

true, then it was both good and bad. Good and bad in that she was tempted to meet Cooper face to face. Bad and good in that she also thought it best to leave things as they were. Virtual. Incorporeal. A friendship she could conduct from her Toshiba without having to shower, stare at the closet for something to wear, tame her wild curls with the poodle brush, or make idle conversation while her heart bled. If she felt crowded or bereft, she need only disconnect.

The phone startled her. It rang in five places at once, in a progressively piercing treble. Roberto leapt over Kitty, yanked the pink receiver, and zoomed into Bembé's new room, whispering into the mouthpiece with his moon head down and his body stiff with complicity. All eyes followed him, even Bembé's, who had appeared to be asleep.

The boy looked up and smiled, squeezing Victoria's hand against his cheek. She was drawn to kiss him on his nose and eyes, and before she could tell how it happened, she found herself sitting back on the settee, cradling him in her arms—his head tossed against her exposed breast for all to see—murmuring a Ladino lullaby she had learned at her mother's side, drifting in a daydream, musing about California and Cooper and Francisco's face and this clement child who had taken to her like a homeless puppy.

"What a serious mug. You'd think somebody died. Must be a patient, no?" Sara looked at Kitty.

"Maybe it's that physical nurse of Roberto's, wanting to ask if they're feeding her boy. . . . She probably just found out the kind of thing Kitty eats, rabbit food! Maybe food you wouldn't feed a rabbit. Carrots, lots of carrots and sprouts, lots of sprouts in plastic containers! So no wonder the *schwartza* would worry! Who can blame her!"

"Shush, Abram. ¡Por favor! No empieces." Sara gave him an elbow.

"I don't understand what you're referring to," protested Kitty. "I do eat! I eat every day! And so does Bembé! We eat very well . . . and not just carrots. In fact, sometimes I think we eat too much!"

"You see, Abram! She just told you she does! Kitty eats very well. She just doesn't like certain foods! And she's entitled!"

Sara had asked Victoria about Kitty each time the holidays rolled around. It amazed her that her son's wife left her food practically untouched after ordering huge quantities, and that she never cooked, not even for Christmas or Hanukkah. Victoria had assured her there was nothing wrong, explaining that women of her upbringing—*Mayflower goys*, she had labeled them for Sara's sake—weren't brought up to *like* food. *It's a puritanical thing; they're not supposed to give way to their senses.* She would not worry her mother, or mention the week spent with Francisco, Kitty, and Roberto in Aspen, how Kitty's regurgitations in the adjacent bathroom had kept her up for hours. Victoria could still hear that rubber plunger sound, sucking and heaving and finally coughing and spitting dry till the last of the Caesar salad had been tossed into the whirling bowl.

"Roberto gets all kinds of business calls," said Kitty, steering the conversation away from the subject of gastronomy. "Patients too, of course. But we try to discourage them unless they're about to have the baby right then and there or something. . . . Even then, Roberto directs them to the emergency room. It's tough for a doctor, you know, to be always on call. . . ."

"Roberto is delivering babies these days?" Sara acted incredulous. Victoria smiled. *Nobody's fool.*

"Why, yes, mami!" exclaimed Kitty. "Isn't that what obstetricians do? Roberto's brought many children into this world." She called her mami, the way her own children did. It came in handy when Sara's inquisitiveness got her goad. *A left hook and a kiss.*

"You goddamn bastard! You scumbag! What the fuck do you want?! Just say it! What do you want from me? I warned you the police are on to you! So get the fuck outta my life or I'll have my friends track you down and personally cut your balls off with a rusty blade, you goddamn faggot!" Roberto's whispers had suddenly burst into shouts. His threats boomed in sudden thunder over the living room.

"I wonder what's wrong," said Sara.

"Nothing, mami. Don't worry. He can handle himself. It's probably business. You know people talk like that in business. . . . It's nothing nowadays. Everything is rage this and rage that, haven't you heard? Office rage, road rage." Victoria felt Bembé tugging at her blouse. He smiled at her like a cat, aquas half-closed, his whiskers rubbing against her.

"I never heard of such a thing. Nobody spoke to anyone like that in business," said Abram, "no one spoke to me that way either. Not even, you know, what's his name who bought the plant? Levy, that's right. Not even Levy, and you remember what a dirty mouth he had? You think he's okay, Kitty? Maybe he could use your help?"

Kitty's lips quivered. Her tick took over. "I don't interfere with his business," she declared, digging her nails deep into the palm of her hand, "but I wouldn't worry. Vic is perfectly right. Roberto is a tough man. And I'd just as soon not get involved in all that man talk, you know. So, frankly, I don't listen. . . . I think that's the only wise thing to do."

In a moment, receiver and mouthpiece made a crashing sound. Roberto reappeared arching his brows comically, spreading a smile across their faces—all but Bembé's, who lay buried in Victoria's breast.

"Robertico! You sounded so upset! I never heard you talk that way!!" Sara grabbed his hand and felt his face for symptoms.

"Naw, it's nothing, mami. I'm not upset. That guy on the phone, he thinks I'm upset. . . . And that's as it should be. I doubt if he'll get any sleep tonight."

"Do you mind if I ask you who this person is?" asked Sara.

Roberto laughed. "Mami! I thought you'd never ask!"

"All right, you wise guy. Go ahead, don't tell me. See if I care!" Sara worked her coy look with gusto.

"Oh, it's okay, mami. The jerkass was my broker, you know, the guy at Morgan Stanley. Trying to sell me on shorting a stock after I'm through telling him I don't want him moving my money around, that I got enough on my hands with the winery this year."

"Some broker," quipped Abram. "I never heard of such a broker that talks to his client like that. Maybe you should switch to Ventura, you know the guy, belongs to the Temple. Larry Ventura, that's the name. I heard he did good by some people."

"Ah, who wants to think about that right now," answered Roberto. "I'd rather go up to the roof for a swim. Do I have any takers?"

Victoria gave him a stone-faced look. *Are you serious?* She concluded that the rubber-stamp family pow-wow in honor of Bembé had drawn to a close. Her parents had been rattled enough for one evening. Her only regret was leaving Bembé behind with her brother. She would ask to take him with her for the night, or at least to see him again. But she'd need to get past Kitty, who was sensitive about her possessions, even if, as Victoria registered, she had not shown an ounce of physical affection for the child during the entire length of their visit.

"We'll give you a ride down to SoHo, *m'ijita,*" said Abram. "Don't want you taking some taxi with one of those guys with diapers on their heads for a driver. You know what Jackie Mason says, they're liable to lose their way, take you to Queens in the middle of the night!"

"Abram, stop with the slurs!" Sara slapped his leg. "Ask Victoria if you don't believe me! It's not safe to speak that way, I keep telling you."

"Ach! There she goes again," Abram addressed Victoria. "You see how your mother attempts to interfere with the U.S. Constitution? Maybe you can do me a favor and explain my inalienable rights to her someday?"

"Okay, you guys. Let's exercise some more inalienable rights and get going. They're going to shut down the pool if Roberto doesn't hurry. . . ." Victoria put her best face forward. It was only ten. She would rather walk the whole length of Fifth Avenue by herself. The cool air would detoxify, transition her into her midnight tryst with Cooper.

At the door, lingering with good-byes, as Sara and Abram usually did, Bembé hid behind his father, playing peek-a-boo with Victoria, who found it difficult to tear herself away from his many dimpled faces, popping like jacks-in-the-box from left to right, right to left, above the head and between the legs of her brother. She noticed thick water beads across Roberto's nose and upper lip. He reeked of fear. His hands and lips were frozen when they kissed good-bye. *This was not the cool cat she usually left behind. He was just a man, thin and gaunt and stripped naked by his real or imaginary assassins, trembling on the edge of the world with a ferocious wind blowing at his back.*

Four

VICTORIA HAD NOT YET DARED TO actually look into Francisco's mahogany armoire, the repository of his sketches, journals, family photographs, and other objects of comfort. In part, she was loathe to go through anyone's things—even a dead someone's, since death itself could be relative. Who's to say the survivor has not also died, while remaining visible to the surrounding eye.

Mostly, she had clung to the idea that as long as she didn't look, there was a mystic possibility that Francisco was simply hiding in the armoire, that he was there—at least his ethereal body, but still a solid presence—and watched her through one of the termite-treated panels from inside.

But this time she was looking for a special picture, one she had decided to e-mail Cooper if he ever asked about seeing her photograph again. She found a poem of Francisco's folded in the album where he kept her pictures. *Yo me recuerdo*—a long caption under Victoria's colorized sepia photograph, a baby picture taken by her father in 1970 with the old Hasselblatt he had managed to smuggle out of Cuba.

She wondered why Francisco had never shown her the poem but reasoned that he might have been intimidated. She was, after all, a celebrated poet. Then it struck her that the poem was not a poem, but her husband's way of crying on his pillow over what they had come to euphemize as her *situation*—Francisco called it *the* situation in order to avoid any finger-pointing on his part, and thus hold frigidity itself the culprit.

Not that she was frigid—*an absurd term for a warm-blooded mammal*—far from it. It was just that she found the moment of intimate surrender impossible to consummate with Francisco in the room. Still, he who was so deft a lover, so persistent, so patient and self-forgetting, had become overwrought with self-doubt over Victoria's inability to climax. Then, one day, perhaps by serendipity or by unconscious design, there had appeared a silver lining in the cloud, an unorthodox solution to their paradoxical problem.

One night, en route to the bathroom, after hours of intense and frustrated lovemaking, Francisco got a glimpse of his wife in the mirror. Unsheathed from the mummified state he had just left her. Prone. Tightened haunches, arched over a pillow. Legs spread eagle, luring the phantom lover. The neon sign across the street cast and magnified her shadow on the wall. Victoria aroused herself gently, more gently than he knew how. Her hand was long, thin—*a white gull's wing/ swooping over a bed of minuscule mollusks/ plucking and lifting the catch/ then plummeting again.*

Francisco reached for his empowered member—*a thick rhizome, obdurate, exacting like new growth.* Unwittingly, he began imitating Victoria's shadow play, keeping time to her doved hand, chasing as she parted her veneris, patterning his strokes on hers, feeling her sultry middle rise, arch, crest, succumb effortlessly to her silent bidding.

That night, Francisco felt the wonder of a woman's touch by his own hand. For the first time, after months of drought, he watched his wife climax. Her thunder was grave, pure, fierce—a pitch he'd never known in all six months of passionate pursuit. She whispered his name, and he understood she'd felt his presence—*Francisco, come here, come inside me, guapo!*

And so, the *situation* ceased for all intents and purposes—or at least became acceptable. For all six years of marriage until his death, they loved frequently—the Sag Harbor wharf under a harvest moon; the stenciled floor, across a stretched canvass where he later draped her torso; the kitchen counter, with her congenital dancer's legs coiled around his hairy middle. Francisco liked experimenting, dreaming up quixotic trysts—but perhaps that was merely a way of searching for *the key that would make his wife's surrender unequivocal/ pressed down and running over/ the way his Spanish soul demanded it/ like Rioja grapes bursting in the middle of his field.*

Still, they were fervent and passionate about one another. And yet, would he leave her for another? And if she really loved him, how could she possibly bar the most intimate, most precious gateway?

Once, he had asked what she fantasized about when he left the room. *You. About you,* she'd said and watched him wince. *Then, why? Then why not with me?*

Victoria had planned to explain someday. . . as soon as she was able to. It was part of the monthly inventory she kept, a *List of Matters to Deal With* that ranged from the banal to the fundamental, a spiral notebook where she marinated lines that later surfaced in her poetry. She had hoped to overcome the *situation* before having to discuss it, so as to speak of it in the past. *And now, as with so many things, too late the fallow rope.*

Victoria had had lovers, suitors, and paramours before him. With some, she actually forgot herself—three, to be precise. But all three had been strangers on the way to their real lives. An Israeli soldier on furlough at the King David Hotel in Jerusalem. He translated for her at the bar before he heard her impeccable modern Hebrew, learned in New York, at the synagogue on East Seventy-Sixth Street, where she was confirmed and where the same rabbi who had taught her the Israeli natural dialect ultimately refused to marry her and Francisco because he would not convert. *Convert from what? he said, anarchism?* The soldier never took off his boots and left almost as abruptly as he had arrived.

The second was a poet she had worshipped in her teen years, who answered the letter Sara made her send along with the eighteen poems that later became the yarn and spindle of her first anthology. *Eighteen is an important number in Judaism. Always send eighteen.*

This major poet, this man many years her senior, rotund from frequent visits to the Kleine Konditerei on the West Side, with chocolate stains on his tie and the wrinkled eyes of an earthen Buddha, became her mentor. He produced an agent, bequeathed her his publisher, and made love to her like clockwork, in silence, on the days he taught at Columbia—*sipping Jack Daniels from Viennese glasses/ under Miles Davis' undulating trumpet/ John Coltrane's seductive saxophone/ blowing Round Midnight or Stella By*

Starlight—between five and seven, twice a week, on his way to New Haven, where his wife of thirty years waited up in bed listening to Martha Argerich play Mozart.

Victoria thought she loved him then, but she was not yet twenty and years later reconsidered. *It was he, not me, who'd heard of love/ And when I had fully suckled, he weaned me, turned his gaze/ insisted I could fly/ loved me because/ I was his sporting kill/ and rather than cannibalize/ he chose to set me free.*

The third voyager had been a pale, sad, handsome Sicilian aristocrat, a character actor of fifty she met at Cine Città in Rome the year she went to Europe on a Guggenheim.

At age twenty-nine, as always, Victoria was a high-voltage beauty. *La Electrocutadora*—the *electric chair*—Francisco coined the term because he said no word previously conceived could describe her. Her rare genetic blend of ancient and modern civilizations at crossways had favored her with a flamenco dancer's body—firm, sinuous, perpetually tanned, the liquid color of *añejo* rum; fruitful breasts, as full, warm, and upright as scarlet Cuban frutabombas; copper-red, spiraling, electric hair; and a dazzling, exotic face—narrow, oval, *a Giotto virgin on a triptych*—with features at odds with one another and yet in perfect sync—large, concave Byzantine eyes, dark as chestnuts yet luminescent; small, pointed nose; broad, luxuriant lips, absorbing, perfectly contoured—*lips that always made him see her naked.*

The encounter with the Italian happened just two days before she met Francisco for the first time, at the Piazza di Spagna. The Italian—his name was Gino, or Gianni?—had, with hardly a suggestive or disrespectful gesture, propositioned her to come to his bachelor room on Via Margutta. She had agreed simply because she had not felt a man's body in months and because he seemed, in a word, *safe*.

He made love to her in satin black blindfolds, cross-dressed in a gold caftan that Elizabeth Taylor was said to have worn at Richard Burton's side during the filming of *Cleopatra*. The tiny room shook with a full production of *La Bohème* at La Scala. It was barely large enough to contain the rococo bed and the Bang and Olafson stereo he treasured *piu che la piu bella donna*.

She found his antics laughable. And yet, she was there, play-

ing a part in his ludicrous charade. And, *yes, yes, yes*, she came—
if not *for* him, certainly *with* him. How could she ever have
explained such a thing to Francisco, the one man she fell in love
with, fully conscious and all grown-up?

Perhaps it had been the anonymity or else the practical impos-
sibility of such liaisons that had freed her to give to others what
she could not give to her husband. Still, she repudiated the pat
psychobabble answers to complex questions. She cherished their
intimacy. She dreamt of their nights where *they lay intertwined like
orchids/ their airborne roots nourished by his breath.*

If there was a reason or at least an original cause that led to
this thing they had come to label her *situation,* she would have
guessed it had to do with the phobias she had been prey to since
childhood, courtesy of Roberto, while her parents labored at the
Galletas Factory under the belief that Victoria was safe in her
room, being read to by her brother. But that, in itself, did not
answer why or for how long—why her and how long before she
would cease suffering for her brother's sins? *Some questions have
no answers, the Talmud says.*

Victoria held Francisco's poem with both hands, read it again.
It was her fifth go-around, looking for hidden meanings, *spending
newly minted time with him, since the poem had, for an instant, defied
his death.*

It was not exactly a feeling of betrayal, but close. Surprise, too,
that Francisco would have kept a secret from her. Of course, again
she reasoned that his pride would have stood in the way of revealing this. *And he would have known that the poem, as poems go, was
derivative, unrestrained, ultimately submersible. All true lovers keep
secrets from each other and all true lovers who were ever false/ shed
but one tear for Cressida. Still, it hurt. And how well—or at all—does
one ever know another?* This was a subject she had meant to bring
up with Cooper—the keeping of secrets, lying by omission, the
tacit acceptance of little white lies within one's own fold.

Cooper:
    October morning, somewhere in time, in mezzo del camin di
    nostra vita . . .

Entry. . . . What? Predawn entry. I shall call this PREDAWN ENTRY, like those missiles they stick in the middle of the Nevada highways . . .

Dearest Unknown: Or shall I say most known, since you live in me because night and day it is you who roams freely about my thoughts, appearing at will with a sweet bluebird of happiness in your hand, even as I struggle to get the probate behind me . . . even when those vultures, Francisco's lawyers, insist that I join a class-action suit—and for what? Will American Airlines' filthy money resurrect the dead or hand me back a life I took for granted? And me, the woman you call Penelope, am I in your thoughts, too, as you go about your day—doing who-knows-what. . . . Are you a banker, a baker . . . perhaps a hermit like the Unibomber, disillusioned by illusions? What is your house like? Do you live in a cabin? Are you near my brother's winery in the mythical town of Santa Ynez with a "Y"? Are you as wide and long as a lumberjack with a full square jaw? Are you a dwarf, a paraplegic, an old man reinventing his life? Are you a young man, wise, as Solomon never was, pretty as a woman in disguise?

Perhaps I should begin with one of your prophets, St. Paul: To the unknown god whom I ignorantly worship . . . except, dear precious interlocutor of my sleepless nights, to me you are no god. But godly, yes. Your reassurances—especially last night's— are manna in the desert. I could not have dealt with my brother otherwise. I kept your words and the thoughts of you branded in my mind throughout the whole ordeal. I say branded and suddenly realize I must be predisposing my thought to Santa Ynez, where cows are probably branded between farms, ranches, and chaparral spaces . . .

Last night's message. The one I was too tired to answer: "You have refused to send me your picture or even give me a number where I can hear your voice."

Cooper:
For one so familiar with voices drowned by night, you know it is hard for me to imagine—or try to imagine your voice— because the hunger for the other makes me ravenous to hear him, not you. Does that arouse jealousy in you? I do sometimes

*feel jealousy when you mention her, your beloved, the one you
are probably writing to when you write me—as perhaps I do,
too, writing him but calling it you, affirming the two worlds
need not know of each other, that we can love the dead and yet
be intimate with the living without hint of betrayal, in parallel
existences, in past or future lives unseen, unknown to each other.*

Victoria read the message on the lithium screen and cringed.
It was not anything she was prepared to send him. She highlight-
ed the paragraphs and pressed delete with dispatch. She started
from scratch:

Dear Cooper:

*It was grueling, to say the least. So long since I spent so much
time with my parents, brother, and sister-in-law. Or anyone, for
that matter. There's always an underlying tension when all of us
get together—things we are allowed to mention and things we
can't, people we can bring up or can't. I guess it's partly being so
aware of who's NOT there. The tangible absence of my husband
and my older brother. But my brother's child is a joy—a most
unlikely joy. Deaf-mute, hydrocephalic. (A water head. Wouldn't
want to make you get the dictionary at this late hour. Do you
still write from bed?)*

*(I have to sit up to think straight.) I have been meaning to ask
you about you and MJ and whether you ever kept secrets from
one another. Just turned up something my husband wrote and
never showed me, so it's been on my mind. I mean, I wonder
sometimes how much we really know anybody at all, or if we are
all individually alone. . . . Did we make these people up? There
was a great Italian poet once . . . his name was Quasimodo . . .
Salvatore Quasimodo . . . you know, he won the Nobel Prize for
a single poem so short and yet so incredible . . . well, here, I will
translate . . . the poem said, "Each one is alone on the heart of
the earth/ pierced by a ray of sun/ and suddenly it's night." It
sounds much better in Italian.*

*My brother wants me to go to California to help him out with
one of his businesses—I should say his other business. He's a
physician. Owns a winery out there. We could finally meet,
Cooper, if it is true you live there. And yet, the very thought*

scares me witless. Right now you are my best friend, and I don't even know what you look like let alone what you're really like in the three-dimensional world. But I feel I know you better than I've known others because we really speak. I mean, we know what we are feeling, and what we are feeling is hard to describe to others who are not us.

Anyway, Cooper, I want to be up front about it because I may even go there and not see you—but still write you, even if you're only a few miles away. Does that sound wacky?

Dear Penelope:

Not wacky. Scared shitless, maybe. Yeah, I kept lots of secrets in my life. Most of the time because I learned that people don't like the sound of the truth. Survival mechanism. My old man used to tie one on once in a while, and he'd whip me good with that hard old leather belt of his if I as much as looked him crooked in the eye. I learned real fast not to ever say nothin' I didn't absolutely have to. Then, there's all these self-righteous asses in the world, no matter where you go, all the way from the Everglades to Alabama and clear out here to California, who decide they don't like the way you look or the way you live or who you love, you know, that sort of stuff. And too many crazies. Crazies are on the increase, as a matter of fact. So, you put it all together real quick and you get that old zip-the-lip disease. Pretty soon you get so comfortable with your cover-ups, you start believing them. Or part of you does. Then one day something happens and, say, you lose your mate or a child or something, and you realize it was all a bunch of hooey. I mean, who are we kidding? Like Popeye, remember? I am what I am and that's all I am. That's what I've told myself, anyway. If possible, I'm going to try to go after getting as honest as I can—but for myself, not for anyone else. So I figure it's my god-given right to lie as long as I have to, or at least not spill the beans just 'cause the other guy wants me to, because, you know, Penelope, in the end there's no one worth either lying or telling the truth for, 'cause something or someone will want to get you in the end. Look what the IRS did to Willy Nelson. . . . "Gotta be me," like ole blue eyes and the one-eyed guy used to sing. Both dead, too. All we got is us, right? Or however you say that.

Which reminds me. Sure, I still have to get up to look your big words up. Pretty soon the dictionary is going to run out of pages at the rate you're going. Wow. You must be some kind of big professor or something. That's how I figure you. So I'm thinking more like college. Have you guessed what I do for a living yet? Been giving you hints. Wanted you to guess. Wondered how you'll feel when you find out. How about my hair? I already guessed you've got red hair, the wild kind—and you didn't have to say it, so score one for Coop.

As far as secrets go, with MJ, too, we kept secrets, so don't feel bad about your husband (you called him that again). Well, maybe his name isn't F, anyway. I understand. Myself, I couldn't say MJ to strangers for a long time after she went. Afraid they'd take her from me, or what little of whatever of her I've got left, I guess, in some strange way.

So, yeah, I think it's pretty normal for people who love each other, I mean people who are together, not just kin, to keep a few secrets. As long as they're not bad secrets, I mean, like fooling around stuff. Most of the time, I reckon we just do it 'cause we're afraid the other person won't like us anymore if they find out. But see, with us, Penelope, being that we started off at the bottom, it sort of doesn't bother me. I mean, the worst has already happened to us, right? So, I think there's a better way. My grandma used to call it shooting straight from the hip. Did you ever hear that old song about "freedom's just another word for nothing left to lose"? Girl who sang it, she used to have red hair, too. Died of an overdose.

*So here I go. Been saving the best for last. What! *&%!!!! You think you might be coming to Santa Ynez?! Your brother has a winery here? What winery? You'd rather not say? That's cool. But if you do, I sure as H would love to know. There's better than a Chinaman's chance I know it.*

And, like I said earlier, it's not that I think you're wacky if you come and don't see me, even though we spend half the night writing back and forth to each other (don't tell Momma). It's just that I've been thinking on my own that, well, I sure would be glad to meet you for real. Not that this isn't real.

*And, as a matter of fact, something really weird came up yes-
terday. Turns out I may have to go to New York to fill in for one
of the guys who works New York. It hit me like a ton of bricks
because I've been thinking about New York and visiting you and
then pow, out of the blue comes this call. It's the first time the
boss ever asked me to go east of the Rockies, so it felt like, you
know, some sort of omen or something. What do you think?
Another thing: can you get AOL Instant Messenger so we can
talk real-time instead of e-mailing back and forth? They got a
new thingamajig now where people can see each other, too.
Cooper*

*PS: That poem was dynamite in a way, but a little too down,
'cause maybe it ain't necessarily so. That dead one-eyed guy I
mentioned before, he sang that, too.*

Cooper:

*I think you have to take back a phrase you just used before I
write again. It's bigoted and incredibly stupid, and I can't believe
you used it. It makes me furious. Penelope*

Dear Penelope:

*Whoa! Something I said? Are we having our first fight and we
ain't even seen each other once? Okay. What phrase? I'll take it
back if I have to. Confused.*

Cooper:

*It's a prejudiced remark against the Chinese. If you want to
know the origin, it meant that Chinese Americans had no chance
of becoming citizens during most of this century. So that kind of
chance was no chance at all—which is what you meant, right?
In a kind of roundabout way. Penelope*

Dear Penelope:

*Wow. That's awesome. I didn't even know it had anything to
do with Chinese people. What a dumbo. Had no idea what Chinaman meant in there. Just something I picked up somewhere, I
guess. Glad you told me. I'm not a bigot, even if I am probably
something of a hick by your standards. My grandma taught me
that everyone's God-made and, anyway, Penelope, I know what*

*prejudice is like. I'll tell you someday. So, I take it back. You're
not Chinese, are you?*

Cooper:
  No, not Chinese. Jewish. Cuban-American. You?

Dear Penelope:
  *Christian. No denomination. No church. No rules. Nature
lover. White. Widowed. Not bad looking. Good heart. Strong
hands. Good aim with a rifle. Not a baby boomer. Not a gener-
ation alphabet soup. Somewhere in the middle. No drugs, just
hooch. Jack Daniels if I can be choosy. Maybe you folks call me
Gentile—at least that's what some people I work with call me,
but they say no offense. So, what do you say?*

Cooper:
  *Okay, you wise guy. That was funny. And BTW, I don't think
you're a hick at all. Have no idea what you do. Sure you want
me to know? I didn't mean we shouldn't keep secrets from each
other. It's different with us. In a way, secrets are good. Don't think
I could have trusted writing you about F and everything else I
rant about in the middle of the night if I didn't feel anonymous
in some strange way. The thought that you might be coming to
NY makes me glad, but also a little farmisht (don't bother to
look it up in your dictionary. It's Yiddish for befuddled. Befuddled is something akin to weirded out. . . . You mind if we think
this over? About meeting, I mean.*
  *PS: No AOL thingamajig. E-mail via carrier pigeon goes fast
enough. Sometimes a girl needs time to think at center court.*
Penelope

Dear Penelope:
  *What if I just surprise you? I mean what if I just e-mail you
telling you I'm at a corner bar somewhere in the Big Apple? Is Central Park still there? May be better than a bar. Say by that big fountain where you cross from the West Side to the East Side, around
Seventy-Second Street? Wouldn't you come down to meet me?*

Cooper:
  Since we're playing Tell the Truth, I should probably be hon-

est and answer probably. I'll sleep on it. You too. Good nite.

PS: You hadn't mentioned you'd been to NY. You know that fountain, eh? Bethesda Fountain is the one you mean. Funny you picked that out of the blue. It used to be one of my favorite places growing up. Used to beg my parents to take me there whenever they brought us into the city. Remember the boathouse? The lake? There's a willow tree right on the water's edge with my brother's handiwork all over it. Or I should say his gaping hole. It was still there the last time I looked, a couple of years ago. We should have known he was going to be a surgeon. Instead of carving a heart or some girl's name, he just gouged a chunk right out of it and wrote his own name. David, my older brother, was incensed. He loved trees and nature and all sentient beings. I think he'd probably be working for Green Peace or some such group if he were here. He really got mad at my brother for that. Told him if he ever found him doing something like that again, he'd turn him in to the cops.

Dear Penelope:

Only been to NY twice in my life and it wasn't real good. MJ was from there. Didn't I tell you? She wanted to go back when she took ill. Wanted to see her folks on the upper West Side of town. Matter of fact, that's where she x-ed. Swore I'd never set foot in that place again (no offense to your city).

Cooper:

Sorry about that. I know how that goes. I'll never fly out of La Guardia or JFK again. Good thing there's Newark Airport or I'd be stuck.

PS: My brother's child is coming to stay with me all weekend. I think my brother may be trying to bribe me because he knows B and I hit it off. He really wants me to go to California. Funny. You may come here and I may go there. There's a writer I like a lot who calls this kind of synchronicity "patterning." His name is Nabokov. Did you ever hear of him?

Dear Penelope:

Say, I like that! Patterning . . . I'm guessing like lots of colors that blend together. What's synchronicity? Don't know the writer, but think I heard the name somewhere. Coop

Dear Cooper:

Look it up. Good night, knight.

Five

IT HAD BEEN SO LONG SINCE DAVID had tasted game or papayas or
water that didn't taste like sewage. He was a large man, with muscles like twisted hemp across his arms and shoulders and eyes the
color and density of crystal aquamarine. The stranger at his side
could tell he was not long on words. And, because her profession
made her unusually perceptive, she guessed that this man of middle years, dressed in a Cuban guerilla uniform, had spent a good
portion of his days crouched in a two-by-two cell, straining his
nose through a crack in the fortress walls and bathing in the
humid loam of mint-green tobacco fields that were once his—or,
at the very least, were his because he and his class were privileged
to live within the gates.

But Dolores was probably less intrigued by the fact that she
was certain her visitor was dressed in a uniform belonging to a
young soldier he had probably targeted at close range with a blast
to the head, than by the idea that this man, this handsome man of
trenchant features as imposing as a marble Zeus, endowed with a
penis so long and girthed and ardently strapping, had never been
with a woman before. Or if he had, it had most likely been furtive
and fleeting, perhaps through a hole in the prison wall, and not
long or tender or amorous, as she had been instructed to provide
for him on the day he knocked on her door and whispered his
code name: *David Ben Gurion, Mitzvah Brigade*.

Not that Dolores Calderín y Echemendia would have a clue
who David Ben Gurion was. Still, she had an innate intelligence,
this brown sugar *goyeh* of high, imperative breasts and hourglass
curves that David had hooked and moored for hours until at last
all virtue had vanished from him and he fell asleep on her nipples

like a nursing babe.

For years, he had dreamt of holding a woman like Dolores, arousing her with his unquenchable sorrow and longing, lying down by the still waters of her untroubled self and returning through her to the person he used to be, before the *milicianos* ambushed him with a fishing net.

The guards didn't let him keep the magazine that Felipe, his second cell mate, had left behind the day the brigade leader drowned him in a hole of liquified pig shit. That would have been 1984, he thought, and the magazines had pictures of papaya-breasted girls with *mamey* lips and soft rosettes that looked like Dolores. They left newsprint on his tongue, turned his peter into a silver snapper wrapped in parchment, made him weep with loneliness once his seed spilled along his chest and navel.

And on this day, on his forty-second birthday, he would be rewarded with a double *mitzvah*. He would be liberated from the dark cell he'd come to know as home, and he would lie with a woman, a pretty woman, one that looked just like the ones he'd loved in the magazines for most of his reproductive years. And he would fuck her until his hunger and his anger and his unbearable desire to dissolve into a universe of stars were quenched, and she would not vanish nor tell him to stop nor offer resistance to his persistent member. Her legs would open wide, and she would crave his manhood with fullness, fierce and fearless and eternal.

He was a silent lover who needed to mount her with the full length and breath of his weight and look deep into her eyes without so much as flickering or tightening a single muscle on his chiseled cheeks. His fervor seemed reserved for the massive member and *toro* balls that struck against her buttocks, opened and plunged deep in her until her immeasurable pleasure gave way to excruciating and then delectable pain, and blood spilled under them in a long, thin river, staining the sheets she had bleached for their tryst, signifying that a virgin no longer resided at 2833 Calle Galiano.

They stretched against the headboard, legs apart, letting the ceiling fan caress them, his arm a vice around her neck, her freshly manicured nails grooming the thick raspberry hair across his chest and middle. She had kept the only LP record she possessed playing full blast—a vinyl Celia Cruz: *Amalia Batista/ Amalia Bay-ombe/ Qué tiene esa negra/ Que amarra a los hombres*—and now the music became audible again.

"Oye, señor . . . de ve'da' que me quita'te la vi'jinida' . . ." He had grown used to her Spanish in prison. *Maid Spanish.* Clipped, high-pitched, elliptical, spirited like Andalusian flamenco dancers. *Mr. did you know you took my virginity . . .*

"Fat chance," he said smiling. "I bet you don't actually remember who took your virginity, do you? How old were you, fourteen?"

Dolores bolted straight up, a cat electrified against a high prison wall. She stood over him, planted one strong, prehensile foot on his chest, unfurling her head of curls, glaring at him with both hands on her hips, impersonating a fully dressed fishwife, ready to haggle with street vendors along the Plaza de la Catedral.

"Whoa! What's that for?!" He slipped out from under her.

"What it's for is that *sinvergüenza* of Manolo didn't tell you, did he . . . that son of a . . . he didn't tell you! He kept it all to himself to make me the laughingstock!"

David pulled her down on him, slid her breasts flat against his nipples. He put a finger to her lips and grinned. It might have seemed incredible to someone else that this man who held her in his arms would be capable of smiling, but not to Dolores, who believed in miracles. This man, this stranger, this sudden lover who had almost rotted his whole life in jail, who ate feces and drank urine and was forced to perform circumcisions without anesthesia or even a shot of wine—and to perform them on grown men, *gusanos,* whose next punishment would be castration, and then finally to watch helplessly, gagged and tethered, while brutes and donkeys and trained goats mounted their wives and mothers on a makeshift stage for all the guards to gape at and laugh at and clap. This man, this stranger who had appeared at her door and spent half the day inside her, making love to her like a lover because he'd never had a lover . . .

"What is it that *so and so son of a son and so on* didn't tell me, *Dolores de amores,* that made you as jumpy as a jumping bean?" Again, the grin.

"¡Esos descarados!" she blurted out. "They didn't tell you I was

a virgin! They said I was a whore, right? Is that what they told you? Those *hijos de la gran puta!"*

David's aqua eyes grew overcast. He drew his face in like a sail. "They didn't tell you, right? They didn't tell you I was a virgin!"

David sat up, covering his middle with the bloodstained sheets. Dolores rolled on her side and looked away, facing the wroughtiron balcony where she had hung the wash.

"Dolores. Why?"

"Why what?"

"Why did you do it? Why did you accept giving yourself for the first time to a stranger?"

"Seems weird, right?"

"Yes."

"Something only a whore would do, right?"

"Yes. At least you might have told me."

"Well, my mother was a whore because that's what she had to do to feed us when we were standing in those food lines where in the end there was no food, just rationed slop, while the Czechs with their thin mustaches and the Russians reeking brine and sweat passed by in their limousines, chewing sausages as fat as their stubby fingers, and drinking vodka in fancy glasses and offering food . . . in trade. So, maybe if my mother was a whore, then that makes me a whore, and Manolo was right to pull the big joke on me!"

He had split her in two like a fruit, like one of the girls in his magazines—the magazines the guards at Guanacabibes ultimately made him chew and swallow without a sip of water. All at once, he saw her for the young girl of twenty that she was. *Was she really twenty? Could she be fifteen instead, and unusually ripened?* She could have been his daughter. A daughter he unwittingly defiled.

David would keep his own counsel. No need to explain that although the Talmud might hold him blameless in this instance, he held himself accountable. No need to betray that he accepted this gift from the brigade because Dolores was a Gentile, and preferably a whore, although one whose hygiene could be vouched for.

Dolores watched him fold inward like night-blooming jasmine. He closed his eyes, turned his back to her.

"Oh, don't feel bad, *señor*," she rested her head on his shoulders and crisscrossed her arms.

"Don't call me *señor* . . . please."

"What do I call you? I know you won't give me your real name."

"Melech, call me Melech."

"What's that? Doesn't sound Russian."

"It's Hebrew for king."

"King? You want me to call you king? Wow, that's even more stuck up than *señor*, if you don't mind my saying so, *señor*."

"Don't call me *señor*, please! And Melech is a good code for my real name. Maybe I can tell you some other day."

"Fat chance."

"Why do you say that?"

"Because we both know you're hauling your ass out of here this very day, and you're going out there to some foreign land, and you're never going to set foot in this place again. And me, I'm going to stay here with all the rest of the *desgraciados* till the *caballo* croaks or some American president finds out where he dropped his balls."

"Fair enough. But you still didn't answer me, Dolores. Why did you do it? I've been too . . . well, too out of it, out of the stream of life . . . certain things that may seem normal to you may not make sense to me. . . ."

"I don't know."

"You don't know? You agreed to have a stranger come to your bed and deflower you without even a tender word . . . And you don't know why?"

"It's not like that, *señor*. I mean, *merengue* or whatever you called yourself, king. I accepted because Manolo told me they had treated you really bad up there in Guanacabibes and you were going to fight for justice, for all of us. . . . And, well, I guess I wanted to contribute something to the *revolución* . . . I mean the real *revolución*, the one that's going to give us clothes and something to eat and medicines and a new record player and those tiny records the Spanish tourists carry around in their sacks."

"Dolores! Are you saying that you did it for the *revolución* or that you did it for no reason at all?"

"You're like a mad scientist or something, king. Don't you know several things can be true at once? Like knowing something and yet not knowing it?"

"I know about that."

"I meant, even though I did do it because I wanted it to count for something, I also wanted to give it to somebody who hated the *caballo* and his people, and not to some dumb *miliciano* who would just come in here one day with his rifle and filthy green underwear and decide he'd like me over my mother or something. . . . This way, even if some dumb *miliciano* does come and take me, at least he doesn't take-me-take-me. He can't boast he gave me bloody sheets . . . like this, see?"

"I see."

It was the way he felt, the reason he had endured those years in isolation, rehashing how a simple *mitzvah*, a simple act of charity, had gone awry, wondering why his family could not help, and ultimately believing that even his mother had abandoned him. He would not be defiled. He would survive, if only to deny his executioners the satisfaction of buckling under their filthy feet.

"But maybe you don't see," said Dolores, looping her fingers on his chest, stirring him with her gossamer, imprecise touch.

"Oh? I think I do."

"Okay, you do. But maybe not the whole thing . . . the reason why I said I didn't know why in the first place."

"Then tell me." He faced her, suckling her lips, harnessing his hardened member, easing it between her legs, swelling, jimmying its aching, circumcised head in once again.

"I don't know . . . because I let God tell me when I should do things . . . when to say yes and when to say no. And today I said yes. And that's the part I don't know why." She held up her end of the conversation *in flagrante coitus* like a seasoned consort.

"I see. I see! I really see! *Bashert! Bashert zein!*"

"What's that? It's not Russian."

He laughed.

"Not every strange sound is Russian, *Dolores de amores*." He was feeling his way inside her now, pulling her to him around the waist, pushing gently, the way he would have earlier, had he known she was a *señorita,* scattering her petals once again, this time deliberately.

"What does it mean, those words you said?"

"*Bashert?* It means fate, *bashert zein,* to be fated. It's Yiddish. Jewish."

"Exactly. Fate. I believe in that. *El hombre propone y Dios dispone.* I skip the first part and let Him decide without giving Him trouble or contradicting him. Just let Him dispose. Know what I mean?"

Again, he laughed. This time, feeling a double joy, fucking her differently, fervidly, for the first time.

"Yes. I believe that, too . . . and I believe in this, whatever this thing is you make me feel. . . . And I, do I do the same to you?"

"Oh, yeah. For sure. Feels great. You must be a great lover. I mean, even though it's my first time, I know you must be a great lover."

"Great lover? Where did you hear that phrase?"

"My mother. She says that to the Russians. Or she did. Now she says it mostly to the Gallegos from Spain and the pink-faced Canadians and even the communist *Yanquis* who come here and no one stamps their passports."

Dolores had suddenly taken the initiative. She had rolled over, straddling him, pushing herself up with both arms, her full, pendulous breasts brushing against his face and lips, taking him in like a deep breath, stroking the full length of his shaft.

"It's you. You're the great lover, *amores,*" he whispered, letting himself go, releasing his seed with a sharp quiver, fingering the unfamiliar stream flooding his eyes, rolling down his cheeks, licking her mouth. Dolores surged and pressed against his thigh and ravished sex like an aftershock, reverberating, ricocheting, and finally impaling herself on the man who would always be her first lover.

They had a brief afterglow, a little death before the white-knuckle knock they'd been listening for. He leapt out of bed, reached for his uniform, cocked his loaded Glock. She motioned him to calm down, batting both arms down. *No hay peligro.* Don't get so fussed, you're safe here. . . .

"It must be the guy . . . you know. The guy who's supposed to take you . . . away."

He nodded, smiled apologetically. How could he explain he had lived so much of his life looking for executioners in the shadows, shadowboxing walls and stagnant air.

"Let me wash up. And you, Dolores, get dressed," he whispered. "Tell him just a minute, will you?"

She nodded, stood up, her body firm, voluptuous like the girls in the magazines, only infinitely more so.

"Be right with you!" she chimed in the direction of the door, which was barely five feet from the bed in the tiny, turn-of-the-century subdivided apartment on Galiano and San Rafael, right in the heart of downtown and only a few blocks from La Habana Vieja, the old part of Havana, which had reminded him of Wall Street on the way in, with narrow cobbled streets, gaslights, and street vendors. La Habana, so beautiful once, was now a tarnished whore, peeling, unpainted, dying of neglect.

"No *problema*," said the accented American voice on the other side.

Their eyes remained fixed on each other as they dressed, he in the dead soldier's uniform and Dolores in a sleeveless print that cupped her breasts and clung to her with static electricity.

"You know him?" he whispered. He didn't want the man to hear him until he had a chance to check him out.

"I've seen him a few times. Works for Manolo. So I guess he works for your people. My mother calls him 'The Shadow' because all he does is come down and take people out, but he never hangs around long enough to finish a cup of three-cent coffee."

"So you're saying he's never, you know, been to see your mother?"

"No. Definitely no. She says she's not sure if he even likes women."

"Right. Well, it's probably better if he keeps a low profile. The walls have eyes, no?"

"That's for sure. Everybody's watching. Even when they let you get away with things and maybe they even know there's something illegal going on, but they are still watching. It's just that they decide to let it go for one reason or another."

Again, the same lilt and manner of the nannies and servants at his parents' house. Any of them, but particularly one whose name he could no longer remember because it had all happened so long ago, light years before he got ambushed, thrown in jail, and sentenced to labor camp.

"Guess you better let him in," he said. They were washed and dressed—if splashing soapy water on your face and privates from a tin bowl constituted washing.

"What's his name? Do you know?" he whispered.

"Yeah," she whispered back, "it's a real Yanqui name. Manolo calls him *Cúper*. He says he's a famous actor, *Garry Cúper*. I never heard of him. Did you?"

He smiled, prodding her gently toward the door.

"Hi. Please to meet you. Cooper, right? I'm your man."

"Figured."

Cooper was a head shorter than David, and at least ten years his junior, with strawberry-blond hair that instantly reminded him of his sister, Victoria, whose book of poems the guards had also made him rip with his front teeth and swallow dry a page at a time.

David scanned his face, his eyes, his round shoulders, and unusually light frame for a man in his line of business. There was something about this Cooper. Something. Face as smooth as a baby's bottom. Bones small for a man his height. A carefully modulated, slightly southern voice, pitched purposely low and yet not resonant.

"Would you like a cup of coffee?"

"Oh, no thanks, *gracias*," he answered in English. "Fact is, there's an earlier transfer, and we gotta make hay while the sun is shining. Got to make it to Caibarién in under two hours." He had spoken for his man's benefit. Dolores did not understand a word of English, although she got the gist.

"So, you have to go now," she said, avoiding eye contact with David for fear of making a fool of herself.

"Guess so," he answered, eyes fixed on the scuffed tile floor.

"Well," said Cooper, "I got a green Chevy parked in a safe zone around the corner. Boss wants me to swing by quick for you and lock you in the trunk till we hit the coast. Yael Herzog is our captain today. We'll be going in her boat. Think you can handle the trunk part? I'll stop from time to time to let some fresh air in. Boss figures it's safer this way."

"I guess so," he answered. He no longer suffered from claustrophobia as he had during the first years of incarceration, when the sound of his own breathing scared him. "I'd prefer to lie on the floor. That's what I did this morning when we made the break. Manolo drove me all the way here. . . . You think there would be a problem?"

"Never know," said Cooper, "but we can give it a go. So far so good. Fifty-five round trips and the suckers don't even know I exist. I'll bring the car around. Need to have you waiting downstairs, though, ready to make a dive for the floor as soon as I open the door and cover for you. There's a blanket you can duck under till we're out of the last *reparto*. That okay?"

"That's fine."

"Where are you going?" Dolores asked David, knowing that just as he could never give her his real name, he couldn't betray his plans. She had often watched Manolo and her mother hide *gusanos* in their underground railroad and then turn them loose to shadow men like Cooper, who whisked them away into oblivion.

"*Aliya*," he answered.

"*Aliya*," she repeated. "Is that a country or a city?"

"Both," he said. "It's the promised land."

"I think that's enough, sir, if you don't mind." Cooper tapped the toe of his cowboy boot on the floor.

"Right," David said, "sorry."

"Does that mean I'll never see you again, king?"

"No. It doesn't. It means I have to take care of some unfinished business. Go a couple of places. Start working and studying. Living. Mostly living."

"Will you come back for me?" Dolores was breaking all the rules. Manolo had warned her. Her mother had been against this arrangement. But Dolores was sure she could handle it. She had given them her word.

People come and people go—that's how Manolo put it—*and we stay. So we can't give a flying fuck about them as people. They are soldiers. Pawns. Strangers who help us in our cause and throw a few American dollars our way so we can stay afloat till the monster dies of old age or one of his mistresses rams a cigar down his throat and chokes him.*

"I'll be back for you, *Dolores de mis amores*. But it may be a long time. Maybe you'll get tired of waiting . . . so maybe it'd be better not to wait. . . ."

"Never," she said. "I'll wait. *Ahora y siempre*. Now and forever."

Cooper kept to himself the first half of the trip, and David fell asleep within minutes of departure for a destination so secret that not even Cooper had been fully briefed. It was the Ben Gurion Mitzvah Brigade's way of running a tight ship during rescue missions that demanded split-second decisions and the kind of loyalty no single human was capable of. No one soldier was ever given the full plan. No real names. No meticulous plan or itinerary. Each man or woman was a link in a relay race leading only to Nisan Ben Nivas, the Brigade's mastermind.

Ben Nivas had disappeared since starting the organization five years earlier. It was rumored that he had undergone plastic surgery so thorough that even his own grown children would not recognize him if they saw him. As a pilot in the Israeli Air Force, he had flown hundreds of rescue missions, from Entebbe to Iraq, Argentina, Russia, and South Africa. Now, as a civilian and highly decorated retired general, he continued his underground commissions around the world, wherever a Jew committed to *Aliya* was unjustly imprisoned or detained.

David had grown accustomed to sleeping wherever it was safe, and the floor of an old Chevy that qualified as an antique was as good as the dirt and brick floors he had slept on for the past eighteen years in the company of small brown mice and flying cockroaches. He had hundreds of questions for his guide, this man Cooper with hair like Victoria's, except it was buzzed tight around the ears. But he had learned to wait. There would be world enough and time to look for a million answers that had haunted him for eighteen years.

"Say, that was pretty risky what you did back there with that girl."

Cooper's modulated voice startled him like the guards with their pointed Russian rifles did whenever he was taken to the Interrogation Tower.

"What do you mean?" He attempted to focus as he climbed up onto the back seat.

"Don't get up yet! We've got about another twenty miles before we're in the clear. . . ."

"Okay. By the way. My name is David, Cooper. Didn't want to mention it back there."

"I know. David. That's what I meant about being a little risky. We have orders from the Cap not to mention any sort of name or destination, not even to people who work for us here, like Manolo and this girl Dolores and her mother. . . . It's tough what you've been through. The Boss briefed me yesterday. Man. Eighteen years, huh? Eighteen fucking years in this cesspool."

"Yeah. Maybe some of it won't sink in till later."

"That's exactly right. I've seen it happen. I've seen the glacier take years to melt . . . and, man, when it melts, watch out for the flood. Takes a whole mountain and ten houses on top of Malibu with it right into the Pacific Ocean. Happened to me once, though not the same as you and the others I've helped out of here. But that anger was real. Whew! Makes you want to punch through walls and shoot a whole fucking magazine into a hamburger joint full of strangers."

"I hope it's just because you're younger than me, Cooper. I never cared for fighting. If I had stayed angry, I don't think the two of us would be here today. The frustration alone would have killed me. Maybe . . . I hope I'm not one of those people you mentioned, the ones with the glacier flash floods. . . . Wasted enough time already . . . "

"You're probably right. You probably worked a lot of it out back there in Guanacabibes. That's where they stuck you, right? I've transferred a few people from there. Men and women. Some of them said all they'd eaten in twenty years was rice and beans. Tortured them, too, the bastards. One of them, a fellow who used to be a lawyer, they gouged his eyes out with a meat hook of some sort. You're lucky they didn't hack you, too. Bastards. Saw them shoot a pregnant woman once, back in Camagüey Province. They performed a caesarian right on the street, right where the bullets had ripped her open, and stole the kid, the fetus. Maybe for parts, like one of these crazy automobiles they got down here. Museum pieces from the 1950s. Bastards."

"Yeah." David had made a covenant with himself. If he ever got out alive, he would bury that part of his life the next day, as one would a cadaver according to Jewish law, sit *shiva* for the prescribed seven days, and only visit his memories once a year on the *yortseit* of his escape.

"So, sir, about you and the girl back there, I just wanted to say that there's gonna be plenty of girls, but that you're gonna have to hang cool till you get the lay of the land, no pun intended . . . you know, like a sailor who's been away from land and starts seeing mermaids riding dolphins and falls in love right and left, doesn't know which ass to grab first. . . . Like I said, plenty of girls, but we can only marry one. Least one at a time. You with me back there, David?"

"Yeah."

"Good. It's hard in the beginning. God knows I've seen this in the five years I'm in this line of work. Before then, too, in the infantry in El Salvador, right before the fall. But most of those guys I worked the jungle with came away real messed up. Still run into a couple of them now and then, walking the streets around the town where I live, or down in Santa Barbara, where the rich folk play nice, meandering in La-La Land, yelling at the air in all that filthy hair, seeing pink raccoons and stuff. Though for Jewish people, it's different. Most do pretty good, especially the ones who just want to go over there to Haifa or Elat and settle. They get families right away. Everyone over there acts like they're family, and that's what I figure keeps them from going over the rainbow when they come out.

"Or maybe it's something else. Maybe it's their faith. For me, my anger kept me from flying over the cuckoo's nest. I figured I needed me if I was going to get some justice and give some justice to whomever had it coming, if you know what I mean."

"That's good. So you're not Jewish?"

"No. But I . . . well. Everybody's got their little piece of real estate in hell, anyway, Jewish or not. My girlfriend's Jewish, though. And I've been to Israel eighteen times and counting."

"*Mazel tov.* She's a nice girl, your girlfriend?"

"Yeah. Real nice. Smart as blazes. Gotta look up every other word she writes me."

"She's away?"

"Lives in New York. Me in Santa Ynez, in California. The Lompoc Valley, we call it."

"Yes, I know it. Had just been offered a job a few miles north, up near San José, when I took a wrong turn and wound up here."

"No kidding? That sucks."

"Do you know anything about my family? Are you the one who's going to be briefing me?"

"No, sir, I'm not. That would be Yael, your transport today. But the Cap has this whole procedure. Decompression, he calls it. Says a man needs a cool head to handle a hot dog, so whatever it is you need to do or find out about, they're going to give it to you easy. Ever been to one of those health spas . . . I mean before you wound up here?"

"No. I was only twenty-two."

"Well, I think you're in for a whole lot of fun, more fun than a barrel of monkeys. Believe Yael is going to be taking you to one of them. Put you through a whole bunch of medical tests, you know, like they do to astronauts who've been to Mars or something. Get you in shape first. Eventually, you might be doing this sort of thing I do myself, unless you're a specialist in some field or something. Are you?"

"Rabbi."

"Really? That's cool. You took a correspondence course in jail? The rotten skunks let you do it?"

"Not exactly. But yes, you could say that. *A correspondence course.* Funny. Your boss, I guess he's your boss, he's getting me into rabbinical school."

"Cool. Reform?"

"Yeah. Reform. You know from Reform? Your girlfriend has been teaching you things, eh?"

"Not my girlfriend. I knew that way before her. Learned it from my wife. She passed away, my wife. She was Jewish, too. But her folks were Orthodox. Threw a fit when she married me, but later on they all made up, and her dad, he said I was okay for a *klainer gornisht.* Know what that means?"

"Yeah. Pretty good for a little prig. Know any other Yiddish words?"

"A few. MJ—that's my wife—she spoke it, or at least understood most of it. Grandma was from Poland. Came during the
Hitler war. . . . You know what, sir? Glad to hear the scumbags
didn't kill your sense of humor. You look in real good shape to
me. . . . Other guys I helped pull out ain't so lucky . . . you should
see them. The walking dead."

"I've seen them."

"Yeah, I can just picture it. Last time I came down here, the
guy couldn't even open his mouth to talk. He was scared anything
he said would trigger a butt in the head or something. . . . Guys
back at home base told me he went totally dumb after that . . .
never spoke another word again . . . and he was a fine lawyer, too,
or so they told me. . . . Said they beat the guy and worked him over
so bad, there wasn't a clean spot on his body. Had scars on top of
scars. . . . They worked you pretty bad, too, no doubt. . . ."

"I got a few scars, too. . . . few broken parts here and there . . ."

"You hurting?"

"Yeah. You learn to live with it . . . bastard . . . a bastard kicked
my guts in . . . can't think about it right now. Want to look out.
Can I look now?"

"Not yet. Gotta keep it airtight here. All kinds of *milicianos*
snooping around, where you least expect them. . . . I swear I've seen
them crawl out of the bushes . . . sneak by under your feet . . ."

"Cockroaches."

"Yeah. Worst kind. Palmetto bugs, kind that can fly . . . that's
what my grandma calls this kind of vermin, palmetto bugs. She
lives in Florida, so you could say she has a special kind of feeling
for them . . . like fear and loathing."

"Say, Cooper, speaking of family, any idea about my family . . .
you know what happened? Got any idea who double-crossed me?"

"No sir, I don't. That would be Yael and the Cap. I call him the
Cap. He laughs. Should call him the General, he says. . . . You
heard what he did back in Entebbe, right?"

"I'm not sure."

"Nobody told you about him? I mean, when the Cap original-
ly got word to you in the camp?"

"No. It was tight in there. Couldn't trust anybody. I just got
word from one of the guards that someone knew about me and

that they were coming for me. I thought he meant someday, and it turned out to be the very next morning. This morning."

"Real rough getting out, huh?"

"Dug a hole under the wire with my bare hands and made a run for Manolo's truck when the guard gave me the signal. Unfortunately, I had to take a fellow, another guard. A Fidelista."

"Yeah. I've had to take a few myself. One less."

"Say . . . Cooper? That's your name, right?"

"Yes, sir. Friends call me Coop. Except my girlfriend. She likes the whole name. You can call me Coop if you'd like."

"So, Coop, I have a question for you. Why do you do this? It's a dangerous profession."

"Yeah. You can say that again. Guy before me got blown up by a hand grenade in the middle of the ocean, in U.S. territorial waters, ironically. . . . The grenade had some sort of time release device . . . and the courier before that got his cock sliced in a meat grinder 'cause he wouldn't squeal, wouldn't spill the transport's coordinates they were after. But the truth is he didn't know. We just know what the Cap wants us to know, but these meatheads down here, they don't get it. And they shoot you just the same if they feel like it, so it's better not to know. At least we keep someone else alive."

"Not all meatheads. Most of them aren't. Just not able to fight back. I was born here, did you know? Not far from here, I guess. In Miramar. Are we going to be driving by there? I was only a year old when my parents got out, so I just know Miramar from black-and-white pictures . . . didn't get a chance to visit when I got down here. . . . *Milicianos* were waiting for me and the rabbi I came down to get . . . think they were expecting us . . . hell."

"I heard Havana used to be paradise. I've seen pictures, too. Limestone palaces, wide boulevards, beautiful girls, music. Now look at it. The armpit. Only cool thing's the old cars, but tell you the truth, they sicken me, too. Collector cars. But look at them. Run worse than rules."

"I wish I could look. All I see is tops of buildings and blue sky."

"Well, keep on not looking. Just passed a gang of them a minute ago. Toting their toys. Only reason we got past them is 'cause someone back at the head office greased their paws. That's another great thing about the Cap. He knows how to grease them. They think I'm a gunrunner or drug dealer for the *caballo*. They have no clue what kind of cargo I got with me this time. . . . Wouldn't want to see their faces if they knew I was driving straight to a submarine."

"Wow, a submarine? Is that how the Mitzvah is getting me out of here, in a submarine?"

"Yes, sir. Did you hear of the Tekuma or the Dolphin and the Leviathan?"

"No."

"Well, let's just say they're what you'd call luxury subs. Made in Israel."

"Amazing. You're getting me out of here in a submarine?"

"Yeah. Whatever works at the time. Back in June, the Cap got one of you out on water skis, right under Fidel's nose, at some country club. Got word that Yael will be your transport today. Don't know what she looks like. Never laid eyes on her . . . I just take you to Caibarién, drop you off at the pier, then the Brothers pick me up and I'm on my way back home, via Air Canada. . . ."

"The brothers?"

"Yeah, Hermanos al Rescate, Brothers to the Rescue . . . Cuban American ace flyers . . . they work tight with the Cap . . . that's how come he recruited me. I just happened to be doing a small job for them, driving a wine truck . . . and just found myself helping one of them out, a total fluke . . . and, well, you could say the rest is history. Going on five years now. "

"How come the Israelis recruited you?"

"Just lucky, I guess."

"What else?"

Cooper laughed, covering his mouth, mindful that he had to look alone in his car.

"So you're not a coward. What else?" David joked.

"Yes, sir, like I said, you're gonna do just fine . . . probably up on your feet and walking around like nothin' happened . . ."

"Wouldn't be so sure . . . but that's nice of you, Coop. Bastards tore me up pretty good. . . ." David shot up his arm from the floor of the back seat, displayed the charred and punctured flesh from fingers to elbow. "Got a few others like this, only inside, gut . . ."

"Bastards." Cooper shook his head. "But keep it down, sir. They got eyes all over . . . sometimes I swear they got the birds and the fish working for them . . . okay?"

"Okay."

"Sorry."

"Me, too. . . . So, are you going to tell me how come the Israelis recruited you? I'm very curious. Been so out of it for . . . how long? Almost twenty years, I think. Used to keep good track of time . . . but then they started moving me around, from one jail to the next . . . sometimes I didn't see daylight for weeks."

"Did you ever hear of the Navajo Trackers, during World War II?"

"Navajo?"

"Yes, sir. More than 3,600 Navajo men and women joined the armed forces during World War II . . . highest percentage of the entire population in the armed services of any ethnic group in the United States."

"Really?"

"Well, Navajo Code Talkers were a special group of Indians during that war. Used a special code based on the Navajo language to transmit messages, so Emperor Hirohito couldn't decipher American messages regarding time and place of attack. Complicated syntax and tonal qualities of the Navajo language totally screwed up the linguists and so-called educated know-it-alls . . . so Indians helped win the war. . . . On top of that, like the whole world knows, Indians ain't chicken when it comes to heights . . . natural born aerialists. . . . They built bridges, leapt from tall towers, you know, that sort of thing . . . make sense to you?"

"Kind of. You're like one of those trackers? You know Indian . . . I mean, Navajo or something, and transmit or decipher messages?"

"Chumash."

"Chumash?"

"Some people never heard of us. Central Valley, California. Ring a bell?"

"Sorry. Told you I've been . . . hell, I'm starting to feel like a walking ghost . . . hope it doesn't kill me once the numbness wears off."

"Don't be so hard on yourself, sir. Easy does it. You're gonna do fine. That's how come the Cap doesn't let us blab . . . and I just did."

"That's okay, Coop. Thanks for telling me. Thanks . . ." David
sank into the bottom of the car in a fetal position, clutching his
stomach, breathing shallow, and blinking to squeeze the tears
from his eyes without reaching or wiping them.

"You all right back there, sir?"

"I will be in just a minute . . . get these gut wrenches once in
a while . . . it'll pass . . ."

"Won't be too long now, I hope. . . . May have to take a side
road though . . . just passed a convoy . . . heading south, I'm guessing. So they're gonna have to go the scenic route for a while . . . it'll
be all right, though. Done this a dozen times . . . there they go . . .
wish you could look at them . . . all bunched up and scrawny. . . .
They got more rifles than ribs. Fidel ought to put more flesh on
them instead of all that ammunition. How're you doing? Ain't
gonna quit on me or nothing, are you? You made it this far, right?"

David sighed, strove to catch his breath. "Not to worry. I'm not
planning to wimp out on you. Got a couple of scores to settle
before I do . . . feeling better now."

"That's good. Ain't lost nobody so far . . . you wouldn't want
to spoil my record . . ."

"You're a good man."

"Thank you, sir."

"One thing I don't get though . . ."

"What would that be, sir?"

"Well, forgive me . . . but like the old Jewish joke goes, it's
funny, you don't *look* Indian. . . ."

"Well, that's a long story, sir. Real long story."

"And you can't talk about it, did I guess right?"

"Yes, sir."

David laughed. "We had a running joke in our family. . . . Has
to do with why my father's side of the family has blue eyes when
we're Jewish...don't know if you'd understand. My mom used to
say 'A pogrom is a pogrom . . .'"

"Yes, sir, I do get it. To the victor go the spoils, like the saying
goes. Indians were raped, too . . . Chumash, Navajo, Papago,
Lakota Sioux, Oneida, Kummeyaay, all the Pueblo Indians. . . .
Genocide's been going on four hundred years and it ain't stopped
yet. Indian people have always been on the edge of survival, where

they could end up starving or homeless. People don't want to hear about it. On the other hand, they love the stereotype . . . you know, that we're sacred, that we protect the Earth."

David groaned, then managed the words: "Yeah, it's lousy, amigo. . . . Cell mate I had once called it hell . . . said this world was Planet Hell, that everyone here died and went to hell . . . and the hell of it is we're given hope and think we can get out when actually our fate's already sealed. . . . Levi Gonsales was the poor guy's name . . . guard cut his balls off with an ice pick, the poor slob bled to death. . . . But you know what I was just thinking? I was just thinking I feel lucky you're the one who picked me up . . . was just thinking maybe it's not all hell . . . *Qué suerte tiene el cubano.* Know what that means? Means the luck of the Cubans."

"Figured. Took Spanish training down here for three months before the Cap set me loose. . . . My girlfriend is Cubano, too."

"Jewish *and* Cuban? *Mazel Tov!*"

"Yeah. You know what the Cap calls them?"

"What?"

"Havana Negilas. Funny, huh?"

"Yeah. More like Havana *hak flaish.*"

David readjusted himself on the floor, keeping to his fetal position, attempting to fill his lungs. He was too tired of this banter and sudden reentry into the world of the living. His mother would have forbidden him to talk. Then, again, she would have forbidden him to come down in that motorboat to get the *rav* out eighteen, maybe twenty years ago.

Dolores de amores had sapped his reservoir. How was he to know he would meet a girl prettier than the ones in the magazines, who gave herself to him for the very first time? How was he to know when this, too, had been his first—even if it felt as natural and *haimish* as if he'd been a master lover all his life. *Ahora y siempre. Dolores de mis amores.*

Six

The rose of pink desire
withered to ivy
capped by a
dusting of snow petals
left over
from his last ice age.

IN HER BOTÁNICA, REDOLENT OF frankincense and Florida Water, Ideliza Mercado loomed like a golden papaya, like an African princess from the Congo Basin basking in her radiance, lost in the avatars of her private pantheon. But here, with her large head and Vaselined hair pressed against the picture window, she looked like so many a survivor from the Middle and the Caribbean Passage.

For an instant, Roberto mistook her amber Nefertiti eyes for one of the lights over the operating table. By the time he turned his face toward her, it was too late. The procedure had begun, and there was a second scheduled back to back. She would have to wait.

He could not fathom how Ideliza had made it into the clinic's private quarters, past his receptionist and nurse assistant, two floors down via a private elevator. Then again, that was the thing about Princess Papaya. Her heathen gods had blessed her.

Usually, it was the air quality and room temperature that occupied his thoughts. Too cold in summer, too hot in fall and winter. After years of prying lives or moribund newborns from women's cervixes, he was still troubled by the airborne, steam-radiated fetor of blood and vitals. His assistant, apprentice, and anesthesiologist was a twenty-five-year-old, Panamanian-trained gynecologist who went by "Dr. Joe" because he had an unpronounceable last name.

Dr. Joe was a natural court jester—he winked, mugged, and stretched his cheeks during the whole procedure and usually succeeded in distracting Roberto from his physical discomforts long enough to last through sutures.

Only, today the younger man could not guess the reason for Roberto's extreme disquiet, how limp-naked he felt knowing Ideliza was watching him rummage for life under the stirrups and the Leron sheets Kitty had bought to redecorate the office. His last glimpse of her before the operation had caught her face stuck like a suction cup against the glass-sealed wall.

"So who's the pretty dame, *compadre*?" The patient was under. Dr. Joe was always careful to refrain from conversation until at least the intravenous Valium had taken.

"I don't . . . someone I know. I just don't know how the hell she was allowed in here."

"Oh? I'd say she got here by limo, that's my bet. But who is she, anyway? That's what I'd like to know. Looks so familiar. She's a dish, whoever she is, I tell you that. Look at those knockers, straight up and hard like a pumped-up stripper. Couldn't find the chart anywhere. Looks thirty, maybe thirty-one? She married?"

"Oh . . . you mean the patient!" Roberto rolled the latex gloves tightly over his hands and reached for the scissors.

"Duh, dummy. Hit me with a feather. Yeah, the patient! Any other person of the female gender lying buck naked with a pair of knockers making eyes at you and with a belly full of fluid big enough to drown a swimming pool?"

Good. Dr. Joe had missed Ideliza. *Perhaps that's how she managed to elude the nurses.*

"Oh, her," said Roberto, checking the suction catheter for power, testing the brand-new ultrasound equipment from Germany, preparing to dive. "She's, you know, God, yeah, what's-her-name, Mrs. Alberstein. Didn't you meet her last week? Mrs. Alberstein. Nice lady. Think she's more than thirty, though. Chart says forty, and they usually lob off twelve years for starters."

"Twelve years? Twelve?"

"It's the Chinese birth sign thing. Year of the monkey, year of the dragon, you know. Happens every twelve years, so they keep their sign but roll the birth year forward. Twelve years."

"Son of a gun . . . Hey, looks like the nice lady's ready to take, Doc. Still blows me away why someone so loaded and bodacious waits this long to make up her mind. I wouldn't . . . but then again, like you people say, thank God I ain't no woman. . . . She married?"

"You care?"

"Maybe. Yeah, why not?"

"Let me get this straight, Dr. Joe. Now that Miss Biddle-Whatsie-Mellon-Duke ditched you, you decide to start dating patients?"

"Well . . . " He was mugging under his mask. "I could think of worse than dating a pretty lady like this one . . . or another one just like her. Maybe both!"

"Dating them, eh? When? Before or after you nooky-nooky their you-know-what, you bum!" Roberto laughed. The young man's sway was working. Roberto was starting to feel loose enough to ply his trade.

"You're good, kid, but do me a favor and keep the comments down. . . . Didn't I teach you the human mind is a funny thing?"

"Ah, Doc, you're so right, you're so fucking right! But just tell me something: Is she married?"

"Surely. To Mr. Alberstein."

"No fooling?"

"Ask her yourself . . . but hold off, will you, kid? Here, help me out. It's going to be a tight one . . . zero dilation here . . . twenty-nine weeks and counting . . . *oy vey* what a feeling!"

"That Mr. Alberstein must be a real big fellow. Think the lady here has a Dallas Cowboy in her stadium . . ."

"More like a renegade cowboy."

"Renegade? That's cool! Somebody should put music to it, like Loretta Lynn or what's his name . . . '*Renegade cowboy . . . Come to youah momma and don't you be coy*' . . . can't you just hear it? Wow! Renegade cowboy! What a cool name!"

"Not that cool, you *coco loco*. It's just something my sister would come up with. She has a way with *woids,* like my dad would say."

"Yeah, you're right. Sounds just like her . . . hey, doc, here, I think she's steady now. Can you start extracting . . ."

Roberto followed the ultrasound. He wielded the forceps, found the legs, and began pulling them out into the birth canal. With sleight of hand, he worked his fingers to deliver first the opposite lower extremity, then the torso, the arms, and shoulders. Finally, he felt the head, lodged in the cervical os.

"Damn these . . . zero dilations . . ."

"Yeah. Just like on Tuesday. Mrs. Wallace. Man, that was some head. . . . Thought you'd have to leave it in there for good. She doing okay?"

"Well. Doing well. Doing well here . . ."

Roberto glanced at his chart. He began orienting the fetus dorsum, spine up, and sliding the fingers of his left hand along its back.

"Got him!" he whispered. He'd succeeded in hooking the shoulders palm down with his ring and index fingers.

Dr. Joe slapped a pair of blunt curved Metzenbaum scissors on Roberto's right hand. It was their halfway mark.

Roberto was beginning to feel the sweat crown his head. Large beads burst across his nose and upper lip, sealing his face tightly against the surgical mask. The baby was moving. He checked the ultrasound. Heartbeat bleeping high on the screen. Feet kicking. Fingers clutching together. Arms flinching. Roberto had delivered Mrs. Alberstein's issue—torso, arms, and legs, anyway. Everything but the head.

He inhaled deeply, holding his breath, bathing his diaphragm, then rushed the air out in a single blow. He advanced the tip of the Metzenbaum, curved down, along the spine. *There!* He held the base of the skull firmly under his middle finger, forcing the scissors into the foramen magnum.

"I'm in!" he whispered, jamming the skull, fanning wide the scissors to enlarge the opening.

"Catheter!" announced Dr. Joe, holding the suction tube while Roberto inserted it through the hole hewn roughly but deeply by his precision tool. Dr. Joe had learned to follow Roberto's moves with military rigor. And, with military rigor, he cleaned up after him step by step, scooping the coagulated waste into disposable plastic bins. He watched as Roberto inserted the tube and evacuated the brains and remains from the skull.

"All sucked out," declared Roberto, easing his hand, pulling out, breathing deeply once more, "skull went south."

Roberto never removed or disposed of the babies. He left that up to Dr. Joe. Mrs. Alberstein's chauffeur and private nurse would pick her up before twilight.

At last, he could turn his attention to Princess Papaya, whose face had remained a gargoyle pressed against the glass during the entire twenty-minute procedure. He unstrapped his mask, pulled the surgical green over his head, motioning to Ideliza with his index and middle fingers to take the elevator back up and meet him in his office in, *count them*, fifteen minutes.

"What was that?" asked Dr. Joe.

"What was what?"

"I mean all that hand gesturing. Is someone here?"

"Oh! nothing, skip it, no big deal."

"Check."

"Hey, Dr. Joe, come here. You want to know the lady's real name?" Roberto leaned over, whispering in his ear.

"No shit and no fooling!" Dr. Joe turned high pink. "No wonder she looked familiar! Wow! I must be out to lunch. You know I own every last one of her fuckin' CDs? Unreal!"

"Well, get her to autograph them," said Roberto, walking away from the scene in the direction of his shower. "Maybe she'll sing you 'Melancholy Baby.'"

Princess Papaya turned her gaze the moment he entered— showered, dressed in a white sweat suit, and rubbed in Guerlain Imperial. She was silent, resisting his stare while he circled her, trying to force eye contact. Finally, after minutes of silence, he threw both arms in the air, walked to the opposite side of the room, and looked out on the corner of Fifty-Seventh Street and Ninth Avenue.

"All right, all right, Princess! I give up! What's going on? And why did you come during my operation? Do you have any idea how nervous you made me back there? I almost botched the job!"

"That was no operation," Ideliza whispered. She kept her head down and her gaze fixed on Roberto's calfskin penny loafers.

Roberto moved toward her, then made a sudden detour. He double-locked the office door, pressed *do not disturb* on the intercom, then returned to Ideliza with arms outstretched.

"Well, whatever the reason you came, Princess, it's good to see you. I think about you, you know. . . . I think about you here a lot, right there, as a matter of fact." He pointed at the buckskin leather couch.

She sat down next to him in silence, and he reclined with his head on his left hand, staring at her, stretching his legs across her thighs, using his right hand to coddle the ensuing erection under his sweatpants.

"Where is Bembé?"

"Ah! Is that it? I told you I would be keeping him another week! He's doing great, Princess! Working that new computer I got him like crazy. I got him another teacher, a real wiz from the Dalton School . . . so the kid's as happy as a pig in . . . !"

"Where is Bembé?" she repeated.

Roberto rose up halfway, rolled his legs off her, and crouched in the opposite corner of the sofa.

"He is with me, Princess. And you know I'd like him to stay with me until you help me solve the . . . you know, the situation of the calls and the threats. . . . And besides, Kitty is, you know, very hung up since she lost her yummies . . . the kid does a world of good to Kitty. You'd get a kick if you saw her . . ."

"I did."

"You what? What do you mean? You did what?" He was up, pacing in front of her.

"I went to your apartment house. She came to the door. I asked for Bembé . . ."

"What? Just like that? The doorman just let you go up like that? You didn't tell my wife who you were . . . right?"

"I told her I was your physical therapist's personal maid."

"Good." Roberto sighed, moved beside her.

"She told me Bembé was away, with your sister."

"Just for today."

"One week, your wife said."

"Okay. One week. Do you think you can find the fuckers who

are calling me and putting the squeeze on me in one week? I think
it gives you plenty of time, no?"

"Robertico, you blackmail me with your own son as ransom
so I can, as you put it, 'put the squeeze' on the *orishas* and make
them tell me who is hunting you down?" She was looking straight
at him now.

"Princess! Not blackmail! Maybe desperation, call it desperation! Here! Look what came in the mail today!"

He handed her a FedEx envelope with the lyrics to a song by The
Police: "Everywhere you go . . . everything you do . . . I'll be watch-
ing you!" Under it, in red ink, a sign-off: "ONE OF THESE DAYS,
DR LOBO, I'LL BE WATCHING YOU . . . DEAD, REAL DEAD."

"Roberto, I want Bembé back."

"If that's all you care about, if you don't give a shit what happens to me, after seeing this stupid letter, then go get him yourself! You got into the clinic, didn't you? And nobody saw you,
right? And you went up to my apartment on the twenty-fifth floor,
and the doorman didn't stop you, right? So what's to keep you
from finding him yourself, you know, doing the phantom thing
you do? Why should I help you with this if you don't give a damn
that someone is out to get me, that there's probably a crazy hit
man somewhere in this city having fun with me, trying to drive
me crazy and then shoot me?"

"What you mention about the phantom thing, it's not the
same. Not the same as knowing everything the *orishas* know. It's
just a blessing, an *aché*, a power certain *santos* give us for our protection. It was that way long ago, when the Lucumíes had to hide
from the white man's eyes . . . and besides, Roberto, Bembé won't
let me come."

"He won't let you *come*?"

"He is . . . well, as you know, he has *aché*. Bembé has a very
strong thought. Someone must have hypnotized him or . . . I don't
know. I can't seem to tune in to him. He is blocking me."

Roberto exploded in one of his bombastic laughs that made
heads turn in restaurants.

"I knew it!" he said. "The kid has a crush on my sister! And
he's having so much fun, he doesn't want you around! Is that a gas
or what?"

Ideliza smiled for the first time.

"You are right, Robertico! It just came to me! Of course, that *angelito diablo* is playing games with me because he found a nice lady he likes, and like the fine little gentleman that he is, of course, he wants his privacy!"

"Okay, Princess, so now will you work with me? Bembé stays with Victoria, and you get rid of those people or that man, whoever it is!"

"But Roberto, I have done *trabajos* and I have prayed and made sacrifices, but the *orishas* are not telling me anything. They are acting deaf about this, deaf like Bembé, you know, who hears everything and nothing."

"But, Princess, it's not possible! Why won't they? Isn't there something you can do for them to soften them up? Something they like a lot? How about a Macanudo or a Partagas cigar?" As incomprehensible as it might have seemed to Sara and Abram and to Rabbi Shapiro, who officiated at his Bar Mitzvah, Roberto believed that if she tried, there was nothing her gods would deny her.

"You are a knucklehead sometimes, Roberto, doctor or no doctor. You think talking with God is just like punching a button or making some deal at the flea market, eh?"

"No. I don't think one way or another. I told you I don't know anything about talking with God. My brother used to be the one who knew all about that sort of thing, and the bastard, he kept that part all for himself . . . but then look what happened to him for fooling around with that God. Shit. . . . I have absolutely no clue, Princess—what can I tell you?" He buried his head in his hands.

"Don't be sad, my angel," she whispered. "I have invited a very big *babalao* for dinner at my house this evening. Perhaps he will help. He is a very good man."

"Good." Roberto glanced at his watch. His next patient lay in wait on the polished steel.

"Oh, shit, Princess. I've got another operation scheduled in a couple of minutes! Please do me a favor this time and don't look, okay? Can you find your way out the same way?"

"That was not an operation," she said calmly, her large body rising on its feet, turning toward the door.

"Oh, c'mon, Princess! You, too? Don't tell me you're like one of those maniacs who march up and down outside the building here, trying to block my patients, making my life miserable with their born-again crap!"

"Human sacrifice," she continued calmly. "God and the *santos* do not want that. You will have to stop."

"Princess . . . *you* stop, please. Don't be insane."

"You will have to stop." She said it three times, and each word filled the space like a mantra.

"Well, I can't stop right now, Princess! Have a patient waiting and gotta go! But listen, don't worry about Bembé. My sister loves him. He's having a great time, treated like a little prince. But please, do something with your *babalao* tonight, will you? Promise? I don't care if you have to put a curse on those bastards and kill them! Or at least let me know where they are and who the fuck they are, so I can take it from there! I got a contact through Dr. Joe who can take care of it for me . . . but first we gotta smoke them out! And tell the *babalao* I am a generous man, okay?"

"Yes, *mi ángel*. You tell Bembé his mother loves him and misses him very much. And tell him Chucho the professor has been asking for him and wanted me to tell him he found a new virus."

"A new virus? What, that second-grade teacher is suddenly Albert Einstein? What kind of virus? "

"A machine virus. You know, something to do with computers."

"Oh! All right, I'll tell him. Princess, please, you know . . . and I hope I can come see you one day this week . . . tomorrow, maybe?"

He kissed her lightly on the mouth and shut the door behind her. He was sure she would elude his staff. *Why couldn't she just find the scums?* It struck him that this had been the first time he had seen Ideliza Mercado in daylight, away from her altar; that this had been the first time he had been with her and not lain in her folds, desperate to vent himself inside her; that this had been the first time his cock had not stayed hard the whole time next to her.

He reached inside the elastic waistband of the sweatpants, lay on his back on the buckskin couch, still warm from Ideliza's touch, and began stroking himself—gently at first, then, when he had grown solid and his member shot up to his navel, he jerked it quickly, expediently, knowing Dr. Joe was likely to ring for him any second, rushing his come over the issue of *Ebony* magazine that had come in the mail, then disposing of it in the paper shredder.

"Princess," he whispered, eyes closed, stretched on the couch, the last throb.

Seven

Victoria marveled at finding herself with Bembé under her special *chupeh* for a whole week—*Widow and misbegotten child/ halving the* Times *like bagels/ across the kitchen table.*

Sara and Jacob would have pointed to her special relationship with Bembé as the miracle that caused her bolted portals to suddenly fling open—a *mitzvah*, a merciful respite that stilled, at least momentarily, the newsreels in her head, watching Francisco fragmenting midair. And if not a *mitzvah* or a minor miracle, then a quickening, a retrograde shift, the flutter of a butterfly in Borneo, Elijah's fiery chariots, some random act of kindness that suddenly lighted on the frosted SoHo loft, where she'd spent months gazing at the lineup of her husband's luminous canvases. On gray days, the paintings were masked traitors because they had survived him. On days of partial grace, they turned to icons because they had been present at her altar and, like her, still bore the ember of Francisco's fire.

Her heart welcomed Bembé with the joy of a man stranded on a desert island, suddenly sighting a ship light years overdue. She cooked him her seven favorite with foods on the first day—*yuca con mojo/* lentils/ fried plantains/ warm borscht besot with chives and sour cream/ beef shank/ *quinoa* and guacamole. *Do you like this? Do you like this?* She kept asking, even as the child dug in with both hands and even licked the dill and meat juice with face and tongue pressed flat on the plate.

She lit the Shabbat candles, served *challah*, showed him how to pull the bread, and gave him a diamond-studded Star of David to add to the four strands of multicolored beads—each a surrogate of a particular *orisha*—and the resplendent eighteen-carat medallion of Obatalá, god of the heavens, guarding his narrow, ebony-buffed breast. At first, the thought that it should join Bembé's amulet jamboree struck her as sacrilegious. Then, on second thought, amusingly whimsical. She imagined her father's predictable reaction—*so, last I checked with the* rebbe, *the Star of David is not a graven image*—and then her mother's response, walking away, waving her arms at him, biting with gusto into *meshugeneh gens, meshugeneh gribbenes,* one of her most popular Yiddish phrases.

She put the chain around his neck and watched Bembé hold up his new lucky charm in the mirror. Propping himself up on the toilet seat, he leaned at a sixty-degree angle and stretched to look at it in the medicine cabinet. Suddenly, she had a flash of herself, age nine, sitting in the third row of the Belasco Theater, enthralled by Tammy Grimes' zany rendition of "Home Sweet Home," a paradise where saints and sinners, Gertrude Stein, Cellini, and even Bellini meet. Even back then, she was awestruck by the notion that all thinkers and all thought eventually must meet in the One.

Years later, when she began research on the Kabala, it was this same idea that brought her comfort—*Each of us emerges from Ein Sof and is included in it. . . . God's presence fills the entire world.* So, it was right, perhaps, for King David's star to make the acquaintance of messengers from another time and place. *And where better than on this gentle creature's heart.*

Victoria made Bembé's bed with the tie-dyed purple sheets he'd pointed to in the window of a store on West Broadway. She folded the edges back like three-cornered hats and fluffed red pillows against the frame. She reclined with him at bedtime, his harvest-moon head deflated on her lap, and sang him lullabies, which Roberto had assured her Bembé was entirely incapable of hearing—*but then/ neither could the venerable Herr Ludwig hear/ when he transcribed his Ninth/ directly/ from the native tongue/ of risen angels.*

She took him to his very first big-screen movie—a special screening of *Modern Times* at the Angelika, where they sat in the last row in deference to the audience and his prominent head. Charlie Chaplin's pantomimes captivated Bembé, and, in turn, Bembé's hand-clapping, head-tossing interaction with the tiny mustached satirist on the screen captivated Victoria.

Midweek, she walked the length of Manhattan at a clip, dart-ing in and out of arcades and ice-cream parlors, dogging the steps of this implausible, miniature member of her bloodline with the aqua eyes of the men in her family and the swift gait of a six-foot man. Victoria slugged in quarters while Bembé piloted flashing video games with the deliberate assurance of a practiced paladin. His fierce concentration and infallible aim repeatedly clinched his final victory over evil forces with acid names that spelled *Metal Slug, Soul Edge, Attack from Mars, Alpha Warriors, Street Fighters, Samurai Showdown.*

On the third day, she asked if he would fill a chapbook with random sketches of his favorite things, and suddenly, like a tourist stumbling upon Tut's tomb, like rose petals unfolding before her eyes, she watched the blossoming of a remarkable artist. With only a stack of drawing paper, a box full of Crayolas, and Francis-co's fountain pen suffused in India ink, in minutes Bembé sketched the streets they'd visited, the food they'd eaten, the faces of the people in line at the Angelika—and he drew a perfect like-ness of Victoria, smiling for the cameras, holding a mango slice between her teeth, with a diamond Star of David on her breast.

Just then, the thought and presence of David appeared so keen-ly in her thoughts that for an instant, she felt her brother standing at her side. Victoria stood in wonder, marveling at Bembé's quick, colorful renderings, at his remarkable details, and at the mastery and precision of his untrained hand. Once, long ago, it had been David who had unearthed her own talents with a question—*why don't you write me your feelings, sis.* With that, he revealed her mis-sion, clarified the voice long sealed in the cellar of the *galleta* fac-tory in Newark. David had been the first to *see* her for who she real-ly was: a minstrel, a poet—*and with his prayer/ my brother lifted the hatch/ that launched my destiny/ And now/ this child/ our marrow scooped/ from kindred clay/ and I/ my brother's keeper?*

For Victoria, this advent, this serendipitous convergence of her life with Bembé's, bore the mystic symbolism of King David, sold into slavery so that twenty years later he'd be positioned to rescue Jacob from famine and the ill-fated, fallow fields where he had strayed—and, thus, guarantee his ascendancy, the twelve tribes of Israel, her very own. It spoke to her of Moses, bound in bulrushes, swaddled and burped in the pharaoh's court, so that years later he could lead Jacob's children to a land where milk and honey flowed like liquid manna in the desert.

And with this wondrous epiphany at the hands of an amazing child, her flesh and blood, the cobwebs that had spun and shrouded her in darkness began to melt like sugar spun into a cone, or the night sky suddenly blinded, defused by light.

The underlying cause of Victoria's spontaneous remission from despair seemed so sacred, when uttered to herself in thought, that she felt bound to encrypt it—like Yahweh, that I Am that I Am, whose name must never be articulated. She gave it the code name *Nexus*. It stood for the bond and light streaming from Bembé's eyes like shooting stars, whisking her bones, airing her lungs, dilating her middle heart.

On Saturday, she lay at his side for hours, drinking him like a fresh coconut, compressing the tender moments with this creature, this spontaneous artist-sage with the milk-chocolate smile, who could render his eyes transparent at will and see all things at once.

By evening, she began to feel the final quickening, the sudden shift on her fault line. First came the glow of his luminous eyes, pointing to the ten *sefirot* of the Kabala, the way by which all things come into being and pass away. Then, the stillness at the point of the turning world, the sacred vision.

She free-fell/ a swirl of doves against the sea/ clung to a silver bucket tilted midair over a canopy of stars/ slept in a waterfall/ a lapis beam drew woman and child inside the magic circle/ her face mirrored in his and in all life in the one infinite Elohim, Lord of the universe/ where there is neither birth nor death nor shadow of turning. . . .

Sitting quietly at his side, smiling at his smile when he caressed her face, she journeyed to that place King David wrote glowed invisible beyond the *shekinnah* of time and space, the helix and sanctity of life.

Like Jacob, her vision had come in a waking dream. She would, at last, release Francisco on his journey like a star, forgive his violent departure, observe his incorporeal body curve and coast through mirror parallels, detached from the pain of his desertion, knowing his presence always at hand throughout all space and longitude of time. It did not mean that she was free of fears or that she had transcended the human condition, but it felt like when a scab had formed, and more. More because despite the contradictions, there was a freedom, a sudden freedom she would not have imagined.

"Do you know that something miraculous happened to me because of you?"

Victoria typed the words and flipped the Tecra toward Bembé, watching him type the word "cool" with his index finger fully perpendicular.

They were stretched out on her king-size platform bed, scanning through the Kirsch-Lobo family album in her trust, introducing Bembé to his relatives "from on the other side"—Cuba, Czechoslovakia, Aruba, Holland, Spain. South and west and east of what?

She laughed and typed: "You know there is no such thing as the other side. But these are your Greataunt Minna and your Greatuncle Zachary, and they're from there."

"Other side?"

"Yes."

"Cool. Are they coming to visit?"

"I don't know. Do you? They were from the 'other side' when they came to America, but now they're dead . . . which, I guess, is another kind of other side. So they're on the other-other side. However, now that they've moved to that other-other side, they're probably said to be from America, which is the side they came from when their souls departed. . . ."

Bembé smiled broadly and swiped his hand over his head with an open palm. He typed back: "But if they visit us tonight, then they get to be from the other side all over again, right?"

"You think so? You'd know better than I. But Bembé, to tell you the truth, 'getting' to be from the other side is not something that people who come from the other side necessarily want. You know why?"

"Who wants to be a stranger?" he typed and swirled the Tecra back.

Victoria arched her brows and gave him one of her high-chin, deadpan academia looks. "On the money . . . but why is that, why don't people like being from the other side?"

"First come, first serve," he wrote back. "No beans left by the time they get to the front of the line."

"Hey! Great serve!" she wrote back, then wondered about the tennis metaphor and wished she hadn't.

Bembé tugged at her hair. He was copying her. "Good shot," he tapped back with one finger, squeezing his right eye into a wink.

"You like tennis?"

"Aranxa, Conchita, Venus, and Michael Chang," he typed back.

"Bembé, wow, computers, video games, and tennis, too! What don't you know? And how come you don't let your father and mother know?"

"My mother knows."

"She does?"

"My real mother. Ideliza Mercado. Roberto calls her Princess. Princess Papaya."

"Do you miss her?" Victoria would have preferred to skirt a matter that she'd found troublesome from the start—the child has a mother. Does he need Kitty or, for that matter, Roberto, who hardly addresses him, who plays with him like a toy and accords him a niche in the wall during his peculiar sexual rituals with his official wife? She stopped short of contemplating what Roberto perhaps used Bembé as during his trysts with the child's own mother.

"I like being with you," Bembé wrote back.

"And how about your mother?"

"Yes, with her, too. She is beautiful, too."

Victoria savored his *savoir-faire*. She might have done the same—avoided the direct response, taken the detours to convey a compliment without sending the bill. It was, no doubt, a cultural fallout, for as unlikely as it might have seemed to the untrained eye, Bembé and Victoria shared a psychological culture in common, a cosmic tree growing downward from its roots above, mirroring the first *sefirah* in the Holy Zohar. Like Bembé, so many of her idiosyncrasies, her predilections, her emotional triggers had been simmered in the Cuban cauldron—even if she was too young to remember and he, in turn, too young to have been there at all—

a souvenir along the scenic route of their common diaspora.

"Does Roberto take you to see your mother?"

"No."

"Would you like to see her?"

"Yes. She is mad as a serpent now, so I have to let her know where I am."

"I'll call her for you, if you'd like. Write what you want me to say. Phone number, too."

"It's okay. I can just let her joystick to my head."

It was the first reference Bembé had ever made to his capacious crown, and he had coupled it with a joystick, an object of affection, which a shrink, no doubt, would have duly noted. But if she understood what Bembé meant—and she did—joysticking referred to a different form of communication, one known to the *iluminados* and prophets of yore, as well as to those today who may brush past us inadvertently.

"She's been trying to send messages to you, and you've kept the phone off the hook, eh?"

Bembé gave her a gurgling smile, tossing his head back, and holding on to his sneakers with both hands. It was the sort of mischief that any child of nine might have enjoyed, playing peek-a-boo with his mother, hiding in a hall closet or under the landing, following the Gypsy circus for a day.

"So, you've been away long enough and now you just want to take all your toys and go home?" Victoria was mugging as she wrote, insistent that Bembé understood she was teasing him and, most importantly, was not at all hurt.

But if he did decide to leave now and, more portentously, leave Roberto's house and render his entire adoption null and void, then what of her? It was just the sort of thing she had been parrying for a year. Attachments. Human or not. She had turned down her mother's present on her birthday for just that reason—a black standard poodle puppy named Jellybean, which she would have otherwise adored, bonded with like a member of the pack, in complete disregard for time and mortality, thoroughly believing herself and anything she loved to be immortal. She thought of Edna St. Vincent Millay's poem and told her mother she'd rather wait until next year—*Pretty love I must outlive you/ and my little dog*

Llewellyn, sitting here . . . dogs live longer than love does. . . .

Cooper made sense because he had tossed her a tether in space, offered a way back to cruise control, and still remained incorporeal, a part of her imagination, as real or unreal as she could handle on any given day—although of late Cooper had begun fleshing out, spinning closer into view. This change in their homeostasis had unsettled her, even made her consider stopping the midnight e-mails.

The possibility of Cooper's visit had unleashed feelings of abandonment. It was one of those Byzantine twists of thought that only Francisco could have understood, and then explained. The idea or possibility of attachments meant the sure promise of abandonment.

The boy had been brushing her face with his eyes, smiling gently, looking at her face like someone reading the weather map. She had lost sense of her own mental wandering, had begun climbing back into her shell right in front of Bembé at the thought that he might leave or, rather, at the unequivocal thought that he would certainly leave.

"I won't leave you," Bembé wrote and then grabbed her hand, urging her to read. Victoria swallowed hard.

"I know, Bembé," she wrote back, "but you have a mother, right? And you probably miss her by now, and she probably misses you, too. I know I would. Would I ever."

"But we can stay friends . . . that's cool, right?"

"I would hope so! There are still lots of things we haven't done, places we haven't been. Like Coney Island, for instance. Did you ever go to Coney Island? I used to love it when I was your age. My father used to drive us there in the summer, in his convertible with the top down, and we used to go to Nathan's and eat hot dogs till one of us, usually your father, got sick from gorging and stuffing down all those hot dogs and chunks of cotton candy and swilling down Dr. Brown's celery soda . . . did Roberto ever tell you about that?"

He shook his head.

"My mother doesn't want me to go to Coney Island. She says it's dangerous. Maybe not before, when you went."

Victoria let out a laugh loud, enough for the vibrations to startle him. *En los nidos de antaño no crecen pájaros hogaño,* Cervantes wrote . . . *no birds grow in the nests of yesteryear.* "Of course! She's right, Bembé! Your mother is a very smart person, too! I forgot how things change. Better think of somewhere else to go next time, right? How about the Metropolitan Museum? That's still there, and it's a great place, a real super place, especially for an artist like you."

Eight

On her tongue, a Torah of love
—Proverbs 31:26

ROBERTO HAD ORCHESTRATED HER TRIP with surgical precision. As usual, Victoria abdicated the throne of responsibility—a lifelong habit that had made schoolmates taunt her and call her JAP, and prompted Francisco to label her nervous, as in *ay mujer, no te pongas tan nerviosa!* She would go for the ride, be a tourist, bask in the curious confluence of events: a man she needed to flee, a miracle child, a sojourn in southern California amidst Merlot and Chardonnay—grapes she despised for their May wine German fruitiness and diet-light bouquet.

Roberto's lips had quivered when she finally took him up on his offer. She watched his eyes narrow and slit with incredulity, and then shoot up with concentrated halogen—*a deep-sea diver probing the reefs. . . .* As to a sudden wanderlust in search of a geographical cure, except for her recent and extraordinary sojourn with Bembé, Victoria had not even ventured to the movie theater two blocks away or taken a weekend off in Aruba since Francisco's departure. This time she'd actually trumped him: there was no way for Roberto to know Victoria was running from a man who spent nights with her across a lithium screen, a man due on her doorstep minutes after her plane's departure.

She began a travel journal in the Sabra limousine on the way to the airport, driven by a chauffeur named Efraín. Efraín González. Cooper had suggested she start a journal as an antidote against anxiety amnesia, symptomatic among survivors—although since

89

Bembé's advent, she no longer felt the broad-hand, explosive fear that had swept in like a Bedouin storm a few months back, *like sand and sawdust in the wind.* The monster had changed stripes, perhaps even its native habitat and hiding place. From its new vantage point, it was no longer nameless or faceless. She could hear its ticking heart. It had a shape and a face and perhaps an unavoidable rendezvous with her. Victoria had named and tagged it, like a hunted deer in the back of the Chevy he said he drove. *Cooper.* She wrote longhand, elliptically, to keep from looking out, to keep from knowing the journey and being frightened by the distance and the thought that she would not see Bembé again for a while. . . .

10 A.M.
Roberto outdid himself this time. Must be whatever mess he's digging himself out of at the moment. Or maybe it's Bembé, or Bembé and me, or Bembé and me and Bembé's mother. Outnumbered? Some sort of payola? Fear his sister and mistress will both drop him at once and then rat on him? Doesn't fit the profile. Even Francisco had to admit that my brother didn't give a fig or fennel about what people said or thought of him, as long as they did what he wanted. He doesn't need money from me— makes wads at his clinic, and Abba and Mami gave him most of their savings to get David out of Cuba. Plus, Francisco sold the house in Bridgehampton so we could throw in our share. Mr. Teflon Man. Someone used to call him that . . . who? Don't remember. Mr. Teflon Man. So, he bought himself a vineyard. . . . Well, I can't believe he really feels he needs me . . . social mountain climbing baloney . . . What real use for me there . . . besides, he hates to share the limelight, anyway. . . . Isn't that right, Francisco? Not here to answer. But damn, I'm asking, anyway. Another reason you shouldn't have flown off in that plane. Not our fault. Not your fault, I know. I've let you go. . . . Well, I'm letting you go. . . . I wonder if you can see Bembé from wherever you are. I guess I'm asking for a sign . . . that's too much . . . the child gave me enough. I love you, Francisco, and now I hope I've learned to stop mourning you. I did last week and felt great . . . then suddenly I want to take it back . . . but it's not true. Something did happen, and I'll hold fast to that. Who said every

crisis was a crisis of faith?

A basket of fruits and vegetables, ruguleh, even range chicken from Zabar's, delivered to the plane before departure—a very classy brother act, taking measures against botulism and E. coli because I'm sent off "alone."

5:15 P.M.

The sun-buffed surfer, cum chauffeur, cum party boy, at Santa Barbara Airport, parked in the no-load zone in a black Mercedes, announcing repeatedly that Dr. Lobo gave him orders to make me feel as comfortable and Relaxed as possible. Relaxed. Relaxed. Ex-laxed.

Lupe, housekeeper and cook, imported from Sonora, arms laden with Leron linens.

Bar and fridge stocked to overflowing, so much the door got stuck.

9 P.M.

An HP printer, new in the box, in my bedroom, so I can travel light. The Land-Grant ranch, Lobo Vineyards in Santa Ynez . . . all this just for minding a shop that doesn't need minding because the winemaker/manager works it like his own—it was his own once, it turns out, before he fell on hard times and Roberto bought him out and kept him on, a serf to his own domain. Mr. Hollister. I only just learned that, mind you, from the driver. And now I have to meet the guy. Tomorrow. But that doesn't mean I have to let on I know. I don't know. What do I know? He's Mr. Hollister. I'm not. What if I want to turn back? What if tomorrow—tomorrow, when it's morning again and I can look out and see what these night phantom scarecrow rows of irrigated trenches look like, tomorrow, when I finally get to stare at these Santa Ynez Mountains, the ones Cooper goes on and on about, how they're like the Golan Heights?—what if tomorrow I just want to up and leave the movie house? Just leave in the middle, catch a plane back? Go see Bembé, invite his mother to stay with us if I have to . . . is that selfish or just plain stupid? But who's to stop me? And tonight . . . tonight, what do I tell Cooper? Do I tell him I'm here because he's there? Because I'm not all there? Because I can't face the thought of meeting him, of meeting his face and his teeth

and his hair? Because I can't stand the thought of losing him? I
used to laugh. . . . My father and I used to laugh . . . he showed
me a headline from the Post, long time ago: 'He killed her
because he could not live without her...' an old joke, I know. So,
what do I tell Cooper? Did he take his computer with him? I don't
know if he owns a laptop . . . plenty of places to check e-mail in
Manhattan. Maybe he can use one at his hotel . . . what hotel? I
don't know where he's staying, in case I want to call him . . . but
I wouldn't, anyway, . . . I wouldn't call him. I'll just log on tonight
like nothing's wrong, like I'm not here, in a place . . . what place?
A huge vineyard in the middle of nowhere with lots of little animals, invisible animals, gophers, moles digging the roots, country mice cleaning their tails on the parched earth, owls blowing
mournful rings like the Casino Indians used to . . . I mean the
Indians with signs all over the airport, when there weren't casi-
nos around, just cowboys and Indians and movie studios . . . Chumash Casino, Bringing out the Winner in You. I'll tell him the
truth. And then what? Then what, I ask myself. I don't have to
answer that . . . I can, say, let the Chumash chips fall where they
may. . . . I never heard of Chumash before. Apache, Pueblo,
Geronimo, yes . . . but they were here, and here they are and here
I am. . . . Poor guy, how could I do this to him? Do this to Willy
Nelson's shadow self. Willy Nelson: someone else I'd never heard
of. Maybe I had. It's not me. It's the one who can't do otherwise
right now. Martin Luther: Thus I stand, I cannot do otherwise.
Wise guy. I mean me. Let the chips . . . let the chips chirp if they
want to. They're in the country. I'll never tell . . . maybe tomorrow, I'll just go back . . . who's to stop me?

Nine

HAD SHE ALLOWED HERSELF TO DRAW A picture of the Cooper she imagined, the way Francisco did regularly for sport on the way to some social event or to a first encounter with an art dealer—bunions, warts, sebaceous eyebrows, liver freckles strewn like galaxies across his subject's chest—she would have guessed the man who looked into her and ambled in her space to be of an entirely different genus. His e-mail drawl. The Willie Nelson country songs. His guns and liquor, and a child in Florida in cracker territory being *reared* by grandparents—*Cooper's countenance betrayed nothing of that.*

He happened at the rear door with the breeze of an old friend who just dropped by for coffee—*smiling with neck tucked in like a dog's tail/ knocking gently on the glass pane with fingertips/ not knuckles/ did he take for granted/ here was not a woman/ but a patient/ a gazelle with cilia and nerve ends so rent/ that the slightest strident sign or sound would make her bolt for the wooded forest?*

Victoria scanned his face, took in all she could gather for present and later de-scanning, strived to read him like tea leaves at the bottom of a cup before letting him stand head to head under her transient roof.

But the screen door shadow-played on Cooper's face, and in a moment he had made his way inside, long before she'd had the option to either study him or undo her imprudent invitation. A thin-boned man, about her height, his face was as smooth as a choirboy, hair as red as hers and buzzed close. He wore a button-down madras shirt, worn jeans, and clean snake cowboy boots.

Small hands bisque on keyboard/ cheekbones/ erect square jaw/

gaze hidden behind eyes and brow/ rotogravures of young Amelia Earhart/ posing for reporters before her plane took flight.

Cooper's inside betrayed his air-and-water carapace/ He moved like stone/ shoulders and mouth lead-measured/ the swagger of his space as resolute as someone twice his size/ His voice, too, shadow play/ deep set/ yet inconsistent in range/ an alto exhaling basso profondo.

Mostly, it was *his eyes*—the very thing Victoria feared. Eyes that trapped her nuances, craved for reassurance, followed her when she expected him to lead. Eyes as hungry as hers, with not enough food to go around.

"So, I pictured you just the same, and you had a totally different suspect." He had taken up residence on the leather couch under the Lobo marquis.

"What makes you say that?"

"Same thing that told me you'd answer a question with a question." He smiled—*an Anglican parson proffering butter cookies.*

Victoria eased her eyes on his—a soft landing. She coiled into the companion leather chair across from his.

"And what's that?" She felt protected by the western penumbra, the Santa Ynez Mountains, reflecting their copper waves above his head.

"*That* . . . is that you thought I looked totally different, but I didn't."

"Not exactly." Victoria sipped the Cabernet Reserve that Lupe had designated for dessert. "True, you surprise me . . . but then again, I told you. I made up my mind not to imagine you . . . as in virtual rules . . . remember?"

Cooper was featherlight. His liquid body filled only a small portion of the couch. His wineglass shone untouched. He'd only eaten the vegetable portion of his heated dinner, cut carefully around the ostrich meat medallions cooked rare and manicured with rosemary sprigs.

"I did imagine you pretty much the same . . . but then again, I'd had the advantage of having seen you . . ."

"Oh? How was that? Thought we were even-steven . . . you didn't sneak a digital camera or something in my e-mail, did you?"

Cooper shook his head. He was poised in his space. Victoria

wondered if she would have to be the one to move, should the chemistry be incontrovertible, then quickly dismissed the thought.

"Naw, nothing like that. Did you ever hear of remote viewing . . . something the government has been doing for years? . . ."

She bobbed her head in a question mark. She had and she hadn't. "You mean like the experiments the Russians and, I guess, the U.S. have been doing . . . spoon bending and telepathic messages across walls and stuff?"

Coopper nodded. He stood up, helped himself to a glass of apple juice from the small fridge.

"Guess you don't like my brother's vintage, eh?"

"Aw, it's not that . . . just don't drink wine these days . . . anyway. Yeah, you're right . . . remote viewing is something like that . . . only more . . ."

"And you saw me?" Victoria surprised him with her cut-to-the-chase. She took others' premises for granted when engaged in conversation.

"I did."

"Really? And how did you do that?"

Cooper stroked his chin, squeezed his blues tight, smiled with eyes shut. "Like this . . ." He opened his eyes distant as snow, with ambers burning. "I can just project myself into time . . . best way I can explain it . . . and I look for the image that is before me . . . the image I'm supposed to see next . . . and I open my eyes, letting the Lord do for me whatever He needs to do. And so, I see what I'm going to see. That make sense to you, Penelope?"

She nodded her head. "Yeah, it does. . . . Cooper, while we're here . . . well, listen, my name is Victoria, you know that by now probably . . . so you can call me that. Is your name Cooper, really?"

"Yeah. Cooper. Really Cooper. I like Penelope, though . . . got used to it. Is that okay?"

"Sure. Who cares . . . I'm from New York."

"Like, just don't call you late for dinner?" He chuckled.

She shook her head. He caught her thought like a hunter. "From the flick of my Bic you can tell I'm a hick?"

"God! I can't believe you just said that. My seventy-year-old father is always talking about the same commercial . . . it's uncanny . . . you don't seem old enough to remember it. . . ."

"I am, okay?"

"Okay?"

"Yeah. I may be slightly younger than you, but nothing worth a commercial . . ."

"So . . . Cooper, you saw me. . . . You did remote viewing and you saw me . . . really?"

"I did. I saw you the third or fourth time we e-mailed . . . and I thought you were pretty cool-looking, too."

"You rascal." Victoria eased into her chair, as Cooper had possessed his. "So why did you keep asking me for a Polaroid?"

"Well, nothing wrong with that . . . wanted to make sure I saw what I saw. You realize humans use only ten percent or less of our brains, Penelope? There's lots we can do, and lots we are going to need to do to survive the new times coming on this Earth in the end times . . ."

"Oh. Oh . . . you sound like one of those Armageddon preachers on television. . . . Listen, you know I'm a nice Jewish girl, right?"

Cooper cocked his head, pierced his blue eyes on her brown.

"Like MJ used to say, what does that have to do with the price of eggs in China? She was Jewish, too, by the way . . . New York."

"I don't know . . . guess it scares me to hear someone . . . I mean about doomsday and Christian Armageddon and stuff. It feels political to me, a little threatening. . . . You probably don't know what I mean."

"Think I do . . . pogrom stuff. . . . Say, Penelope, want to take a little walk outside with me?"

"Outside?"

"Yeah, just a little ways down . . . enough room to look up, straight up, I mean . . . something I want to show you . . ."

The desert sun had dropped cold. Her cotton T-shirt might be too thin under the night sky. He read her. "No need to put any *serape* kind of stuff on . . . I think you'll be warm enough. . . ."

It was a full moon, and it flooded the canyons, shimmered over the grape leaves, blew a silver breeze in its wake. The chirping stopped as they moved toward the wine trenches. The invisible creatures who'd kept her up all night held their breath.

Cooper walked at her side, leading with each step forward, brushing his shoulder against hers, silent and yet present in mind and scope. About ten minutes into their pilgrim walk, he came to a sudden stop, looked up and east toward Orion, crooked his arm around her shoulder. Victoria smelled his ear and neck, vanilla thin with lemon. They stood still at the still point of the turning world, the only two people under the purple sky.

"Makes me feel close to the Earth here . . . moon climbing over the hills, like standing in front of a large fire pit filled with rocks the size of a man's head, icy air whipping our necks, shifting from one foot to the other, waiting to enter the sweat lodge. . . . Ever see a sweat lodge? Round, canvas-covered cave, about four feet high and twelve feet wide, where folk around here come to sweat the fire, purify themselves. . . ."

"Sacred ground . . . I know what you mean, Cooper. Abraham used to walk the land he claimed for himself and his people . . . walk it foursquare, declare *the ground I'm on is holy ground* . . . guess like Shalom Alechem said, all spiritual seekers join hands under the seas. . . ." Her eyes fell on his face, softly as moonlight.

"I wanted to be here with you, feel together how infinite and vast the galaxies and universes are. . . . And yet like the psalm, you know, how mindful the Creator is of each of us. . . ." He faced her, letting her shoulders go, detached as the moon. "I don't mean I wanted to show you. I mean, I wanted to be here with you. . . ."

"Why?" She found herself smiling defensively, conscious of the river pull between them.

"Why what? Why why?"

"Why you wanted to walk and show me . . . or know this?. . . . It's lovely, by the way . . . what a beautiful place this is." She caught herself. It had not occurred to her until now that there could be a lovely place left in the world.

"Because sometimes it's the only way to strip all the lies away . . . you know, all the fears . . . something humbling about putting on the whole armor of God, which is no armor at all, like my grandma used to say. . . ."

"But why?" She did not mean it as a challenge. She was asking herself what she was doing there, wanting what the stranger wanted, engaged in some ancient druid practice with a man who was not at all what she had imagined him to be, and, thus, in a way was even more the stranger.

"Because we . . . because we deserve to know each other outside of all the stupid trappings . . . you know . . . Christian, Jew, male, female, tall, short, black, white . . . and just stand under the moon and stars and breath free without even electricity to shape what and who we are . . . and then . . . guess what?"

He sat down on a rock that seemed to plunge to a purple valley, stretched his hand, helped her to his side. They looked away into the silver-washed Santa Ynez Mountains, listening to each other's voice like words streaming from a radio.

"What?" She turned to him, caught his look pierced by sky light.

He smiled, breathed deep, answered in silence.

"Did I ever tell you my favorite poem in all the world?"

"No."

"It was written by an Italian, Salvatore Quasimodo. *Each one is alone on the heart of the earth/ pierced by a ray of sun: and suddenly it's night.* . . . That's it. That's the whole poem . . . isn't that cool?"

Cooper drew closer to her, with arms to his side. He bent his head, caught her lips in flight, clung like a butterfly, with silk wings over her, kissing her kisses without holding her, caressing her in silence with tongue and breath. He made love to her without undressing, and she came on his cupped hand thrust deep between her legs, and then again, naked by the moonlight stretched on the grass, parting like a river to his lips and tongue and chin and urgent fingers. She felt his cry on her and held him fast and came again against him, feeling his fire walk across her middle. They would have stayed out the night, slept on each other until the sun woke them.

"There are coyotes and wolves and even mountain lions in these parts," Cooper whispered in her ear.

Victoria untwined herself, sat up straight, a column in the dark.

"You're kidding, right? Tell me you're kidding."

"Nope." He had remained stretched long across the rock, his head propped against his arm.

"Let's get out of here." Victoria was standing.

He rose, drew his arm around her waist.

"If you insist," he said, "your place or mine?"

They walked hand in hand back to the house, and this time Victoria heard the night creatures echo their chirp against the mountains. They did not stop until they reached her bed, where they made love again and did not sleep until almost dawn.

Ten

LUPE FOUND THE TWO MAKING BREAKFAST, heard the merry sounds of a new couple's laughter and bantering like hens and roosters in her backyard long before she reached the door. The gentleman seemed quiet to her, and not unfamiliar, although she could not place where she might have met him. Victoria wore a different face from the day before, when she had seemed so angular and gray to Lupe, so nervous during her shopping, so equivocating in her choices.

Cooper had received a message through his beeper that seemed to require mathematical deciphering. He sat funneled in his jeans and loose shirt, elbows on the kitchen table, reading numbers off his beeper and transcribing them to paper like hieroglyphics on an ancient tablet. He said some numbers aloud as he carried them to paper, then transposed their sequence in a logarithmic pattern. Victoria brought the bagels and cheese omelets to the table, then sat down beside him, looking on at his mysterious I-ching. Her hair was dark mahogany, still wet from the cold shower she had taken by herself after Cooper had failed to warm up to her invitation.

"You go," he'd said feigning stupor. "I'll get up as soon as you come out."

Victoria waited for her new lover to explain what he was doing, but his concentration seemed to erase her out of sight. Lupe continued the cleaning she had started the day before and asked if she might be needed to drive Victoria into town this day.

"Oh . . . gee, I don't know," said Victoria. "It depends whether Mr. Cooper has his car with him or not. . . ."

Lupe waited silently for her decision. Her eyes gave her away.

She was not a strict religious woman, but her discomfort was apparent at being the sole witness to this obvious morning-after between two strangers, or, at the very least, two unmarried lovers who did not know each other very well.

Cooper was shaken by the silence. He traced the conversation backward, piecing together that Victoria was wondering if he had come by car. She had only seen him at the door and not at the front entrance to the ranch, where cars were parked. But Lupe knew, undoubtedly, whether his car was there or not.

"Uh . . . sure, I did. Got my Chevy out there . . . thought you'd seen it. . . . If you have something to do that's really pressing, maybe Lupe should take you in. . . . I . . . I'm just getting some instructions about a job . . . think I might have to skip out and go down to L.A. this afternoon."

"Oh." Victoria didn't mean to sound like a spurned lover, but that is how she registered to her own ears. She hastened to make it light, to make it known she was reasonable in her expectations. "That's just as well . . . there is a ton of stuff I have to buy to start getting this place in shape. . . ."

Cooper smiled into her eyes. He'd caught her midflight. "But that's not to say I can't be back here tonight . . . if I'm invited, I mean. . . ." He ignored Lupe's presence, squeezed Victoria's hand, kissed her like honey on the mouth.

Victoria laughed and pulled away. She looked to Lupe for condemnation or approval and got neither. The young matron with beads around her neck had turned her eyes to the vacuum cleaner and to the small attachments her *patrona* had bought the day before.

Cooper turned back to his hieroglyphics. He was so open about whatever it was he did, yet so secretive. Victoria made her mind up to ask him about it soon if he did not volunteer on his own. He began eating the omelet as he transcribed the messages with the casual ease of a husband reading the morning newspaper.

A bark that grew insistent, then turned into a howl, turned their heads up. Lupe shut off the vacuum cleaner to discern where the noise came from. Victoria went to the door.

"Oh, it's nothing but that old dog of Mr. Hollister's," said Cooper, "that German shepherd ninja dog of his . . ."

"You know the dog?" Victoria was startled. Lupe squinted her eyes, trying to place where she had come across Mr. Cooper before, but still she could not place him.

"Sure I do! Told you I live just a few miles up as the crow flies . . . and I did some work for Mr. Hollister a while back. . . . I brought in a cargo for him from San Fernando a few times . . . nice gentleman."

"I get it."

"Get what?"

"You wrote you did a lot of traveling, and Mr. Hollister mentioned yesterday that he gets his workers from the San Fernando Valley. . . . So I guess you really are a truck driver, just like the guys in the songs you sent me. How come you didn't tell me before?"

Cooper smiled.

"You didn't ask. And you didn't guess. Remember I asked you to guess, but you didn't want to. . . . Guess now you want to . . ."

"I guess I do." Victoria winked, amused.

"But Penelope . . ."

"Yeah?"

"That's not all I am, you know."

She laughed. "I know, you're a lot more."

"Yeah, but I don't mean that. . . ."

She waited for him to explain. He didn't. "Some day, maybe sipping a lemonade and sitting under a palm tree, I'll tell you . . ." He had finished transcribing his message, closed his notebook, and packed it in his back pocket.

Again, the dog barked, then cried and howled deep—a young wolf calling the pack. Lupe went to the door. She frowned, looked for signs of the shepherd, saw nothing, shook her head.

"Sounds serious. Is he always like this?" asked Victoria.

"Not at all, *señora*," answered Lupe. "He's usually quiet as a mouse. . . . There could be some poachers out in the field. . . ."

"Poachers?" Victoria had a sudden glimpse of herself in a cowboy movie. *Who ever heard of poachers?*

"Naw. Not a chance at this time of day," said Cooper, sipping the cup of Cuban coffee Victoria had prepared. "The dog is obviously bothered by something, but I doubt if it's poachers. . . . Besides, there isn't much to poach here . . . harvest's all done. . . .

Hmm, good *cafecito*. . . ."

"You know Spanish?" Victoria looked at his eyes whenever she addressed him, and he always received her.

"*Un poquito.*"

"How come?"

"Oh, been here and there . . ."

"How come you know the word *cafecito*? Did you ever have Cuban coffee before?"

Cooper smiled. "Oh. Let's see . . . maybe about a thousand dozen times. . . ."

"Really?"

"Really."

"Where did you have it, in Cuba or in Miami?"

"Both."

"Recently?"

"Recently what?"

"Did you have *cafecito* in Cuba recently?"

Cooper moved out of her stare and began collecting his jacket, beeper, and sunglasses. "Depends what yes means," he answered.

"Oh, I see," she said, "that part is reserved for the lemonade under the palm trees, eh?"

"Touché." He laughed.

"Well, did you know you can get struck by lightning if you sit under a palm tree very long?"

"Only if it rains."

Again, the shepherd's howl and cry. This time Mr. Hollister's voice called out for him. Then, the loud ring of the kitchen phone.

Lupe held out the receiver for Victoria.

"Yes . . . oh, yes, I accept . . . Ideliza? . . ." Victoria covered the mouthpiece and whispered to Cooper that it was Bembé's mother, calling from New York.

"Can you send Bembé to spend some time with me here? . . . It's really great . . . think it would be a great experience for him. . . ."

Ideliza's voice boomed through the plastic. Cooper could not make out what she was saying—and not because his Spanish failed him—but he could tell it was not a simple yes or no.

"I see . . ." Victoria's face grew still. "Well, are you sure? I mean. How do you know he's missing? I mean, you don't speak to Kitty, do you? Did Kitty tell you? How did you find out?"

Another loud and muffled explanation on the other side.

"Well, in that case, maybe you should come here to be with me, Ideliza. . . . He's probably on his way here, don't you think? I mean, both of them probably are, no? Yes . . . hmm . . . aha. Well, I can get an electronic ticket for you. . . . Let me have your . . . yes, I'll call you with it as soon as I can book a flight. . . . You just show up at the airport, and you can just get the ticket from the machine . . . to Los Angeles . . . then a small plane to Santa Barbara . . ."

Cooper watched her hang up the phone and waited for an explanation. Victoria's air grew suddenly serious. She walked to the bathroom, ran the tap water, splashed her face.

"So?" Cooper was waiting at the door.

"It's just weird . . . Ideliza . . . that's Bembé's mother, she says Bembé has disappeared and that so has Roberto, my brother. . . ."

"You mean they're both missing?"

"Yeah. Says Bembé suddenly left the house, that she didn't see him leave . . . and she also got a call from Kitty, my sister-in-law, inquiring if she had seen Roberto. . . . He didn't go home last night. . . ."

Cooper shrugged his shoulders.

"Well. It seems clear. The kid and the father left together . . . seems natural . . . heard you say they would probably be coming here?"

"Not so natural at all. Ideliza seems worried, that's the thing. . . ."

"Got it."

Victoria looked in her bag for the travel agent's card. She would need to book the flight as soon as possible.

"Are you worried or something, Penelope?"

"Yes. Guess I am. Worried mostly about Bembé, if you want to know the truth. . . . He's a deaf-mute, you know. . . ."

"But his dad ain't, right? And he's probably with his dad, no?"

"Maybe. Maybe not. Anyway, Cooper, why don't you go do your business, and I'll take care of bringing her here . . . and getting some things with Lupe. . . . The other bedroom is just a mess in this house. I don't know if I did right to invite her."

Cooper arched his eyebrows.

"What about tonight?"

Victoria smiled. This much of him she did imagine: his questions were uncensored.

"Well, you just do your business and come back when you're done and we can have supper together and I can have Lupe pick Ideliza up at the airport. Sound good?" She made an effort to smile, to keep their brief life untarnished by daily life.

"Yeah. This will be my last job for a couple of weeks . . . taking my vacation right about now."

"That sounds good. Maybe you'll finally tell me what you do, now that you're taking a vacation? Okay, truck driver?"

"Ten-four, partner."

Before he left, and with Lupe still in their midst, Cooper kissed her like a lover, leaving the imprint of the night before fresh on her flesh.

Past the door, halfway along the narrow path they had walked under the moon hours before, he turned to meet her face. "Two things I ask, Penelope. First, don't worry till you have to. And second, *don't analyze, utilize,* like the folks in AA say. . . . Ponder those things, professor . . . how about it?"

Victoria nodded. She felt a clutch at the throat watching him walk away, disappear around the terra-cotta path.

Moments later, she felt the live presence of his body against hers and began to give way to the million visions and revisions that plagued her doubts and actions. Midstream, she stopped before the cabinet mirror, pursed her lips, and admonished herself: *"Don't analyze. . . . Utilize!"* She wanted to do just that, even if Cooper's Twelve-Step ditty also sounded farcical, as make-believe as the whole notion of Bembé running away from home or Ideliza's imminent arrival.

Kitty was not answering the phone. The machine was off—*perhaps the tape ran out.* If she called her parents, and it turned out Kitty had spared them, as Roberto no doubt had instructed her to do under all circumstances, then Victoria would be giving it away. But if they knew Roberto was missing, then they needed to hear her reassurance. Victoria paced the narrow hall between the kitchen and the living room, facing the new addition windows that looked on the bare rows of muscatel and merlot.

Victoria sent Lupe shopping for essentials while she booked Ideliza's flight and attempted to get some trace of Bembé's and her brother's whereabouts. Her hair had dried and seemed to uncurl slightly on its own in the desert air. She brushed it back and gathered it with a barrette to keep it out of sight. She was wearing the shirt Cooper had brought as a spare and khaki shorts that Francisco once filled.

Victoria laughed out loud. It occurred to her that a rabbi would prove handy at this time. This business of deciding whether to call or not reminded her of Shabbat days back in Newark, when her father and his temple cronies would sit around the kitchen table discussing the Madrash, asking each other what was allowed and what was not. *And then, the Talmud says, some questions don't have answers.*

She tried Kitty again, pacing the hall as far as the wall phone would go. Suddenly, the shepherd barked. This time, not with a cry or howl, but like a sentinel at the palace door. Victoria looked out in the direction of Mr. Hollister. Like shadow play, she caught a fleeting figure in the window, then it vanished. A man's face. Dark hair, deep-set eyes. No more. She put down the receiver, walked to the window, pulled the screen doors open, and stuck her head out to see what she thought she had seen. A strangely familiar mien, yet so ghostly in its flight, she could not even tell if it was a man at all.

"Anyone there?" she asked into the air. The shepherd stopped. No one there.

She tried Kitty again. This time, she answered.

"Well, does Roberto ever stay away without calling?" Victoria cut to the chase. Kitty seemed sedated, which would have been Victoria's guess. That old quiet desperation that Victoria had labeled her with. *Hysterically calm.* That was Francisco's term.

Kitty measured her response.

"Well, sometimes he hasn't called if he's been caught late working or doing some sort of research and perhaps has thought not to wake me, you know, to let me sleep, as sometimes I have trouble . . ."

"So maybe he's just working or doing research somewhere . . ."
Kitty cleared her throat: "Maybe."
"Just maybe? You don't buy it, right, Kitty?"
Silence.
Victoria could not tell if she was crying or taking a sip of gin.
She waited.
"No, Victoria, I don't buy it. I have this . . . this fear that something happened to him."
"What do you mean? You think something happened to him?"
Victoria repeated the words, searching for meaning. Kitty knew more than she let on.
"You didn't call my parents, right?"
Kitty laughed dry. "No, goodness. You know I know better than to worry those dear people in New Jersey."
"Good, I'm glad." *Those dear people.* "Did you call the police?"
"I did."
"And?"
"They have to wait forty-eight hours before a person can be declared missing."
"And how long has it been?" Kitty was making her pull teeth.
"Forty."
"Oh. Good. I mean, you can get them going soon. It's terrible, Kitty . . . I'm sorry. I don't want to worry, and I don't want you to worry, so maybe that's why I don't feel that there's anything wrong. . . . You know Roberto used to scare the whole family with his disappearances once in a while. . . ."
"Yes."
Victoria paused, poured herself a cranberry juice with one hand, holding the receiver between chin and shoulder. The dog barked. She looked out. This time, the ghost figure moved slower. She saw his face and shoulders. *A familiar face.* Suddenly, she was seized by the uncanny notion that the stranger alerting the dog and circling her house looked like her brother David, or how David might look now.
She bolted for the door, made her way out to the side of the house, leaving Kitty holding the line.
"Hello! Who's there . . . anyone there?"
The ghost visitor had vanished. A fog had rolled in around the

terra-cotta path, looped its way round the merlot fields. The shepherd drew to a whimper, then hushed.

"Kitty? Are you still there?"

"Ahuh . . . been waiting here . . . figured you had to take care of something . . ."

"Listen, I'm sorry. It's the strangest thing . . . this dog, Mr. Hollister's dog, he keeps barking sporadically . . . and now just in the last hour or so, I saw a man go by the window right here in the living room . . . so I just had to find out . . ."

"Oh Victoria, you better be careful! Why don't you tell Mr. Hollister, then? It's not safe for you to be there in the middle of the vineyard with some man lurking around. . . . Did you see him? I mean, when you went out?"

"No. He was gone."

"That's odd. Did you ask if anyone was there? How about Mr. Hollister, could that be him?"

"I guess so, but I doubt it."

"Oh, so you saw the man. . . . It wasn't Roberto? I was kind of hoping maybe . . ."

"No. Funny thing is his face, it reminded me of my older brother, David. Isn't that weird?"

"Oh, David? But he's in Cuba!"

"That's what Roberto tells us. I don't know. I'm not saying it was David. I just caught a glance . . . well, two glances. But it looked like him . . . it's not so much the look either. Something in his eyes, a split-second thing..."

"Strange. Well, I think you should tell Mr. Hollister about this. He's responsible for you there, you know. He's supposed to take good care of you. Roberto gave him strict instructions. I heard him myself."

"Oh, don't worry, Kitty. You're right, I will tell Mr. Hollister as soon as we hang up . . . but I'm not entirely alone, anyway, you know."

"Oh, yes, the maid, she came . . . she's there with you, then? She's a good girl. . . . Lora . . . Lura . . . is that her name? Lovely woman. Very able. She took care of us when we were there last fall . . . and speaks English, don't you know."

"Lupe. Yes, she does. Think she was born here." Victoria

braced herself. This was no time for political evangelism. And perhaps it was good that Kitty had not picked up on her strange desire to announce Cooper's advent.

"So, Kitty, I don't know. I feel that maybe there's something you're not telling me. . . . I mean, do you have a reason to worry? Do you think something is wrong? You could call the hospitals, you know. . . . What about Dr. Joe, Roberto's man, I'm sure he can be of help. Did you call him, I hope?"

"Oh yes, Dr. Joe and I have been on the phone all day. He's the one who called the police for me. . . . And he called all over . . . hospitals and places Roberto might be at . . . all kinds of places. . . . I even called Ideliza, you know, Bembé's natural mother . . . she has the boy for a few days . . . but she said she hadn't seen him, that Bembé had not seen him since he dropped him off at her apartment three days ago."

Victoria scanned the windows, looking for traces of the figure, but only the mist rising formed faces on the windowpane.

"But is there something I don't know? I mean, something you're not telling me?" Victoria wondered why Ideliza had not told Kitty that Bembé was missing, too.

"No . . . well, nothing I can put my finger on . . ."

"But something?"

"Well, it's just those calls. . . . Roberto's been getting some calls lately that upset him an awful lot, even if he doesn't tell me about it. . . ."

"Oh, yeah, I remember . . . he got a call that last time my parents and I were there . . . you seemed to think it was a patient. . . . He looked upset, though. . . ." Victoria was surprised at her detachment but knew it was not detachment. It was alertness in the face of danger.

"Well, maybe you're right, Victoria. Maybe Roberto is up to one of his Cuban antics. . . . Anyway, Dr. Joe will be coming by soon, and we're going to go to the precinct together."

"You are going to go to the precinct? What precinct? Are you sure you should go?"

"Yes, I want to. I want to talk to the policemen myself and see if there is any kind of search they can put out without getting it in the papers or something. You know, as a physician, Roberto has to be careful."

"Are you going to tell the police about the calls? I think you should."

"Well, if it comes to that, I will, of course."

Eleven

"WHEN I WAS AROUND TEN, FRESH AFTER MY mother moved us to the Lompoc Valley, I found the word *hermaphrodite* in a book on Greek mythology. . . . I don't know if this ever happened to you, Penelope, but for a flicker of a firefly, I knew what I was . . . knew what girls were, and that I'd been told I was one. And I was, sometimes. I'd been told what boys were, too, and that I wasn't one. But I was, anyway, sometimes. So for just a moment, reading that secondhand book on my mom's night table, I had a picture of who I was. Then I read through to the end of the paragraph and realized it was just a story about some mythical beast. . . . So I told myself I couldn't be that, that it couldn't be who I was. I don't think I was really conscious of gender, at that point, anyway. I was just a person."

Victoria was cradled in the wall, a human niche, sipping the rosemary tea Cooper had brewed, aware that the slightest rustle or shift in her attention might turn the moment, make him recant, stop his daring lark flight. She trailed and memorized his words. Myriad sensations played on her like rapid fire—*loss, fear, revulsion, desire, prurience, disbelief, belief, humor, the pull of pity, even the tender mercy she felt for Bembé.*

Victoria had long stopped examining her deep heart's core or questioning the whys and hows of others. Remaining above water seemed daunting enough. There was no room for Jung or Freud. Still, Cooper had shaken her, made her question herself. His confession seemed to come out of left field, blindsiding her, clutching at her lungs. *There is a deep self that knows truth before it surfaces.* Her erstwhile poet used to tell her that, and back then, she would accuse him of being a Freudian slave.

She had never intended to interrogate him or *force the moment to a crisis. Confessions are double-edged.* Someone hands you their heart, *demands of reciprocity attached.* Her question, the words that had precipitated Cooper's astonishing apologia after an intoxicating evening of passionate and constant intercourse, had been asked innocently enough. She'd held the shaft of his penis in her hand, fingered the soft membrane wedged where testicles should be, and had inquired spontaneously, without reflection, without blame or surprise—perhaps attributing the loss to one of Cooper's secret missions, which he'd hinted at but refused to discuss. She'd never imagined. . . . He had been cautious and private in his e-mails. Not one hint. In bed he'd shown her strength, virile resolve, the whole gamut of masculine imperatives. There was no hint of femininity in him. *Or was there?* Had she looked but refused to see? Could she be so out of touch as to overlook the obvious? And, even so, what did it mean? She could only see him as he was now.

Cooper poured a second cup of rosemary, slipped off his Jockey T-shirt over his head. He paced in his black briefs, semierect, comfortable in his engagingly pubescent body, his thin-haired thighs, and hairless chest with rosettes like women's nipples, a long white scar across his chest and belly button, his smooth, slightly rounded hips and buttocks, his taut calf muscles, his sharecropper biceps and low-hung pelvis.

She signaled with her eyebrows—*And then? What happened?*—afraid that uttering a single sound would bring on self-consciousness, make him halt suddenly when he had long piloted past the line of no return.

Cooper looked away, turning to her eyes in furtive milliseconds, pacing slowly, sitting at the bottom of the bed, bolting to the other side, gazing at the olive Santa Ynez Mountains for echo and backbone.

"Well . . . things really started happening after that . . . and two years later, my body went totally haywire. My hips spread, my voice started to break. Breasts grew, but guess what? So did my beard. I began to get intermittent menstrual periods, and intermittent morning erections. . . . And Penelope, I swear, there ain't nothing worse than getting both at once . . . like getting a blast from a double-barreled shotgun."

He chuckled, looking for her to see the humor and absurdity, perhaps to agree that despite it all, he was no freak. Victoria shook her head, squinted with open mouth, and whispered, "Unbelievable . . . it's the sort of thing . . . I think I . . . I probably would have gone over the edge a long time ago . . . can't believe I'm looking at you now, that you survived all that. I'm just stunned. . . . Wow, only Cooper . . ."

He nodded, squeezed her hand.

"Yeah. It was loony-tunes time. You could say it felt totally unreal . . . and I mean, really unreal. Then, one day, out of the blue, as the Lakota ancestors would have it, clear out of the blue, I remembered the Greek myth book I'd found on my mother's night table and I started . . . well, I was just amazed. . . . It hit me that this thing, this male and female fusion or maybe not fusion, this coexistence that I'd felt all along was in my head and in my head only, and that no one else could possibly know about or understand it. I felt that this thing, my own secret shame and desire, was suddenly becoming visible, becoming real. It exploded outward over my body like war, like a tornado, like some sort of voodoo or one of those Cuban *santería* curses. The book had said it was a myth, but this Hermaphrodite had come and got me. . . ."

"It's incredible, Cooper. In some way, it feels unreal to hear you . . . and yet not strange or anything . . . seems unreal and yet human. Come sit by me a bit, won't you? I want to hear what you did, how you lived . . . I mean, I really want to hear it, but believe it or not, to a certain point, it also scares me a little."

"Yeah. I know. You don't wanna see me suffer, right? Even see me suffer in the past?"

"Yes. How did you know that's what scared me?"

"Uh. I dunno . . . a lucky guess. Just like I know I caught you by surprise and maybe you're questioning your sanity or wondering if you're gay or something. . . . Well, don't worry about that. You had no way of knowing, and I had no way of telling you before, though God knows I wanted to . . . and you're not gay. Not today, anyway. Maybe you got the Indian sign on me . . . just like I guessed I could tell you about it, about my "it," I mean, when I never did tell anyone else."

"You have never told anyone else?"

"Nope."

"What about MJ? She never knew?"

"No. She didn't. I wasn't as grown-up then as I am now, Penelope. . . . And to hit that bottom we've e-mailed each other about . . . you know, that *freedom's just another word for nothing left to lose* mind-frame in order to be able to look at certain things square in the eye. And I mean, not only that, not just to look at them, but let people see me . . . you know, with my defenses down . . . and all those other corny things like *I gotta be me* . . . that babble brook, touchy-feely stuff, you know. . . ."

He trailed off, parodying his clichés. Victoria leaned on his shoulder, squeezed his hand to her chest.

"I guess sometimes people have to die in order for us to finally get certain fundamental things. . . ."

"Guess so. Don't know. Know there are certain unavoidable little trips to hell now and then in everybody's life . . . for sure . . ."

"Cooper?"

"Yeah?" he arched his eyebrows, kissed her lips.

"I don't want you to stop now."

"Stop what?"

"Stop telling me the whole story . . . how you became you. . . ."

"Ah, shucks . . . had a whole 'nother thing in mind . . ."

"Cooper . . . don't stop now. Okay?"

"Okay. Okay. It's still hard, you know, even if I can be a little more relaxed now that you didn't chase me out of your house with a broom or anything. . . ."

"Yeah. Very hard, I know. But I need to know . . . and you need me to know, right?"

"Yeah . . . well, so . . . next. Next came years of doctors . . . so many I can't count . . . and medications, and tests, and enough blood drawn from my arms to feed a whole legion of vampires. In the end, I was diagnosed as having something called . . . are you ready? Secondary congenital adrenal hyperplasia. And, to the doctors' annoyance, I developed a very bad allergic reaction to these things called corticosteroids, which are the drugs of choice to treat my so-called condition.

"The stupid thing is that every new doctor I went to would refuse to believe that I had this intolerance and insist on testing me with it anyway, and I would always faint and fall all over myself in front of them. One of them, I remember, yelled at me. He said, 'You're not supposed to be having this reaction!' I finally got so mad I screamed back: 'Don't tell me what I'm supposed to have! I'm a human being and I have a Physician's Desk Reference of my own!' So, anyway, since I couldn't tolerate these corticosteroids, he decided the next line of damage was simply to put me on high-dose estrogens and hope for the best."

"Where was your mom in all this? Did she know about it? She must have . . ."

"My mother? Well, she was sort of different, as moms go. Back then, she had joined a whole group of separatist feminists . . . we lived in this commune . . . and, needless to say, she was very distressed when her 'daughter' began to grow chin whiskers, body hair, and a cracking voice. Told me flat-out she could never love a son. I did have a real nice grandma down in Florida, though . . . still do . . . and she was real sweet to me, accepted me as I was, told me God didn't make no mistakes. . . . But I didn't get to see her in those days . . . not much anyway."

"That sucks about your mother. Look what she would have made *me* miss! I'd have to sue her for alienation of affection!"

Cooper laughed. "Jewish humor? Always breaks me up."

"Me, too."

They exploded in laughter into each other's eyes, then exhaled whatever air was still trapped between their ribs from holding their breath.

"So. Where were we? Your mother was a pig." Victoria registered how at ease she felt with him, despite this most improbable scenario.

"Yeah. My mother was a Piggly Wiggly. Maybe worse. Later, and I mean years later, I found out I'd had what's known as the primary version of CAH, ambiguous genitalia, at birth, and that my mom and the doctor had agreed to pare down my penis as much as possible and shoot me with female hormones and make me a girl. . . ."

"My God." Victoria finished the tea quickly, poured herself another cup. She was visibly shaken, but Cooper, midway on the high wire, continued his fire walk step-by-step.

"Anyway, as it was, the estrogen made me psychotically depressed and dangerously hypertensive. It also made me ovulate, for the first and last times, and, get this: I got pregnant."

He caught her eyes, clung to them like moths. Victoria didn't flinch. She would practice Lord Byron's admonition: *suspension of disbelief.* In Hebrew school, she'd heard a Treblinka survivor tell unspeakable tales of carnage and torture. The woman maintained that ever since the Holocaust, Jews can never be surprised by anything again. *Look everything in the face without fear or weakness, everything.*

"So? Are you grossed out yet?"

"No. I'm not. I guess you were still a girl then. . . . I mean, yeah, it feels weird, but not ghastly . . . not . . ."

"Freakish?"

"Yeah. Right. Freakish. Not freakish, I mean."

"Whew!" Cooper smiled, wiping a finger of relief across his forehead.

"I mean . . . you don't have some secret baby stashed somewhere in the chardonnay fields being raised by mountain lions or anything, right?"

They laughed, breathed in tandem again.

"No. Not a chance . . . but since I was sleeping with heterosexual men in my teens . . . I should say, in a desperate effort to be normal, not because I liked it, it was inevitable. . . . It may crack you up to find out that my mother was overjoyed I was having an illegitimate child at thirteen, malformed uterus and all. As it was, my internal organs held out for eight months and then spat out a premature child—a normal boy, strangely enough."

"Jesus H. Christ, Cooper. You must have felt so awful."

"I did. Anyway, I wasn't in any shape to bring up a child . . . that's my son I wrote you about. My grandma brought him up. I didn't see him till he was full grown. By then Grandma introduced me as his dad. We get along real well now, but you know, I say to myself, maybe later . . . don't think I really know him as my son. But back then, when he was born, I had so many mixed-up feelings, I couldn't tell you which was worse . . . I guess the worse was, well . . ."

"That you thought you were a boy . . . or that you *were* a

boy . . . I mean, I suppose that was it, no?"

"In a nutshell, yeah. But there's always lots of barnacles, other issues hanging on when you're slaying invisible dragons and stuff, I mean.

"So, fast-forward a few years later, the doctors took me off the hormones. The hypertension was just too much, and everybody thought I was going to croak. So, I asked the MDs, *what now?* Don't believe they had a clue. One of them put me on an anti-androgen, which didn't seem to do much except make me run to the bathroom all the time. And then, plain and simple, I was dropped. . . ."

"You were dropped?"

"Yeah, MDs said there was nothing else they could do for me. I think that's when I started to crack, right after they took me off the hormones and hung me out to dry. I spent nine months living in a little cabin on the banks of the Chumash Wildlife Sanctuary, going nuts. My body was withdrawing from all the medication, and I had psychotic mood swings, real depressed, had some very scary uterine hemorrhages. I ran naked in the snow. I talked to trees and peed at them with my little pecker like a water pistol. I let my body do what it wanted. I remember screaming out that Hermaphrodite the Greek God had made me this way, and that I was going to be natural, just be myself and screw the world. . . ."

"Wow. I can't believe I'm looking at the same person, Cooper. Did you get some sort of insight in that cabin?"

"Well, it was a nice fantasy to live like a hermit . . . till I wound up in the hospital from bleeding and depression. Anyway, cutting to the chase, finally, at that same hospital, Endocrinologist Number Seven decided to test me to see if my problem had been that they were trying to make me a girl when they should have let me be a boy, and he gave me a shot of testosterone. Well, let me tell you, Penelope, one shot of that testosterone, and I felt like the sun had come up. My depression lifted, and I ran around like a maniac, fixing things I'd had no energy to do before. 'Whatever that was,' I sang to Number Seven, 'I love it! Give me more of that!'"

"Did he?"

"'We can't,' the bastard told me. I asked 'why not?' Told him it solved the problems. I didn't bleed. I didn't get depressed. I didn't have violent mood swings. And the jerk broke it to me this way. He said, 'Cooper, you're not a transsexual. Regular doses of testosterone of that magnitude are indicated only for transsexuals.' According to his big books, I was an *intersexual*, and the treatment for intersexuals consisted in pushing them as hard as possible back toward the gender they had been raised. I guess they were covering their asses for the next time some doctor reassured some worried parent of an intersexual baby that as long as they treated the kid in stereotypical ways, everything would be all right. . . . I mean, no sex-changed intersexual would come bouncing out of the woodwork yelling, 'Oh, yeah?'"

"I would have gone totally ballistic. One hundred percent ballistic."

"I did. Kept asking him to give me the frigging testosterone. The MD said there would be what he called *unacceptable* side effects if I took this drug. So you know what I did?"

"Punched him."

"I said to this character, 'Look, I've been living as a woman with facial hair and body fur for years now. I can handle it. Besides, I don't care if I turn purple and grow horns, personally.' But nope. I wasn't a transsexual, and he wasn't gonna help, and that was that. So, being not too dumb on my grandma's side of my family, I left the doctor's office and thought fast. Transsexual, eh? I'd read enough and knew the routine. Was I one or not? I thought I felt male, but I wasn't really sure what male felt like, except I liked girls and I liked to do boy things, like hunt and fish and kick a ball around an empty field. For that matter, I didn't exactly know what feeling female was either. I'm still not exactly sure how anybody feels male or female. Are you? Anyway, I couldn't stand the way I felt without the testosterone, bleeding all over and feeling kind of crazy, so I reasoned the thing out all by myself. Transsexuals get mastectomies. Okay, I never liked my androgynous breasts anyway, I can do that. Transsexuals get hysterectomies. Well, considering my prior difficulties, ditching my malformed uterus wouldn't be a problem either. I liked having muscles. I did want to have my budding, suppressed penis develop, wanted to feel with it what I felt inside when a certain woman's body aroused me. . . ."

"Far out. I'm stunned."

"Yeah. In the process, I started looking stuff up. I learned I was missing a required enzyme, called 5-alpha reductase, and that boys who are born with this enzyme deficiency are often assigned a female identity at birth. Happens thousands of times a year in hospitals all over America. However, since pubertal genital tissue is sensitive to the effects of testosterone, such a child can experience what MDs call *masculinizing puberty* and genital growth— assuming that their gonads have not been removed, which mine were not. That's how come I was having erections and the menses at the same time and could only pee standing up. No one had ever bothered to explain any of this. . . . The biggest bombshell came when doctors at Cottage Hospital in Santa Barbara finally told me who and what I was. Turns out the main doc there, some sort of brain, wrote a report saying I was, medically speaking, an intersexual who was a *True Hermaphrodite*, with a DNA chromosome karyotype of 46 XXXY, called *mosaic.*"

"Incredible, Cooper. But maybe it made it less confusing? I mean, you felt like a boy, you knew you were a boy who had just been born with two sets of genitals but with a boy's heart. . . . I mean, it's not like you'd ever thought of yourself as a girl, right."

"Yeah. Guess so. Actually, I found out there are different kinds of intersexuals. Learned all kinds of words and medical terms that talked about me from this doc. It was funny to see yourself defined and explained in strange words like *karyotype, mosaic, alpha reductase, androgyne* . . . big words that hold the key to you, but have no meaning or feeling in my head . . . and in the end don't seem to explain anything."

"I know what you mean. An Egyptian hieroglyphic that contains the recipe for some rare elixir, except no one can crack it."

"Yeah! That's exactly right."

"So?"

"Well, turns out some people appear to be males but are biologically females, and then other people with female physical attributes are actually medically, or I guess, biologically, males. Then there is a whole group whose external sex is what the doc explained as *indeterminate*. And there is the group he said I belonged to . . . those of us having external characteristics of both, with the DNA chromosome of what he called both *karyotype* sexes. . . ."

"So, were you relieved to find this out? I can't imagine what it must have been like . . . my hell has been in a totally different zone, and I guess . . . well, let me tell you this, Cooper, it shuts me up totally. Feels like . . . f-u-c-k, what was I whining about . . . know what I mean?"

"Sure. But don't feel that way, Penelope. Everybody's own hell is their own, and feels bad no how . . ."

"Right. Reminds me what my brother David used to say in his mock British accent, *comparisons are odious.*"

Cooper laughed, shook his head, wetted his lips on the teacup's rim.

"So, did you feel better to find out about yourself finally? I mean, just to know you were not just crazy or something?"

"If you want the honest truth, Penelope, back then, before I became the man I guess I was, I was angry that I couldn't just be me, couldn't just be honest and say, 'No, I'm not a woman or a man, I think what I am is a somewhat masculine androgyne, and can we just turn me into that?' But that wasn't an option. It's still not an option. I see both male and female cultural roles as a crock. So I swallowed my rage, said the right things, and got the drugs."

"'How can I know what I think till I've said it.' Compliments of E.M. Forster."

"Oh no. What does that mean? Don't tell me you're gonna make me look something up! I just shot my wad with all the big words I own!" Cooper smiled broadly.

"It means, I guess, that you didn't want to really be a boy till you became a boy . . . that nothing is understood until demonstrated . . . metaphysical stuff, I suppose."

"Yeah, speaking of metaphysics, I think that was the road to a kind of peace that brought me to myself, the spiritual teachings of the Native American people, especially the Chumash in this area. They're the ones who helped me and maybe got me right bright enough to meet someone as terrific and high falutin' as you . . . gorgeous, too."

It was the first physical compliment he'd paid her. It surprised her, stirred her, kindled a feral, impious desire to feel and stroke his fashioned penis inside her again, this time knowing who this man who called himself Cooper was and had been. He drew her to him, standing on his knees, caressed her full breasts, kissed her nipples, sucking for milk with his tongue, whispered against her skin, slipped his lips slowly to her hidden equator.

"This is sort of metaphysical," she quipped, stroking his ready member nestled inside the black briefs. "I mean it's . . . it feels slightly out of this world . . ."

"That's what I wanted to tell you . . . Walker Between Worlds . . . did you ever hear that phrase?"

Cooper split the elastic band of her panties with a single jerk, tossed them aside, rubbed her cool skin against his, caressed her buttocks with his fingertips, slipped a firm hand between her thighs, then skimmed his solid member inside her, fucking her in syncopation to their coos and conversation, arousing each to an impending climax, then holding back in Tantric elegance, stopping and going, rising and fucking hard and long again, conversing at ease, using their verbal banter as both aphrodisiac and bunting, swelling their lurch and sway and fever pitch until neither one could prolong the ecstasy a moment longer.

"For example, did you know that the concept of a gender gamut, completely separate from biological sex types, is something totally accepted by native cultures? Many native religions call people like me *berdache*."

"I didn't know. But it makes sense. . . . Speaking of doctors, and all the bad luck you had with them, at least you found a real good doctor in the end, Cooper. . . . Whatever he did, or she did, she did right. I think you're quite a man . . . a lover man. . . ."

"He. He gave me the right hormones, then cut me open and cut me up, closed up the uterus, reconstructed me using my own original pecker, which did grow more on its own, but needed help. It hurt like hell, hurt for months on end . . . I thought I was turning into a morphine addict, but I didn't. In the end, I just took the pain and flushed the pills down the can. Say, Penelope, that . . . feels real good . . . we can't have babies, you know . . . but I can feel you . . . you feel real . . . gave me such a big boner . . . you like this? Yeah, feels good . . . this . . . like this . . . Penelope . . ."

"Do you have any idea how crazy you are driving me, Cooper? You make me . . . think I'm going to have to . . . can't believe you stay so hard, keep . . . you're driving me completely insane . . . fuck, Cooper, I've never wanted to come so much in my entire life . . ."

Cooper eased his thrusts, pulled out despite Victoria's protestations, slipped his hand between her thighs, kissed her softly, pressed himself against her stomach, guiding his large, obdurate member, stroking it between her breasts. Then, once again pressed urgently into her—gently, slowly, relentlessly.

"The Arapaho of the plains believe that *berdache* people like me exist due to supernatural gifts from birds. The creation story of the Colorado Mohave speaks of a time when people were not sexually differentiated . . ."

"That's fascinating, Cooper. I think you're a scholar in the whole transgender and mythical thing, no? You studied hard . . . guess you had a good incentive . . . whatever you studied, I think you learned a lot . . . and I don't mean just book learning. . . . If you keep doing that, I'm going to have to . . . orgasm . . . can you do it with me again? I want to feel you come with me . . . makes me so hot . . ."

"I can . . . in a little while . . . wanna make love to you, Penelope . . . like making love, like fucking you like this . . . slow and easy . . ." he whispered. "I . . . yeah . . . I was telling you about *berdache* people . . . are you interested?"

"Interested, very. The question is, can I stand it in this, shall we say, vulnerable state . . . hard to think straight . . . but it's racy, too . . . like talking with you like this . . . very cool . . . excruciatingly cool . . ."

He pulled away, held her fast in his arms, stroking her, pressing his ravening member between her breasts.

"In the Omaha language," he continued, "the term *berdache* meant *instructed by the moon.* Many myths warned not to interfere with the fulfillment of the *berdache* role. Consequences could be dire and sometimes resulted in death. An old Sioux legend explains that if nature puts a burden on a man by making him different, it also gives him a special power . . . the Lakota call their *berdache winktes.*

"The Mohave call theirs *alyha. Lhamana* is the Zuni word for *berdache* . . . and the Navajo call us *nadleeh.* There are literally dozens of other names. So, for your information, Penelope, Native

Americans consider the *berdache* a gift to the tribe, someone to be honored and cherished. In the old days, and even today, *berdaches* are believed to have great spiritual vision; they were often viewed as prophets. . . . This is . . . awh you are just terrific, Penelope . . . so . . . fucking . . . good . . ."

"I buy that . . . that you're special, I mean . . . don't know if I buy the prophet part yet, since I know from prophets, but it's cool that you're a *berdache*, Cooper. Weird and—but promise you'll never ever make me tell my parents or anyone else in my family about it because they'll have me committed to Payne Whitney in paper slippers—but yes, cool, very cool. . . . You're a gift to this tribe for sure, let me tell you . . ."

"Which tribe? The tribe of Israel?"

"I knew you were smart."

When they could wait no longer, their rapture turned to magma and then to *a hot spring sparkling to the surface, meandering its way under smooth stream rocks.*

It was almost daybreak and they'd been up twenty-four hours.

"God, Cooper. We better get some sleep. I didn't get to tell you, Bembé and Ideliza are coming today . . . at least I hope they're coming today."

"Oh. So the kid went home?"

"Hmm. It's a long story. He didn't exactly go home. Some person, I haven't yet figured out who or how, turned up with him at the airport. She made Bembé call Ideliza from La Guardia and tell her to come meet him there."

"The kid spoke?"

"Oh. No. He didn't. I'm half asleep . . . or maybe totally worn out by Don Juan over here. The woman talked, she called Ideliza, told her she had Bembé with her, and the tickets I bought her. . . . It's all very strange, but I'm just glad she found him, and that they're coming. Will have to figure out what happened when they finally get here. Asked Lupe to go pick them up at LAX. Thought this would give us some time to straighten things up . . . and some time alone together before, you know, they get here."

"Sounds good. I'll help you fix things up if you'd like. They're sleeping downstairs, I guess. That bedroom is pretty grimy . . . think old man Hollister used to use it to make hooch . . . rot gut."

"Yeah. I'd like to throw out the furniture and paint the room blue and get a new armoire and two queen-size beds."

"No kidding? All that before they get here?"

"I'd like to."

"Oh. Oh. Miss Scarlet."

"Wise guy."

"What about your brother, did he turn up? I meant to ask but . . ."

"Yeah, but. . . . You came in like a banshee. . . . Do you realize it took you ten minutes flat from the moment you came back this evening to the moment you had me lying supine on this bed?"

"'Supine'?"

"Yeah. Look it up."

"So, how about your brother, did he turn up?"

"Last I spoke with Kitty, just before you came, he was a no-show. Don't know what to think, whether I should worry or not. I must admit you have a certain influence on me. . . ."

"Like what?"

"I worry less. I mean, I think I should worry about Roberto, but I don't feel so worried. Does that make sense?"

"Yeah. It does. It's just like my grandmother says, 'Making whoopee makes a person feel unconcerned.'"

"Funny. You do a great southern accent, too."

"Comes naturally. In my genes. Redneck to the core. You like that?"

"Yes, like it a lot. You're such a Gentile. Such a *goy*. You have no idea. Someday I'll tell you . . . maybe."

"Yeah. But I think I know what you're gonna say. . . ."

"How come?"

"MJ was Jewish, too."

"You're kidding."

"Nope. Thought I'd told you that. Matter of fact, I'm sure I told you she was Jewish . . . several times. Guess it flew over the cuckoo's nest. That's okay."

"God, I hope it's not some sort of fetish or kinky thing on your part."

"You hope what is not a kinky thing?"

"The fact that you like Jewish women . . . you know, like certain white people only want to sleep with Blacks or Asians?"

"Don't worry. I never thought about it. It's not that. It's you."

"You're a gent, Cooper."

"That's better than Gentile. Say, that woman who called Ideliza with your ticket, what was her name?"

"Funny you should ask. I've been thinking about her name because there is something weird about it . . . it's an Israeli name. Yael. That's the name Ideliza gave me. She had actually written it down to tell me. She thought she worked for me, that I had sent her. But all I did was get my travel agent to get the ticket and hold it for them at the airport."

"Yael? Did you say Yael?"

"Yeah. Yael. Why, does it ring a bell?"

"I've worked . . . I mean done some work for someone named Yael. Yael Herzog. That's the name. I don't know. . . . I'd have to think about it . . . but I'm feeling a little sleepy just now. . . ."

"Okay. Good night."

"Bed bugs bite."

The marine layer and cool breeze from the mountains set in just as they finally surrendered, cocooned in one another's twine, deaf to the shepherd's howls and oblivious to the familiar face watching them sleep from the skylight window above the bed.

Twelve

I am a writer who came of a sheltered life.
A sheltered life can be a daring life as well.
For all serious daring starts from within.
—Eudora Welty

THEY RUSHED TO THE FRONT GATE TO GREET Ideliza and Bembé.

Upright, dressed, and armored, Cooper seemed remarkably measured. He appeared gracious, light-footed, not far from the man she had imagined him to be when he first appeared at the screen door, before they'd lain naked *under a shroud of stars.* Then, as now, Victoria was struck by his *untarnished innocence.* It made him look not the five or six years her junior he probably was, but all of sixteen, a beguiling adolescent, a strapping swain emerging into manhood. *Cooper the* berdache, *the wise man in redneck trappings. Cooper the wanderer between two worlds, sacrificial debunker of gender and false identities.* Yeats' verse came to her lips: *Bodily decrepitude is wisdom; young loved each other and were ignorant.*

Bembé jumped into her arms before they'd made eye contact. He bolted from Lupe's car in a single leap across his mother's lap, propelled by his cannonball head. Victoria held him fast to her, fastening his legs around her waist. She twirled him around the eucalyptus tree by the car paddock and covered him with kisses while Ideliza and Cooper watched from the sidelines, forming an instant bond of laughter and surprise at the wonder of this love affair between moon-headed child and star poet.

"You rascal!" Victoria shouted, exaggerating her facial muscles so he could read her lips. "How could you just up and, poof, disappear like that on your mother and me! You had us so worried sick! Worried sick, do you hear, you little rascal!"

To which Bembé, packed in a blue and white sailor suit from Macy's, grinned and silently declared, "You are so beautiful, Victoria! Let's whirl around the silvery tree again!"

Victoria put him down with a wink, turned to welcome Ideliza—Cuban *abrazos* and two-cheek kisses; fast-clipped Spanish, two pitches higher than Victoria's normal range, salted with *"¡ay chica!"* and *"qué alegría,"* and ending with the burning question that could not keep till dinner: "Any word from Roberto?" Ideliza replied with a silent shake of the head. She said she'd hoped Victoria would have some news for her by now.

"That's so strange for Roberto to be a total no-show this long . . . three days. He always calls home, or calls . . . well, I mean, forget that. Why hasn't he called *me*, since I'm out here at his winery. . . . Do you think we should worry, Ideliza?"

Was Victoria asking for hope or a simple opinion? Ideliza wavered between her private doubts and her natural inclination to put her host at ease.

"Well, I wouldn't . . . *Ay*, I don't know, to tell the truth, Miss Victoria," she answered. "I agree it's strange he hasn't called his family . . . and usually this time of the month he would have paid me a visit. I'm doing some *trabajitos*, asking the saints to tell me something . . . at least where he is . . . maybe Changó will visit me soon . . . especially since, let's not forget, here I am. I've come all the way to Santa Barbara, which belongs to him."

Victoria agreed with Ideliza's concern, disregarding the part about asking the saints.

"Well. We should hear back from Kitty any moment. I left around ten messages on her machine, I think. Let's hope Roberto's back home by now and just too exhausted, for whatever crazy reason, to pick up the phone . . . and that Kitty took so many valiums she can't hear the phone ring either. . . ."

"Yes. Better to wait and see . . ." Ideliza's voice trailed off. She squeezed Victoria's hand, smiled tenderly in her persona as priestess of Spanish Harlem, spiritual counselor, sorceress of the night.

Cooper interrupted them, motioned to Victoria, and pointed

with a smile at the child waiting with arms crossed under the eucalyptus tree behind her.

"Oh, all right!" she returned to Bembé, gesturing with arms and hands, "but only a couple of more times, okay? It's making me see double . . . even triple!"

Cooper escorted Ideliza into the house, stepped in front of her and disappeared, aware of her papaya breasts shooting flames behind him. He carried her trunk into the newly painted blue room with a new queen bed for mother and son. Her trunk was so formidable in breadth and bulk that Cooper's wrist cramped instantly, and he wound up lifting the handle with both arms and dragging it along the floor from time to time.

"Whew . . . gotta be a mummified corpse in there, I swear, nearly yanked my hand off," he muttered to himself, slightly embarrassed as she explained away his seeming lack of brawn.

"So *fuerte*, so estrong, *señor!*" Ideliza raised her voice so he could hear her as he walked back to help Bembé and Victoria. "Do you heah abouh Changó? Your relative, I think . . . but I don't know for sure. The *babalao* would know, but I need my cowry shells. Ju know whah I talking abouh?"

"Yeah, I do . . . Changó. *Que viva Changó*, right? Heard Celia Cruz sing it once, in Miami. Calle Ocho. So, great, you speak English?!" He thought Victoria had told him Ideliza didn't speak a word.

Victoria caught up to Ideliza. Bembé trailed behind, clutching at her belt loops. *Mi casa es su casa*, she said to Ideliza, insisting that she feel at home, pointing to the essentials—bathrooms, shower stall, fresh towels, closets, blankets, medicine cabinet, earthquake preparedness knapsack under the bed.

"Take a breath and rest or shower or do whatever you need to decompress," said Victoria. "I know it's late for you, and you had such a long trip and probably ate on the plane, but Lupe cooked something for us, and I'd love it if we could chat a little. Then we can all get some rest and pick up in the morning. . . . What do you say? I made plans to take us all to see the vineyards around here

tomorrow . . . maybe even drive up to the beach for a swim. If it's
too cold to go in, at least we can look. The Santa Barbara coastline
is . . . well, a lot of people say it's gorgeous. . . . Can Bembé join us
for a little bite tonight also, or is it past his bedtime?"

"Not a chance of keeping Bembé all cooped up in here . . .
boy's too nosy . . . and anyway, he slept all the way. Ay, you know
what is just amazing, Miss Victoria? This incredible country air,
this earth and sky fragrance . . ." Ideliza opened her bedroom window, gazed long into the rows, the vines, and tilted stalks, the
Santa Ynez Mountains refractory of verdigris and purple.

"Please don't call me *Miss*, Ideliza. Just Victoria, okay? After
all, we're practically related, no?"

Ideliza continued color gazing and responded without facing
Victoria: "Ah . . . so you found out about Bembé, eh? How? You
guessed it?"

"Well, let's put it this way, Ideliza: It didn't take a brain surgeon. You know, one look at Bembé's eyes . . . I think even my
mother got it on the first bounce. And, mind you, my mother's in
her seventies and has cataracts in both eyes."

Ideliza exploded with startling abandon—*a rousing prolonged
laughter/ head and headdress tossed in a backward glance/ undulating flamenco shoulders/ fanning a fusillade of ruffles.*

Victoria was swept up in her merriment and music, enrap-
tured by her ease. And while she basked in it, a sudden revelation
came to her, a memory long buried of her brother David sitting
beside her on the front stoop, attempting to explain Roberto's penchant for "brown sugar," *azúcar prieta*, as he put it.

*Roberto likes mulatto Cuban women because they're earth moth-
ers.* He'd tried to make sense of their brother's predilection for
*Ebony Magazine. Because, don't you get it Victoria, they own where
they stand, bless the ground holy like Abraham. A Cuban mulatta
strolls down Fifth Avenue or Calle Línea like some voluptuous bombshell, naked down to her glass house slippers, shuffling from bedroom
to bedroom and all the while giving you the eye.* This native ease, this
unself-conscious sense of place and permanence, grounded Roberto. It allayed his nameless fears, covered his head under the shadow of the Almighty, led him safely through the valley of death. It

was the one aspect of Roberto's hall of mirrors that both Victoria and David could understand—*an antidote to the Lobo family's congenital angst and turgid sensibility, to the malaise of displacement,* which also plagued Victoria, even when happiest and most relaxed.

Bembé felt his mother's rolling vibrations, grinned at Victoria as though he'd heard and understood not only the exchange between his mother and aunt, but her own private thoughts and recollections of a slice of time with David so very long ago. While the two women spoke and Ideliza transformed the room with laughter, Bembé staked out his side of the bed, unplugged the lamp by the night table, and began recharging his laptop and organizing the notebooks he used to paint and to converse with her.

"Well, see you two in a little bit then," Victoria smiled and turned toward Cooper, who had been waiting in the hall outside the bedroom door.

"Thank you, Victoria," Ideliza trailed to a slow stop. "To tell the truth, I don't know why I came or why we are here, but I am sure Changó, or at least Eleggua, will tell me when he feels like it. The country air is . . . well, it's very good . . . *el monte*, where the *orishas* live . . . did Roberto ever tell you about it? About the *santos*, I mean? Did you know this whole city, this whole *campo* and city we're in belongs to Changó? Changó is the *ochá*, the Santería religion's name for Santa Barbara. Did Roberto mention that to you?"

Victoria shook her head.

Ideliza pointed to the colors streaming from the window, named each one after a different *orisha*.

"Changó . . . Ogún . . . Ochún . . . Yemayá . . . and, of course, Obatalá . . . Obatalá, white *orisha*, part of everything . . ."

"Like a color palette . . . white in everything, yes." Francisco always started with white as his base and then succumbed to color. "So. Join us in a little bit, or whenever you'd like. We'll just hang around and munch on some of the finger food. . . . I mean, are you hungry, I hope? I'm starved!"

Ideliza smiled, nodded, then called on Bembé. "Bembé, come here and help me get this trunk upright. Put it on top of that desk." She pointed and Bembé snapped to.

"Oh, would you want Cooper to help you with it. . . . It looks kind of heavy. . . . I'd offer, but lifting is not my main suit. My back goes out on me when I least expect it. . . ."

"*Ay*, no, no. And don't bother the gentleman. He already helped. He carried it all the way in here. Bembé knows how. He's strong."

"Okeydokey. But, Ideliza, *por favor*, call him Cooper, okay? He's not so formal either . . . *¡estás en tu casa!*"

Ideliza smiled. "Yes, I just need a few minutes, Mis . . . I mean, Victoria, thank you . . . you've worked so hard to welcome us today. *Ay*, such a beautiful *campo*, so much green and pale yellow and open country for the *orishas* to romp around in. See those trees, Bembé?" She turned to her son. "Changó likes to hide in trees like that one over there, next to that fence, and smoke his good Partagas cigars. When he smokes, the trees don't burn, because he's the god of fire and lightning . . . and earthquakes, too!" She spoke without straining or facing him so he could read her lips, certain that Bembé could hear with special ears, ears made up not of incus bone, cartilage, and auditory nerves, but of the same ethereal stuff Beethoven's were made of.

"The god of earthquakes, really?" Victoria mused. "In that case, please tell Changó to hold off on any seismic activity while we're in California! You know they have earthquakes here, right?" She caught herself. Perhaps she sounded cavalier, even disrespectful. Not that she would disrespect another's religion—just that she'd never thought seriously of Santería, knew only the urban legends rife with spilled blood and the goring of small animals in senseless sacrifice.

"Oh, yes, earthquakes, huge earthquakes!" Ideliza answered with remarkable alacrity. "Roberto told me about them a long time ago. He wanted to make sure nothing like that happened here when he bought the vineyard. He gave a big offering to Changó before he signed the papers. I did a special *trabajo* with coconut milk and palm oil and lavender flowers for him so the *santos* would listen. Later, he said the grapes came out perfect, even larger and sweeter than usual. I had to laugh. Changó knows how to spit, and when he spits everything grows. And, let me tell you, if anyone can put his foot down on the ground and stop it from shaking, it's Changó . . . Santa Barbara Changó. Personally, I've never felt the earth shake. Have you?"

"No. But my stomach is starting to rumble like there's some kind of tremors going on . . . think it's called hunger. I better go do something about it and help Lupe out before she goes . . . poor thing's been on the road all day, back and forth to pick you up in Los Angeles. . . . And before that she shopped and cooked for a whole army like a pro. Think I better go tell her to go home and get some rest. . . . I'll let you wash up. . . ."

Victoria kissed Bembé's forehead, closed the door, taking with her the image of Ideliza with her nose pressed up against the glass, gazing at the merlot fields, mystified by the *orisha* colors at her window.

She'd had no idea that Roberto dabbled in Santería or that he'd ever asked a *santera* to perform incantations so that his tax-deduction nouveau grapes would prosper and outdo neighboring vineyards for miles around. *Did Roberto's superstitions, secrecy, and mental circumlocutions know no bounds? Who was he?* The answer, as usual, would have to keep. Right now, she had to find out where and how he was. She would try Kitty again.

The thought of Roberto making offerings to Changó clung like syrup. She caught herself humming *How long has this been going on?* and realized it was Ella Fitzgerald's tune—Ella being a chief icon in Roberto's early onanistic pantheon. She laughed at the many humorous tricks of the subconscious, then hung up the phone when voice mail picked up for the umpteenth time. "No answer at Roberto's yet. Ridiculous."

Victoria had planned Bembé's arrival like a birthday party. The new coffee table—rattan, mauve suede and leather to fit its habitat—brimmed with meats and breads and colorful glasses, grapes and dates and *Welcome Home* napkins, streamers and Mexican wood flutes and Mylar balloons. An upright trio of Lobo bottles in a Chumash basket unintentionally divided the meat, dairy, and *pareve*.

Under Victoria's direction, Lupe had fixed special hors d'oeuvres and cooked a full Christmas meal for mother and child who'd come such a long way on their maiden voyage. Roast pork Cuban-style, fried sweet plantains and garlic yuca, along with latkes with sour cream, made according to Sara Lobo's recipe, because the child had grown so fond of Jewish cooking during his visit with Victoria.

Bembé changed into shorts and a T-shirt and joined Victoria in the big room long before Ideliza reappeared. He sampled Lupe's *antojitos* one after another, setting the tortillas, quesadillas, and fried *carnitas* in rows like toy soldiers, taking intermittent bites from each, while Victoria stroked his head, reclining on Cooper, who had stretched out on the new saddle-leather couch and was punching the television control in a semi-daze, skipping back and forth between Fox News and CNN.

When Ideliza finally emerged, she had showered, dispensed with her headdress, and folded her Valkerian tournure into a soft magenta muumuu. Her hair, relaxed by hot comb and Brillantine, was up, beehived, and laced in red and yellow ribbons. A dusting of magnolia-scented talcum had left a piste under her cinnamon arms and open-toe sandals.

"So what happened, Ideliza? Did Bembé simply not go home? How did he wind up at La Guardia by himself? The whole thing sounded so bizarre when you told me. . . ."

Victoria addressed her in Spanish, assuming Cooper could grasp the general idea, although she was not sure he would get the nuances or occasional Cuban slang, a slang that had grown obsolete in Fidel's Cuba but had been frozen in time and codified forever by Cuban *exiliados*.

"That woman called me from the airport . . . she had our tickets . . . she'd taken Bembé. But she was a very nice lady; she put us up in the fancy hotel at the airport, because the plane didn't leave till six A.M. . . . I hope Roberto is paying for that . . ."

"Don't worry about it, Ideliza. I'm just so glad you and Bembé are here. I just tried Roberto again, by the way . . . still no answer."

Victoria joined the finger-food troth. She would not touch the pork and was beginning to suspect Cooper was vegetarian. Ideliza could have the whole roast to herself, if she wanted. Perhaps Bembé would eat it, too. Why shouldn't he? It would keep a few days in the fridge. Good thing Abram and Sara weren't visiting.

"Did Roberto call you or talk to you before you left New

York?" Cooper muted the television, addressed Ideliza, and began keeping pace with Bembé, swallowing one quesadilla after another. His Spanish was flawless, *gringo* accent around the vowels notwithstanding.

"No. Like I told Miss . . . like I told Victoria, I have not heard from Roberto in four days. I thought maybe he had taken Bembé without my permission and it made me mad, but Bembé says he didn't see him. . . ."

"My god, Cooper, you really *do* know Spanish! How come? I can't believe my ears! You kept it from me? I think I'm starting to feel a little paranoid. . . . What else do you speak? Yiddish?" Victoria came to the brink of forgetting herself and her guests.

"I'll explain later, Penelope," he quipped in English, winking cheerfully at her to throw Ideliza off the trail. "I did mention it a couple of times, but I guess you didn't take me seriously. . . . Anyway, just want to . . . you know, let Ideliza tell us what's going on, you know, with these people who put them on the plane, and your brother and all. . . ."

"You're right," Victoria continued in English, "but please remember, the name is Victoria, *por favor*? At least when not in private . . . okay?"

"Yeah, I meant to say Victoria . . . sorry, Penelope." He chuckled, poured each adult a glass of the Merlot Reserve Mr. Hollister had left at the door and handed Bembé a fresh lemonade in the MacDonald's glass he'd picked up for him earlier that day.

"Okay, you arcane and mysterious Janus of many faces . . . I have a feeling there's more at the bottom of those blue eyes of yours than meets the eye . . . maybe a false bottom, like a magician's or prestidigitator's top hat . . . then again, I probably always feel that way about everything. . . ." She laughed at herself.

"Holy Moses, Pene . . . Victoria, don't start making me look things up just now, eh? Presti-what . . . and Ja Noos who?" He mugged, shook his head, flashed her a *Who me?* grin.

"Nothing worth explaining. Just some stupid reference, okay?"

"Fair enough."

They laughed in unison, basking in the warmth of intimate banter. Then Victoria caught herself, shifted gears and addressed

Ideliza in Spanish once again.

"So how on earth did Bembé wind up at La Guardia, Ideliza?"

"I don't know. I just don't know where my boy went, or how he got to the airport." Ideliza was savoring the *antojitos*, making sure she swallowed each morsel before speaking, just as she'd taught Bembé. "I thought maybe Roberto had come in my house and kidnapped him when I was doing a *despojo*, a cleansing for the greengrocer around the block . . . but Bembé says no. . . . He says he just went with that nice lady and a man, the gentleman who waited up with Bembé at the hotel when the lady came to pick me up in a long, shiny black car, big like a bus with only two people in it, the lady and me.

He says they rang my door and when he saw the cowbell shake several times, he let them in because he knows it makes noise and interrupts my prayers. They took him outside where the car was double-parked and went off with Bembé sitting in the back with the man while the woman drove. . . . He said they told him not to interrupt my session. They let him bring his laptop and just took off with him . . . and brought him cream cheese and guava *pastelito* cakes and a six-pack of Coke and a coloring book . . . Pokemón."

"How does he talk to you . . . I mean, how do you know for sure he didn't see Roberto?" Cooper refilled Ideliza's glass.

Ideliza made a hand gesture along her chest, something short of the sign of the cross: "If a mother doesn't know her own child, who does? I simply know. I ask him, and he answers me by painting or writing but mostly by sending me messages from his head."

"I know what you mean," Cooper nodded.

Bembé drank down his lemonade with both hands. He sat on the floor beside Victoria, his laptop close beside him. Ideliza stood up, walked to the front door, and returned to the fields with her eyes again, to *el campo*.

Victoria lifted the wineglass—¡*salud*!

"You have a lot of room out here," said Ideliza, taking stock of the open, uncultivated garden to the right of the house.

"I say we do," answered Victoria. "Especially if you're from New York, like me, and refer to an apartment as a house."

"I was thinking you should plant some nice *hierbas*, some holy and medicinal herbs . . . right out here, maybe in that little corner over there, where it's so open and probably gets a lot of sun. *Cáscara sagrada* bark, jasmine flowers, lemon verbena, valerian root, *hierba buena*, lavender, chamomile . . . you need to do this."

"Ideliza has a point," said Cooper.

Was he serious? Victoria searched his eyes.

"Yes, you need some good herbs here, both of you. For protection and also for medicine, in case you get a tummy ache or cold or some other trickster spirit," Ideliza reaffirmed, looking over the overgrown patch she had staked out.

"Well," said Victoria sighing, "I have to confess I don't exactly have a green thumb. . . ."

"Oh. No problem," exclaimed Ideliza, "I'll do it for you. I have seeds with me . . . even some shoots . . . in my trunk."

"You do?"

Cooper laughed and answered Victoria's rhetorical question: "Yeah, she said she does and I believe her . . . and that ain't all she has in that trunk of hers, let me tell you. Weighs a ton . . ."

"Oh. Great. Well, fine, Ideliza. Go ahead and plant a little herb garden if you want. It can't *hoit*, like my dad would say. So, yes, it'll be wonderful! Does Bembé know how to grow things, too?"

"He's very good at it, when he feels like it. . . . Since Roberto got him the computer, though, he's been a little distracted. Maybe we can get him interested if you volunteer to lay out the herb garden with him, maybe rake and prepare the beds, get rid of those weeds. He'll do anything for you, as long as he can be around you!"

Victoria laughed. She was flattered. Worse, even Bembé seemed to notice.

"Well, okay, if it's not too hard . . . I'll try a little raking and weeding with him. But start without me, okay, Ideliza? I hate to promise and then fink out . . . there's so much other work for me to do around here . . . and I'm feeling so, so distracted with this whole business of Roberto's disappearance and these people I don't know anything about who took Bembé and had your tickets. . . . Don't know if I can concentrate on gardening . . ."

"Tomorrow," she answered, "when it's light and a little warmer . . . it'll do you good."

"Yeah, once you've had some rest . . . or I should say, we've all had some rest. Isn't it a little late for you?" Cooper had been expressing his desire to march upstairs for a while, stretching and yawning to show how beat he felt.

"But, Cooper, I'm still not clear what happened or who these people were who took Bembé to the airport," protested Victoria, eager to tie up the loose ends and growing restless at the thought that Roberto really seemed to have vanished into thin air, compounded by the fact that Kitty had not been home or at least had not answered the phone for a whole day.

"You're right," answered Cooper, "let's see if we can get to the bottom of this. Ideliza, what was the name of the woman who picked you up, the woman you said took Bembé to the airport?"

"Yael. That was her name, Yael."

"Oh. That's right. Victoria mentioned that earlier. Yael, eh?"

Victoria caught his eye.

"It seems to ring a bell with you, Cooper. How come? You said you'd tell me. I don't know anyone named Yael. The only thing I know about Yael is that it's an Israeli name. It's weird. I can tell you one thing for sure, though, my travel agent had nothing to do with it. I checked. She said she just gave a computer order under Ideliza's name, Ideliza Mercado, and specified the tickets be left at the check-in counter. She never saw or spoke to anyone or sent any strange messengers. She swore."

"Yael is someone I heard about in Miami a couple of months ago. . . . Dunno why there'd be any connection . . . she mostly lives in Israel . . . in Haifa, I think. But I think I'll make a phone call. All right if I use your phone? My cellular's juiced."

"Do you have to ask?"

Ideliza continued surveying the garden under the spotlight by the kitchen door. The beam of her eyes hovered like a UFO, turning itself on automatically when animal or human body heat activated its sensors.

"I think I'm going to take a look outside," said Ideliza, "smell the fresh country air a little bit and visit with the spirits out there. . . . It's so . . . *glorioso*." She stepped out into the light-spotted darkness, which had grown cooler with each descending hour.

"Hang on, Ideliza! Here, take this, you'll need it!" Victoria handed her one of the many flashlights she'd purchased earlier and hung by the door, as well as Cooper's jacket. With those papaya breasts, Ideliza could not possibly fit in her slim cardigan; even Cooper's jacket might be too small, but at least she could wear it like a shawl.

"And you, Mr. Bembé Lobo, move over here, next to your silly aunt." Victoria pulled Bembé up onto her lap and cradled him, rocking him from side to side, absentminded and eager to overhear Cooper's phone conversation.

"Yeah, hi, Marty. Cooper here . . . no, nothing like that," he chuckled a business chuckle. "No Amazon or Isle of Pines for me this month . . . took four weeks off to take care of some . . . some family business. . . . Yeah, right. Well, get a family then, man, like I told you before, get a life. Listen, dude, need a favor from you . . . can you check the Cuba list for me . . . can you tell me if that captain, the one who took over my party on the last round . . . can you check and see if she's back on another run? I know, I know . . . encrypted, but you have the code . . . Apache. Hell, yes, Marty, I wouldn't be asking if it wasn't important! No, no hot water . . . all I'm asking for is if she's back in the states, not where or how, okay? Okay, okay. Thanks. Name is Yael. That's all I know. She was the captain who met my party . . . yeah. Right. No, sub. It was a sub. I'm pretty sure. Just find out if she's in the states, like in New York. Yeah, New Jork, you knucklehead." Cooper waited, listened to the voice on the other end, paced the kitchen floor.

"I'm on hold," he announced, looking in Victoria's direction, covering the mouthpiece, "may be a while . . . guy's on his break . . ."

Cooper's interlocutor was back. "Oh, yeah? How come?"

"That's fine, Marty. I owe you. See you in a couple of weeks, down by the dispatch. Say, you know if that check of mine is in the mail? Didn't get anything yet. Fine. Do that. Thanks, buddy."

Cooper hung up, clung to her eyes.

"Well, if it's the same Yael I heard about a while back, it looks like she's in New York, due to stay there till tomorrow, so maybe it is her. . . ."

"So? Where does that leave me?" Victoria quipped. "Nowhere.

What does this have to do with Bembé and the plane tickets? As a matter of fact, I'm more confused than ever. . . . How did this Yael name even come up in this context? . . . Also, Cooper . . . your conversation sounded from my end . . . well, let me tell you, sounded like you were talking to a gunrunner . . . maybe a drug runner. . . . God! Please tell me you're not a dope runner! I couldn't stand it!"

Cooper laughed, dismissed her overactive, city-girl imagination. All eyes turned on him.

"Hell, no!, not at all. You don't have to worry about that, okay? No drugs, no dope, no fooling. I told you I was a straight-laced guy, didn't I? Done told you and told you . . ."

"Whatever. But what was that business about Cuba and subs? You weren't referring to Subway sandwiches. . . . Cooper, let me tell you, it sounded creepy at best. I really think you owe me . . . no, wait, strike that, okay? You don't *owe* me, but I really would like an explanation of what it is you do. . . . If it's some godforsaken boys and their toys . . . CIA conspiracy stuff . . . then let me assure you right up front that I never tell anyone anything and that even though I will probably find it very unsettling, to say the least, and am hoping, even as I speak, that I am totally wrong in my suspicions. . . . bottom line is I won't tell anyone, even if it's totally revolting and it turns out I don't feel exactly predisposed toward you afterwards. . . ."

"Great. If that's not a totally no-win maneuver, I don't know what is. Well, tell you what, Penelope. You're snoopy. Snoopy dog. Plain and simple. Shouldn't snoop on someone's conversation and then make your mind up when you've only heard one half of it . . . just like you should never read anyone's diary. . . . Didn't your mamma ever teach you that?"

"Fine. So, are you going to tell me?"

Cooper smiled. "I'll tell you, Penelope, don't get high falutin' about it, okay? . . . I've been planning to tell you . . . just there were a few other things going on . . . like getting through the whole deal with my life and sex and gender and guts and all . . . but, chill it, I will tell you. Promise. Later. Upstairs . . . okay?"

"You can tell me now. Ideliza doesn't mind if we speak English, and Bembé can't hear . . . at least not the regular way. . . ."

Cooper was still standing in the kitchen area, with the black rotary phone cradled under his arm. He took his finger to his lips, pantomiming his missive.

"Ah . . . Victoria . . . I meant to tell you . . . did you know Ideliza speaks English? Very good English, as a matter of fact . . ." He glanced at Ideliza, turning his caveat to Victoria into intended praise for Ideliza.

"*Sank yoo*," Ideliza acknowledged his compliment in English.

"Oh?" Victoria swam to shore. "That's great! Ideliza, I thought you'd told me a few weeks ago that you didn't speak English . . . on the phone, remember?"

Cooper chuckled. "Maybe the lady just meant she doesn't speak it unless she absolutely has to. . . ."

"Wise guy."

"That is true! I only speak it if I have to! Anyway, everyone speaks Spanish in New York!" Ideliza rushed to set the record straight. "Because I don't like to sound funny. . . . English has too many chewing gums . . . words you just have to chew and stretch so far it hurts my liver lips, like Roberto says. It's funny, he calls my *bemba* liver lips . . . *bemba colorá*. . . . So, Mr. Cooper is right. But, Miss Victoria, I don't mind if you talk privately, man and woman together. It's only natural. Besides, I never hear nothing unless it's my business . . . don't like to crowd my head . . . look at Bembé, what the *santos* did, crowding his head with all kinds of stuff, blowing it up like a blowfish. You see the results. It's enough just to keep what *orishas* have for me straight. . . ."

"Oh, no, I know, Ideliza. Please don't think . . ."

"Don't worry about it, Penelope," interrupted Cooper. Then, just as he was about to admonish her not to turn the faux pas into an even bigger one, he jumped back with a yelp. "Holy Shit!"

Victoria came to her feet, letting Bembé slide to the floor. "My God, what's wrong?"

Cooper was holding the phone upside down, yanking the bottom plate without turning the screws, prying the wires with two clawed fingers and pulling on a single obstinate metal fragment. Finally, it popped in the air, heads-up like a shiny quarter. Cooper held the fiber optic bead, as light and miniscule as a contact lens, between thumb and index finger, then proffered it with arm extended.

"This," said Cooper, "see this? No wonder Marty sounded like a catfish in a tank . . . was about to ask him if he'd sucked on helium or something. . . ."

"This what? I don't get it."

"Well, it looks like a phone tap to me. Wireless. Not the most sophisticated I've ever seen, but not chicken liver either. . . ."

"What would my brother want with a listening device in this telephone? I mean, no one lives here. . . . Hollister is down the path in his trailer shed. . . . No one has actually stayed here for months until I got here!"

"Maybe Hollister put it there."

"What for?"

"I dunno. Maybe to bug you . . . find out what you're up to . . . he's known in these parts as a kind of . . . well, quirky guy, I guess."

"You don't know? You dial some mysterious person who tells you about some other mysterious person named Yael, a woman who, for all practical purposes, abducted Bembé for no apparent reason, and then you find a bug in my phone and you look like you know what you're doing . . . and then all of a sudden . . . lo and behold, you tell me you don't know? Your best bet is that Hollister put it there? That wouldn't be my first bet."

"Maybe he's trying to figure you out . . . find out if you're gonna be in charge around here and whether he's gonna need to start answering to you. . . . Folks 'round here are very sensitive about those things, particularly if a woman is involved. . . . You know, boss ladies, they don't like . . . not much, anyway."

"Yes," Ideliza joined in, "maybe this man Mr. Cooper talks about knows a little but needs to know more, so he put a tape recorder in your phone . . . like me, sometimes the *orishas* just whisper, but I can't hear everything they say, so I have to be patient . . . wait till they're ready . . . but do a few *trabajos,* offer some fruit, you know?" Ideliza had returned from her exploratory walk around her future herb garden and had been standing at the door, observing Cooper dismantle the device and, like Bembé, silently partaking of their banter.

"Yes, of course, Ideliza. Cooper's lucky he has you to defend him. . . . Birds of a feather . . . so, fine, Cooper. Think about it. I mean hard. What other reason would there be for some bug to be just stuck inside my phone? . . . Think about it a lot 'cause I'm starting to feel funny . . . as in *I may throw up.* Know what I mean?" She winked at Ideliza, reassuring her she was only kidding, even if it was plain for all to see that such nonchalance did not come naturally.

"Yeah. Well, don't worry, Penelope. Plain to see Ideliza scored a touchdown on this one. She's right. I am trying to put two and two together . . . but it's not adding up . . . not yet . . . maybe you should give Kitty another call, see if your brother's back home yet."

"It's past midnight in New York. Think I should?"

"I wouldn't stand on no ceremony. I mean, it's your brother who's missing, right? What about your parents, did you try them?"

"Oh God, no. I can't let on to my parents that Roberto's missing. It'll kill them . . . since David . . . well, they're just extra . . . extra, if you know what I mean. . . . But I will have to call them soon enough. No way 'round that one. Otherwise, they'll be calling every hour on the hour, leaving all kinds of hysterical messages. . . . I'm just hoping Roberto has surfaced by then . . . don't think I can handle it. . . ."

Cooper handed her the telephone.

"Well, so glad to know it's not bugged anymore," Victoria quipped and began dialing New York, hanging up and starting over several times because the rotary mechanism stalled under her nervous fingers.

"I haven't used one of these since I was three . . . and you Coop, you probably never even saw one of these Alexander Graham Bell devices before in your life, except maybe in some black-and-white movie. Am I right? How old are you, anyway, sixteen?"

"Getting warm, Penelope." He laughed, then turned to Bembé, who was lost in his laptop, working the mouse tracker in rapid, sweeping circles and ignoring everything around him.

"Hey, what r'ya up to, old buddy? . . . I have one just like this little beauty out in my truck . . . yep. Exact same one. Dell Inspiron 7000. Mind if I take a look?"

He crouched down on the floor next to Bembé and scanned the screen. The child had been drawing a story in sequential panels like a comic book.

"Damn! You're good! You did this yourself?" Cooper pointed to his pictures and clapped to show his admiration.

Bembé nodded, all smiles. Clearly he understood—but how? Victoria had confided that some doctor had paid her a visit—casually dropped by during the time Bembé stayed with her some weeks back. She didn't want Roberto or anyone to know. *Prelingual deafness*, the otolaryngologist had explained—born deaf and dumb, a child so bright. According to him, there was no human way for sound to be perceived by his ears.

"Well, let's take a look . . . hey . . . is this the woman who picked you up?" Cooper decided to write out his questions. He wrote longhand on the scratch pad he carried in his pocket, then pointed to Bembé's picture of a woman standing on Ninth Avenue, leaning against a Cadillac DeVille, smiling at the camera—presumably at Bembé.

"Y-a-e-l." Bembé wrote on Cooper's pad.

"Oh . . . man! So that's what the famous Yael looks like. Not too hard on the eyeballs, eh? I take it you did these melons justice, buddy?"

Cooper wrote in block letters because his own handwriting had deteriorated into scribbles since he'd switched to computers over ten years ago. He pointed at Bembé's drawing of a sharp-nosed, wavy-haired man. Green-blue Caribbean water eyes. Yarmulke and tallith and a book pressed against his chest. Hebrew letters scrolling down to the bottom of the page. The stranger looked gnawingly familiar. Victoria had not exaggerated. The kid was talented, really talented.

"This guy, is he the guy that stayed with you in the hotel? You know him?" Cooper wrote quickly, gratified Victoria could not hear their silent repartee.

Bembé wrested the pen from Cooper's fingers, justified his answer neatly under his question: "King. Melech."

"That's his name? Mr. King? Mr. Melech King?"

"Melech," wrote Bembé again, "Melech or King."

"Oh, I see. Okay. So he told you his name was either King or Mulch, right?"

"Not Mulch! King-Melech!!!!!!!!" Bembé snapped, impatient Cooper was so slow on the uptake.

"Ah . . . duh . . . Gottcha!! His name is Melech, which means King . . . in what language? Hebrew? Yiddish . . . these are Hebrew letters you've got here, right?"

Bembé pointed to Cooper's writing, landing his finger on the word "Hebrew."

"Okay. Let's take a look. . . ."

Cooper drew the laptop to him and began scrolling down Bembé's panels, following his story line, a pictorial account of the child's sojourn with the two strangers who had whisked him off to La Guardia and put him up in a fancy hotel. He studied each rendering carefully, scanning for details, nodding silently as he went.

"Very good, Bembé! Tell you something, you're some artist, for real! A future Picasso? Thanks for the story, buddy . . . think I'm starting to get the picture . . . so, here, let's put it away. Okay?" Cooper clicked on save, then quickly shut off the laptop, bypassing the usual exit protocol. He winked with complicity, explaining: "Hope you don't mind . . . better to wait and show Victoria tomorrow. You mind?"

Bembé lingered on Cooper's face, tracing his high cheekbones, his smooth complexion and soft round mouth with his cool blue lasers. Finally, he took the pen and scratch pad in hand and wrote, "Picasso plus! Leonardo. Lichtenstein. Walt Disney. Chagall. Goya. Daumier."

"Oh, well, pardon me, my feet don't stink!" Cooper gibed. "Not just Picasso. Picasso AND Leonardo . . . all those artists and the whole enchilada, I bet?"

Bembé nodded repeatedly, smiling proudly, his even teeth in a Bugs Bunny overbite. He seemed to dismiss Cooper's invasion of his Dell, and the sharp way in which he'd pulled the plug on his artwork.

"What's going on here?" Victoria surrounded them, scratched their heads hello. "Has Bembé been showing you his artwork?"

"Yeah . . . pretty good stuff. Kid's awesome. Real talented."

"Didn't I tell you?"

"Absolutely. The kid's five artists rolled into one. You get through to your brother's?"

"Nothing. Left a long message on their voice mail . . . the twentieth message or something. . . . I'm surprised the tape hasn't run out . . . maybe it means someone did get my messages."

Ideliza had been sitting on the couch, taking in every corner of the house from her vantage point. She reached inside her bosom and took out a white linen handkerchief doused in Florida Water.

"If the wife doesn't answer, maybe you call his partner instead. Dr. . . . met him once, that young doctor Roberto has working for him . . . he knows something. I'm pretty sure he knows something. . . ."

"Oh, yes, you mean Dr. Joe?"

"Yes, that's right! Dr. Joe. A young man."

"I will call him tomorrow at the clinic, first thing . . . unless we hear from Roberto or Kitty or somebody first. Tell you the truth, I hope I don't have to call Dr. Joe."

"Why?" Cooper stood up, poured himself a soda.

Victoria rolled her eyes, flamenco dancer style.

"Because he's a kind of dirty old young man . . . makes me feel uncomfortable."

"What? He made a pass at you or something? Do I need to feel jealous?"

"Worse."

"Worse than jealous or worse than a pass?"

"He asked me out."

"Oh, well. Heck, I take it you said no."

"Yeah. And he asked me out and he asked me out and he asked me out . . . and finally I had to beg Roberto to call him off, like some rottweiler or something. . . . Guy wouldn't quit . . ."

"Well, next time he'll have to face this rottweiler if he wants to start bothering you again. How's that for a dogfight?"

"The *señor* is *muy macho*. Very strong too!" Ideliza attended her approbation with clapping hands.

Victoria and Cooper exchanged glances.

"I wouldn't say *muy*," Cooper quipped, eyes clinging to Victoria's glance.

"Well. My friends," announced Ideliza, "this *santera*, daughter of *Obatalá*, is going to bed. . . . Good night . . . get some sleep, and Victoria, I want to say something. Leave it on the altar. Leave the worries about Roberto on the altar. Wait for the Almighty to ring your bell."

Victoria raised her eyebrows. *Young Samuel: Speak, oh Lord, your servant heareth.*

"Good advice, Ideliza." Cooper hooked his arm around Victoria's waist, and all four walked together to the foot of the stairs, where Bembé followed his mother into the blue bedroom while the copper-haired couple of identical height and breadth marched hand in hand up the creaking steps.

Thirteen

THE MARINE LAYER MADE IT SEEM LIKE SIX, but Bembé had waited until seven by the door, holding the CD of Celia Cruz in one hand and his Mickey Mouse watch in the other.

"Bembé!" Victoria jumped up, startled to find the child lodged between them on the double bed, finger-tipping the invisible cilia hair along her forearm and blowing softly on her face and eyes to wake her.

Her sudden alarm bell spun Cooper from his web. He opened one eye, found Bembé's marble blues hovering over him like a magnifying glass.

"What's up, man?" Cooper shot up against the headboard.

Bembé smiled, brought his right hand a half circle from behind his back, and proffered his mother's CD, the housewarming gift she'd brought from New York.

"Oh, look! It's a gift from Bembé . . . and Ideliza!"

Victoria took him in her arms, kissing his head, petting his head from nape to forehead—a casual, innocent gesture that also aroused an inadmissible pleasure in her. *Those nappy-haired boys by the Newark station—I'd do anything to brush my palms against their wired hair like a razor.*

Bembé rolled from the bed and motioned toward the stairs with two index fingers.

"Think maybe the kid's trying to tell us something?" Cooper smiled at his nightside companion, kissed her with open eyes.

"Yeah. Good idea if we get up . . . it's seven."

"Shucks. Too bad." Cooper winked, stretching and sliding back on the bed, while Bembé tugged at Victoria's feet.

147

"Hang on, Bembé." Victoria motioned, wrapping Cooper's shirt around her bare skin as she prepared to rise.

"No wonder Bembé was excited! Wow!" Victoria, Cooper, and Bembé had descended the stairs to encounter an impressive, although rudimentary, altar to Santa Barbara / Changó.

Ideliza had hauled the statue from New York, along with gold sword, intaglio chalice, and props. She had spent the early morning going around the vineyard, plucking nature's offerings for her altar.

"Well. Guess that solves the great mystery of the trunk," Cooper smiled. "I swear I thought she had a full-length Egyptian mummy in there . . . well, close, anyway."

"Cooper, shut up."

"Didn't mean nothin' . . ."

"But it sounds like you do! That's enough!"

"No, it don't. Only if you're so politically correct, you don't believe in any form of underwear!"

"Have it your way, Burger King. Let's go find Ideliza and tell her how great her altar looks. I'm starving. How about some breakfast before we start for San Luis Obispo . . . or San Luis, like you call it here?"

"What about your brother? Aren't you gonna call his wife or something?"

"Of course, I am, Cooper. That's the very first thing I'm going to do as soon as we acknowledge Ideliza. It's the one thing on my mind while everything else is going on. Did you think I'd actually forgotten about it or something?"

"Hell, no. Just reminding you. But you had to go and take the clock apart . . . 'cause that's what you do, dissect stuff, dissect words like those squirming little larvae under the microscope. Guess it's only natural, being a poet and professor-type person and all. But just wanna say I'm not working some angle when I just say something that pops into my head . . . know what I mean, Penelope? Wasn't thinking you'd forgotten about your brother or interrogating you about it, just plain reminding you."

She laughed.

"You got me, Cooper. I must drive you absolutely crazy. My brother David used to tell a joke about Freud . . . someone passes him in the street and says 'Hello, Dr. Freud,' and Freud mutters to himself, 'Hmm, I wonder what he meant by that.' I know the joke's not funny anymore, but it's funny to me."

"You're right. It ain't funny. But it's funny to me that it's funny to you. So like the song goes, 'keep on doing what you're doing, just do it one more time.'"

"Now you make it sound like we should take the show on the road, the Borscht Belt . . . ever hear of the Borscht Belt?"

"Yeah. Soup."

"C'mon, Cooper, seriously. Do you know what the Borscht Belt is?

"Okay. How's this? A conveyor belt where they make beet soup."

Victoria laughed. "Well, I'll grant you one thing. I'm impressed you know that borscht is beet soup. . . ."

"Well, what can I say . . . you know about us self-educated folk . . . learn things cafeteria style, a little here and there. Used to know a guy from Russia, actually Ukraine, back when I was doing the eastern route . . . Dmitri . . . his wife used to pack him those beet soups in Styrofoam cups and half the time the damn thing burst and wound up all over his clothes and I swear he looked like a butchered pig . . . messiest guy you ever wanna see."

"Very colorful, Cooper. You're something else."

"Say, Penelope . . . did you know sometimes you come off just like my third-grade teacher, Miss Wilkins, at the res . . ."

"Like what?"

"Like you're the teacher and I'm the dummy and you're glad I get half the answers 'cause I must be some not-right-bright nitwit from nitwit city. . . ."

"God. Cooper, I'm sorry. Had no idea I was doing that. Comes with the territory. Teachers sound like teachers, I guess. On the other hand, maybe that's not what you hear. Maybe I'm covering up. Maybe it's just a mask to hide the fact I'm probably feeling vulnerable. . . . But I hardly think of you as a dunce! Quite the opposite, believe me."

"Yeah. I heard someone on television once. He called it 'the arrogance of insecurity' . . . not that I'm calling you insecure or nothing, please. Just putting two and two together from what you said."

"The arrogance of insecurity. Very cool, Cooper. Touché! . . . Oh, no, Christ, there I go again!"

"Don't sweat it, Penelope . . . not that big a deal . . . I was just blabbing. Like my grandma says, 'don't care what you call me, just don't call me late for dinner.'"

"That again? Tacky."

"Who, my grandma?"

"No, you, creep. Your little joke about late for dinner."

"You think that's tacky? How come?"

"Just is. Tacky is. Like is, is. I know tacky when I hear it."

"Okay. Now that we've got that straight, can we go back to bed now? Maybe shoo Bembé out of there, stick a little note in his pocket?"

Their lips brushed, light butterflies. Then the cinders not yet entirely spent from their night's sojourn burst into flames, spread like wildfire.

"What would the note say?"

"Hmmm . . . the note? How about 'Don't wait up. See ya back when pigs fly?'"

Victoria pressed her nose against his cheek, licked open his lips with a single pass, fell prey to his sway. He drew her in with both arms; her breasts quickened against his shirt. She quivered, pressed closer, relaxed, made way for his importunate, full-blossomed member sheathed in his weathered jeans, seesawing, demanding entry with its obdurate cobra head.

"Okay, wise guy . . . let's not frighten the horses . . . you-know-who is staring right at us." Victoria pulled away, fighting the urge to cast the spinnaker, mast, and mainsail to the wind.

"Ah shucks . . ." Cooper smiled, softened his grip, let her uncouple. He pulled his T-shirt out over his pants and for an instant lost his footing, because she'd taken him past the point of no return.

"C'mon, let's go find Ideliza!" Victoria took Bembé's hand and motioned toward the kitchen garden. "There's always tonight, Cooper . . . promise. . . ."

They sat around Ideliza's altar. The *santera* had placed the three-foot red gesso statue in the corner opposite the kitchen, where it presided over the big room. It struck Victoria that all the while they'd sat together the previous evening, her guest must have been sizing up the house, taking mental measurements, looking for a corner where her gods could have full pride of place.

Ideliza stood beside them, abstracted, ethereal, despite her size and presence. She anchored a *batea* wooden bowl where Changó stood, then meticulously separated each strand of marjoram, basil, and rosemary she'd plucked from the abandoned vegetable garden—sacred herbs parched dry and gone to seed, but with enough oil to scent her fingertips and enough hard roots and twigs to boil a pot for a *limpieza*, a cleansing of the home.

Bembé followed his mother's ballet as she carried a glass filled with water to the brim across the room without spilling a drop. He watched her place a bottle of Tabasco, flanked by three uncut Partagas cigars, at the foot of the Yoruba king who presided over all, flaunting his mighty sword and chalice for everyone to marvel and pay him homage.

"No answer at Roberto's. The machine keeps picking up." Victoria had begun picking at Cooper's boxed breakfast mindlessly, unaware of just how all that food had found its way to the coffee table cum dinner table.

"What about the young doctor, did you call him? He should know." Ideliza was counting the stalks, the sacred pebbles, and the cowry shells she would select for Changó.

"Yes, Dr. Joe. I did. I called the clinic. That insufferable nurse of Roberto's said they'd cancelled all appointments for two weeks, that neither my brother nor the partner is in. . . . Very strange . . . I couldn't get zilch out of her . . . what's her name? Anyway, she kept repeating the same thing over and over, like someone had a gun to her head or something. I kept telling her I was his goddamn sister, and she just kept answering the same thing over and over like a perfect robot. . . . She knew nothing, had no number to reach them at, had not heard from Kitty . . . so weird. . . . I won-

der if I shouldn't call the New York City police myself. . . . What
do you think? Kitty told me she was taking care of it, but now, you
know, 'the lady vanishes'. . . ."

Cooper motioned her closer to him, but Bembé beat her to it,
wedging himself between Cooper and Victoria on the leather sofa.

"Well, what do you think, Bembé? Should I call the cops in
New York? I'm starting to really . . . I mean, I'm worried sick." Victoria looked into the child's eyes, rested on their light and balm,
unsure if he could really hear with his secret ear, looking for sol-
ace in his silence and hermetic wisdom.

"I don't know if you should call the cops in New York, Pene . . .
Victoria . . . isn't there someone in New York you can call to take care
of this from there? Seems like a long way from here, don't it?"

Cooper poured a fresh cup of the weak western coffee he'd
boiled in a tin pot left on the stove. He raised the open box of
Entemanns, offered Bembé a jelly doughnut, and whispered,
"Here kid, pass the ammunition."

"No. I have to take care of it myself. There's no one in New
York. . . . Besides my parents, everyone I can call is a *yenta* in one
way or another . . . know what a *yenta* is?"

"Yeah."

"Oh. Right. MJ."

"Right."

"Anyway, anyone I could call would tell my parents . . . and it
would kill them. They're still sitting *shivah* for David, so how can
I suddenly break it to them that Roberto seems to have disappeared into thin air?"

Ideliza turned from her altar-in-progress, "Perhaps you just
wait, Victoria, and the answer will come . . . the right thing to do.
I do the same thing. I worry, too."

She took her place in the large leather chair that Victoria had
bought at the Lompoc mall with her in mind.

"So, Ideliza, I've been admiring your altar. You know that the
Hebrew people do something similar to this?"

"To Santa Barbara? To Changó?"

"Similar to this shrine you brought with you . . . a tabernacle
. . . in the desert, because they had to wander around the desert,
escape from places where they were slaves, so they took their

altars with them, like a turtle. . . ."

"Yes, Roberto told me," Ideliza nodded. "Both our peoples know suffering . . . from long, long time ago. Longer than the Americans. But suffering is also part of life on this side, in America, too . . . and we have the *santos* to protect us . . . they are so good to us . . . but we have to respect them and treat them good and give them their rum and cigars and drums and *güiros* . . . else, you know, much suffering. Roberto says *santos* are mean sometimes . . . that's what he says, mean. He makes me laugh."

"Speaking of Roberto," Cooper joined in, "you have any idea where he is?. . . . I mean, do you know if there was something wrong?. . . . Pen . . . Victoria says it doesn't make sense that he just bailed out for no reason . . . right?"

"Yeah. It's totally out of character. Did you . . . I mean, Ideliza, did Roberto tell you whether there was something wrong?" Victoria searched her eyes.

Ideliza shrugged and then glanced at the forsaken garden where she had spent the early morning digging dry roots and scattering her seeds. She paused, sipped her lukewarm, watery coffee with both hands, and stared into her cup as if reading tea leaves.

"I don't know." She swallowed hard, her tongue squeezing Cooper's swill, chasing after the faint trace of coffee bean.

"I know a couple of months ago . . . someone called his apartment while I was there, and he seemed very agitated . . . Do you know anything about that, Ideliza? Did he ever mention anything was wrong, that he was having trouble with some people? Do you know any reason why he should be in trouble?"

Victoria knew to give her room, let her speak from her center. In the delicate balance of class, race, religion, and entitlement, her safe move was to let the reel spin out of its own inertia, hit bottom where crabs and eels *scurry across the silent seas*.

"There isn't necessarily a reason why things happen," answered Ideliza, eyes fixed midair, a cat staring at invisible objects of creation.

"Sometimes, yes, and sometimes, no . . ." said Cooper. "Sometimes there is a damn good reason why things happen."

Ideliza smiled.

"Did you know I heard the other day, right on Ninth Avenue,

where I have my *consulta*, that a man from New Jersey slit the throat of a tourist in front of everybody, right at the Port Authority terminal? He told the police it was a sacrifice, so his gods would give him the *bolita* winning numbers."

"What do you mean?" asked Victoria, "the person he killed had the winning lotto ticket?"

"No," Ideliza shook her head, "the man from New Jersey killed a total stranger as a sacrifice to some devil so his gods would appear in his dreams and whisper the lotto numbers for the following Saturday's play. . . ."

"That man was insane, a total *loco!*" Cooper blurted.

"What about those men from Arabia who attacked this country, killed so many people, blew up the big buildings downtown and, like Roberto said, even killed your other husband, too, on the plane? Any reason to do that? And what about Fidel Castro, whipping and punishing the Cuban people and throwing everybody in jail to torture them. What's the reason for that, just so he can talk and look pretty to the Arabians and that little man with the beard and the turbans? Is that a reason?"

"That's another kind of crazy, though. But I agree, insane." Victoria examined Ideliza's eyes for missives.

"Sure, you say insane this and insane that," rejoined Ideliza, "or else you say evil . . . evil this and evil that, that's what I hear on television. I hear those people on the Cristina show on television say the same thing . . . but what's that? It just means they can't explain why people do things, or when they're going to get it in their heads to do them. I mean, how can we know why someone wants to kill a person . . . or when?"

"What makes you say kill a person, Ideliza? Roberto told you he was afraid for his life?"

The *santera* rose, faced her altar, and continued the preparations for her offerings.

"He said people were calling him, saying bad things. He was concerned. I did a lot of *trabajos* for him . . . for months and months, maybe six months. Robertico was afraid."

"Afraid of what? People he knew?" Cooper followed Victoria's lead in a minor key.

"Did it have anything to do with his clinic?" asked Victoria.

"Why would it?" asked Cooper.

"Because he is . . . I think Roberto's main practice has to do with . . . abortions . . . you know."

"Holy Moly. No kidding. An abortionist?" Cooper's eyes grew as sharp as obsidian.

"Yeah, well, an obstetrician, technically, but abortion. I think that's the main thing he does," explained Victoria. "Even read about some demonstration in front of his clinic a while back, in the *New York Times*, right in the metro section with his picture in it. I asked him about it, but he pretended not to hear. I've been thinking that maybe . . . well, who knows . . . you read about abortion doctors being threatened and worse. . . . No one can ever discuss it with him because he'll just tell you he's a general gynecologist-obstetrician and change the subject. But well, I think otherwise . . . am I right, Ideliza? Did he ever mention it?"

Ideliza nodded.

"Only recently. The day I went to get Bembé at his clinic . . . I watched him do a very terrible thing. . . ."

"You watched? You saw him perform an abortion?" Cooper clenched his jaw.

"Not an abortion . . . a grown child killed in the womb. . . ."

"She's probably talking late-term abortion?" Victoria looked to Cooper for confirmation.

"No abortion," insisted Ideliza, "cut in pieces, like a chicken." Ideliza spoke emphatically, head and arms waving. She looked at Victoria for validation but met a sobering stone wall of neutrality. She stilled herself and started back for her room, changing the topic, excusing herself, signaling she had forgotten an offering for Changó by her bedside.

It struck Victoria how Ideliza felt free to speak her mind and yet, in some insidious way, knew how to keep her place, how to make herself a target out of range at the slightest hint of opposition—*a woman shining with inward fire/ emerging from the Middle Passage/ pride and fear intact/ in equal parts.*

Victoria paced the floor and then opened the kitchen door looking for air, space, for inspiration. She caught Mr. Hollister's shadowy figure walking across the pathway toward the winery, where his *braceros* were busy scouring and readying copper vats. *Good. He had not caught her spying.* Muscatel walked at his side, silently, slinking like silk, single-minded like the wolf he resembled.

She turned to Cooper, who had laid out a game of *Warpath* on Bembé's laptop, wired with a joystick and crashing with warning sounds the child purportedly could not hear. She read the banner on the screen: "A real-time, multiplayer game where you race to explore, mine, colonize, develop, and conquer the universe."

"I gather Ideliza is rather dead-set against abortion, forgive my understatement. I don't think I want to go there right now, no way José . . . know what I mean, Cooper?"

"Sure do. . . . Why get hung up on just one method of atrocity, right?" Cooper looked up briefly, then continued to fire against his opponent, crouched on the floor.

"Really? You feel that way about it? I'm surprised. . . ."

"Why?"

"Not sure why. Maybe I thought of you as . . . liberal? For obvious reasons. . . . But please, let's not get into it. I can't stand polemics. No one wins, and everybody screams and winds up hating each other. . . . So, can we talk about it some other day? Actually, I take that back. . . . Do you mind if we never talk about it? That whole pro-life zealotry thing gives me the willies . . . a lot of political baggage, all wrapped up in self-righteousness. The same people who don't mind dropping scud missiles over a whole country suddenly go out of their way to save a fetus that hasn't even been born yet . . . smells like a misogynist rat to me, if truth were told. . . ."

"Sure. Why talk about it, since you already did. . . ." Cooper strained to smile, eased away from his concentric brow.

"Okay, smarty-pants. Now we both know how we feel. Hope Ideliza doesn't go ballistic on me or something. . . . This is the last thing I'm ready for, thank you very much."

"Awh! No way! You kidding? She's a lady, can't you see? It's obvious she bailed 'cause she didn't want to offend you none. . . . You know, just flat unplugged in case of a lightning storm."

"I gathered."

"Mind if I ask you a question, though?" Cooper looked at her, motioned to Bembé to be a little patient.

"Shoot." Victoria put her hands on her waist and stood defiantly over him, bracing herself.

"Would you, I mean you, Penelope, would you ever personally have an abortion?"

"I sincerely hope I wouldn't have to."

Cooper laughed.

"Touchdown, Penelope! Ought to join the Dallas Cowboys! Know what my grandma would say about you? She'd say you give as good as you get . . . know what I mean?"

"Yeah. I do."

"You could have been a lawyer, too, gone to the Supreme Court or something."

"No, I couldn't."

"I think so. Why not?"

Ideliza found her way back to the altar and unwrapped a silver chalice packed in cotton that had been soaked in spices and Florida Water. A scent of cinnamon, frankincense, burnt anise seed, and clove numbed the air.

"Ideliza, glad you're back! I wanted to ask you . . . did Roberto ever tell you that specific people were after him for this thing he did, this abortion business? You think there might be some group after him? Maybe someone holding him hostage or something? . . . To my knowledge there hasn't been a ransom note or anything . . . though I don't know, since Kitty is not answering and that Dr. Joe seems to have taken a temporary powder for some unfathomable reason. . . ."

The *santera* had begun her *limpieza*, the spiritual cleansing for this peculiar assemblage, brought together under the California sky. She placed the chalice before Changó in measured reverence, then occupied her leather chair, fanning herself with a cardboard fan imprinted with the words *Nathan's Hot Dogs* across its heart. Her double-jointed wrists wielded the handle, stoked the sacred potion hovering in midair. She took slow breaths, holding the fragrance in before releasing it.

"I don't know of any groups," she answered finally. "Roberto could not give me the names . . . he said he didn't know. . . ."

"Oh? But he told you there were actually people after him? What kind of people?" Cooper continued firing at Bembé's digital enforcers.

Victoria shook her head. *A wonder something like this hadn't happened to sooner.* "Well, Roberto sure knows how to get himself in unusual circumstances. . . ." She completed her thought aloud, then realized the *santera* had gained entrance, was reading her thoughts.

Ideliza frowned, shrugged, looked straight at her.

"Robertico is a fine . . . a very kind person. A gentleman. No people after him. It's not people after him . . . just some evil eye, some *trabajo* done against him . . . some envious person, because Roberto, he has so much."

"Oh? But I thought you said you were not very happy with him. I mean, you just said how you thought he did terrible things."

"No. That, I did not like. And I am sure he will stop. . . . I told him how the *orishas* felt . . . he didn't want to do it. Not Roberto. Unfortunately, he has too many obligations in this world, where life is so expensive. . . . And growing up rich like he did . . . like all of you did . . . he had to find *sobrevivencia*, a way to keep his wife in that tall building and the Mercedes car and computers for everyone, for Bembé, too . . . and so many things . . . you know. But Robertico is good, *una onza de oro*, as good as gold. If people hate him, they don't know him . . . or if they do, envy blinds their eyes . . . because he is a caring man . . . maybe just proud . . . too proud to let people see he is human. Because he always has to be the strong man. And everybody is always calling him for help, asking for money, for medicines . . . and Robertico, this I can tell you for sure, he just gives them what they need and he never asks for anything back. Just last month, he gave me some prescriptions for people in Miami, and he sent medicines to sick people in Cuba. I took the boxes to El Refugio Cubano myself. Maybe some people hate him because he never asks anything from anybody. And because he is somebody, an important person, a doctor, and that causes envy, too."

Victoria's mouth hung open. She'd never heard anyone voice such undiluted devotion to her brother. There were always *buts* and *ifs* attached, praise that belied faint praise or else came from the mouths of strangers. Kitty whitewashed him, kept his secrets from herself and others. And although she extolled his virtues and cleverness before Victoria, and before Sara and Abram, her laurels came in affected clichés, hollow words, words Victoria suspected Kitty would take back in a bulimic bout the first chance she got. But here Ideliza had praised him whole, from her middle chakra, a lotus blooming to the surface.

Victoria met her gaze silently, perhaps with unconscious gratitude, as if to thank her for speaking well of a member of her family. She watched a tear rise from the corner of Ideliza's eye and roll down her cheek unchecked.

"Oh, my God. Ideliza . . . you really do care for Roberto, don't you?"

Ideliza pursed her lips, then glanced over at Bembé on the floor.

"Is it because . . . because of Bembé?" Victoria needn't have asked.

"Obatalá gave me Bembé when a child was not possible. . . . Once, long ago . . . I let the doctor, you know. . . . Afterwards, he told me the operation had gone bad. No more child for me. . . ."

"An abortion?"

Ideliza nodded, looked away.

"Oh. I'm sorry. I understand."

Ideliza stood before the statue of Santa Barbara and held the silver chalice up facing Victoria.

"Roberto gave me this. Pure silver. I serve Changó Matusalen rum in it."

"Very beautiful. Where did he get it?"

"At a department store. He called it our loving cup, where we mingled our hearts and flesh and blood. . . ."

"Wow." Cooper caught Victoria's eye, then looked thoughtfully at Ideliza while Bembé rattled his empty Coke can—*Coop, it's your turn!*

Ideliza's tears lingered. She rose, wiped her face.

"Oh, Ideliza . . . I'm sorry." Victoria reached for her, squeezed her hands.

Ideliza nodded, still wiping her cheeks and eyes.

"That's not why I love him. Bembé would have come one way or another," Ideliza continued. "Just look at the Virgin Mary . . . the *orishas* can do anything they want. . . . It's Roberto, child or no child. Did he tell you I call him *Ángel*? That's my name for him.

He's naughty and he gave me a nickname, Princess Papaya. Now everyone calls me that. I let him, even if, you know, I know he's teasing me, being a little disrespectful, because you know enough Spanish, you know what the word *papaya* means in Cuba. But that's Roberto, the way he is. He has no noose around his neck, like most people, and maybe looks arrogant to them for that reason, and he kids around too much and people feel insulted because he shows no respect. But I always think, when he's bad, that's not really him. The naughty spirits, they make him do and say things. They're mean to him, turn up the music to keep the *orishas* from hearing his prayers. All his life, he told me, he wants to do one thing, and the bad spirits make him do the opposite. *Ángel*, my angel love, *sí*. We never talk like that, saying *I love you, I love you*, like you see on television all the time. Words mean nothing. Just mouthwash. You, too, Victoria, no? You understand Robertico? He told me how he worried . . . that he was very worried about you when that bad thing happened to you. He felt very bad. . . . I know he cried, but he kept it secret. . . . Robertico . . . You love your brother, don't you, Victoria?"

Victoria nodded. *Yes, I love him, I suppose, if it's possible to have a bitter herb stuck in your craw about someone your entire life and still love him. Yes, because my parents love him. Yes, if worrying about where he is or if something's happened to him means I do. Yes, because he's my brother. Yes, if she could see him the way Princess Papaya saw him, in some parallel existence, in another dimension where sheer compassion can transform memory.*

Victoria worried Ideliza's words like beads between her fingers. Did she know more than she was telling? It seemed at that moment that if anyone had a clue about Roberto, where he was or what happened to him, it would be the one person who shed tears for him.

"Ideliza . . . I know how you feel about my brother . . . and it means a lot to me. But mind if I ask you why you're crying? I mean, is it just because you feel deeply for him, or does your intuition tell you something's happened to Roberto? Is that the reason?"

Ideliza opened her eyes wide, pointed at heaven through the ceiling. "I cast the cowry shells, and they tell me opposite things. . . . I smash open the coconut and, again, the same thing, it comes back top and down . . . that he is alive, that he is not alive . . . that he is suffering . . . that he is not suffering . . . that he is close by, that he is far away. . . . For this kind of thing, when it is personal, a *santera* has to consult a *babalao* priest because, you know, like when Bembé stayed with you, and Roberto kept it from me, and Bembé blocked me out because he fell in love with you, sometimes there is too much static . . . like a big boulder in heaven, blocking the way. But it so happens my *babalao* left for Miami on vacation, or maybe he's moving there permanently, I don't know. . . . So many people getting out of New York, you know, since the bombs . . . so maybe that's Obatalá's answer. . . ."

"What answer?"

"That asking so much is not faith . . . that it takes patience . . . that sometimes just waiting and being still is how we should pray."

A hard, hollow blast shot across the vineyard, echoed through canyons, and rippled down the merlot furrows nearest the house, clanging in their heads like a metal plate. Ideliza and Victoria clutched hands for an instant, rushed to the kitchen door, and searched the fields as far as the eye could stretch.

"Holy Moly!" Cooper jumped to his feet and pushed them away. "Get away from here, away from the door, for Christ's sake, move in!"

"What was that? Sounded like it came from the winery!" Victoria pushed Bembé and Ideliza toward the big room.

"My guess? Probably an S444 Marlin timber carbine rifle, eighteen-inch barrel, Winchester." Cooper stationed himself by the kitchen door, shielded behind the side panel, eyes panoramic, reconnoitering the vineyard from side to side.

Victoria squinted. "You can actually identify the exact kind of rifle from the sound it makes? My God! Cooper, I have to know, is someone chasing you or something? Does this have anything to do with the strange thing you do for a living?"

"No. Not a chance. Clean as a whistle. No one's after me for nothing."

"What then? Jesus, Cooper! This scares me."

"I don't know, Penelope. Looks like whoever it was quit, though. Maybe just cleaning the darn thing and it went off. Let's just lay low a few minutes. It's probably nothing. Tell you one thing I do know, though. It's not a hunter . . . season's done and poachers don't live long in these parts. Central Valley rangers don't mess around."

"Only one shot, not shooting," said Ideliza. "Like Mr. Cooper says, someone just cleaning the gun . . . the man upstairs from me, that happened to him. His wife said he was cleaning the rifle and it just went off. . . . Even Bembé woke up from the vibrations. The policemen were there in no time, looking for terrorists . . . but it was nothing. Nobody got hurt. Mr. Acosta was just cleaning his gun."

"I think I better call Hollister." Victoria looked for the Post-It where she had scribbled the number. She picked up the receiver, began dialing, and was startled by Kitty's disembodied voice streaming through the line.

"Hello . . . hello . . . Victoria? Are you there?"

"Kitty? I was just dialing out! Didn't even hear the phone ring . . . I can't believe it. Where have you been? I've been calling you constantly for two days. . . . Any news?"

"Why, yes, that's what I'm calling about. . . . Roberto is all right . . . we think."

"*We* think? What do you mean?"

"Dr. Joe and I. We think Roberto is all right. . . . We got a letter, a legal document, this morning. Thought you might have received your own copy by now."

"I'm totally confused, Kitty. What do you mean? I didn't get any document. Is Roberto okay? Did you see him? Is he there with you?"

"Not exactly . . . the letter and this long legal document . . . his attorney sent it. Mr. Karras. Did you ever meet him?"

"No. But can't you just tell me what this is all about? I've been out of my gourd, calling you night and day, leaving messages . . ."

A dull silence, then words putt-putting like a cold engine. "Well . . . yes, I'm sorry. I was out with Dr. Joe. . . . It's . . . probably good news . . . though I grant you it's strange, but you know Roberto is not one to do anything simple . . . he's a very complicated man. . . . He . . . he . . . well, it looks like he has been called by the White House, Victoria. . . . I think it's the White House . . .

or anyway, the government. The Pentagon or something . . . anyway, Roberto had to go on a special mission . . . a secret mission . . . as a doctor, you know . . . that's why . . ."

"What? That sounds totally preposterous, Kitty. Roberto has never gotten mixed up in secret government stuff in his life! For God's sake, he even became a Quaker in case he was ever drafted. Do you seriously believe the Pentagon called him? Him? What would the government want with an abortion doctor?"

"Oh, Victoria. That's not fair . . . to talk about Roberto like that. . . ."

"Fine. Sorry. You're just not making any sense, Kitty."

Silence, then a hand on the mouthpiece, a muffled giggle, the low treble of a man's voice.

"Think I better let Dr. Joe explain it to you, Victoria, since you insist on being so ornery. . . ."

"Hello, Victoria? This is Dr. Joe."

"Yeah. Can you tell me what's going on, Dr. Joe? Is Roberto . . ."

"Well, the letter should explain everything . . . we thought you would have received it by now . . . FedEx . . . maybe it's the time difference . . . it'll probably get there this morning . . . the doc is all right, Victoria. He has been called by Washington to help out in what looks like pretty high-level, serious stuff. . . ."

"I find that . . . well, forgive me, not credible. But, anyway, can you tell me where he is and how he is and if there is any place I can reach him?"

"That's the thing. He's off on some assignment . . . the letter says for three to six months . . . and he can't be reached because he is, you know, doing spook stuff. I thought it sounded weird, too, at first, but then I put two and two together. . . . The doc was getting all kinds of calls, was acting sort of secretive the last few weeks, maybe months. Now I sort of get it. . . . He was obviously hiding something, and it's probably the fact that he was being recruited by the president or something. . . ."

"Do you happen to know for sure if he's all right? I mean, did you speak with him? Did he tell you this personally himself?"

"No, not personally. . . . Oh, just a sec . . . hold on a sec . . ."

Dr. Joe covered the mouthpiece. Victoria strained to make out his underwater words: "Oh, hon, can you hand me my drink . . .

in the front room, by the computer? . . . Yeah . . . ice, please . . .
you're a doll . . ."

"Sorry about that," Dr. Joe came back. "Let's see . . . yes . . .
did I see him?. . . . No. I didn't. Nobody did. He probably didn't
know they would be picking him up and probably didn't have
enough time to call. But the lawyer's letter explains the whole
thing, or as much as they let him say. . . ."

Victoria took a deep breath and tried to collect herself. She
slinked down to the floor, feeling all eyes on her, especially
Bembé's aquamarines, shining like neons. She mugged at him,
shrugged her shoulders indicating frustration, then forced a reassuring smile.

"Can you just tell me what's in the letter, Dr. Joe? I haven't
received anything."

"Sure. It's long, though. A lot of *whereas* stuff. Whereas this.
Whereas that . . . you know the doc, a stickler for detail . . . but
basically, in a nut shell, it just says that *whereas* he has to absent
himself for a period of time . . . you want me to read you the whole
thing on the phone? It's long . . . divided into sections. We didn't
read your part very carefully because, well, frankly, I figured it was
none of my business."

"Can you give me a general idea?"

"Right. The skinny. Okay. Well, he decided to pass on Lobo
Vineyards to you, that's one thing."

"What?"

"Just what I said. He bequeathed the vineyard to you . . . guess
he figured since you were there already . . ."

"Why would he do that if he's just going away for three
months?"

"Maybe, you know, since it's a government deal . . . just in case
it backfires or something. Seems to me he just wanted to leave all
his affairs in order . . . but that's just the way the doc is. . . . Doesn't
necessarily mean there's anything wrong, that he's in danger or
anything. . . . Says here in this addendum to this paragraph . . . let's
see . . . yeah. Here. 'Whereas California wine growers harvested
and crushed a record-setting 3.3 million tons of wine grape vari-
eties last year' . . . hmm . . . blah blah blah . . . guess he's trying to
explain that the moneys he transferred to you should be sufficient

to cover overhead and production and all that stuff, 'cause it looks like you're set to get a profit. . . . Oh, Jesus. A hefty profit . . . son of a gun. The doc never let on about that winery of his. . . . Hey, Victoria, you there? Listen, let me ask you this. Did you know the doc was so fucking secretive? I sort of knew, but man, I'm starting to wonder . . . and let me tell you right off that to me the doc is like a father, and it doesn't mean I don't appreciate the guy 'cause I do and I know he knows without a doubt. . . . Well, hey, he bequeathed his whole clinic to me, Dr. Joe, so what else can I say? But holy shit, take this just to show you what's giving me agita . . . I start reading you this and, what can I tell you, my mouth drops. And that's not all that drops. Can you believe the doc's been cutting into women, shoulder to shoulder with me all these years, and not even a clue about this Lobo Vineyards of his? Maybe he's been a CIA spook all along. That's funny, a spook with an OB-GYN license . . . is that the bomb? But it's not just me he kept in la-la land. . . . This is confidential, all right? Even Kitty hardly knows the guy. . . . Did you know he told her he delivers babies all the time? But, what can I say? If the doc said that, I'm just going to read it like he wrote it, if you know what I mean. Why get her all upset, right?"

"What else does the will or whatever you call it say? What about the clinic? Anything about Kitty?" She bristled at the thought of Dr. Joe in Trump Tower drinking her brother's soup and probably sleeping in his bed. She had a sudden flash of Bembé crouched in a wall niche over his newly adopted parents.

"Hey, how's that California sun, Victoria? Didn't you just hear me tell you the doc leaves the clinic to me? Kitty, she gets everything else, you know, his wife. . . . Oh, yeah, well, not everything, far from that. But plenty. Says here he left $200,000 to your parents, living trust kind of gift, transferred into blah blah blah . . . Morgan Stanley account in their name. . . . Wait, there's more in this paragraph about you, too . . . so fucking long . . . let me see . . . oh . . . where did it go? Hang on a minute, will you?"

Again, the muffled speaker: "Hon, can you just hand me the whole thing. . . . I'm missing some pages. . . . Thanks . . . yeah . . . if you don't mind, just a tad . . . thanks, doll. . . .

"Yeah, okay, here it is . . . you there, Victoria?" Dr. Joe was turning leaves, shuffling onion paper in her ear.

"I'm here."

"Right. Well. He transferred funds for you, too . . . says here something or other about Bembé's schooling . . . guess he adopted him legally? Cute little fellow. I met him once. And . . . yeah, here it is . . . for overhead, $100,000 Lobo Vineyards . . . $100,000 for you . . . lots of stuff here . . . must have taken the doc weeks to draft this, I swear . . . meantime, not a word to me about it, God forbid. . . . Oh! Jesus, Mary, and Joseph . . . almost missed this one. You ready? The doc also left $200,000 macaroons to some woman called I-d-e-l-i-z-a P-r-i-n-c-e-s-s P-a-p-a-y-a- M-e-r-c-a-d-o. Is this some sort of joke? You ever hear of this person? Never mind . . . I don't expect an answer . . . but see what I mean? About the bequest or whatever it's called. Very precise. Don't think you'll have any trouble figuring it out. . . . You're supposed to sign the letter Karras sent you, send it back to him. . . . The doc set aside $100,000 for you and another $100,000 for Bembé's schooling . . . says here Bembé Lobo in Broadway lights. . . . Anyway, that's the skinny. Doc's all right, that's the main thing. Kitty and I were just running 'round ragged for a while, calling the police, going up to the precinct, even looking into a private P.I. . . . But then the FedEx package arrived . . . I called this Mr. Karras. He's out of California . . . L.A. He seemed cool. Nice enough. Said there was nothing irregular about it, that he does this sort of thing for his clients all the time . . . like gifting, so there's no IRS problem down the road . . ."

"Down the road? You mean, in case he . . . he doesn't come back. So then it's treated outside probate?"

"Yeah. That's it, exactly. Very smart. Too bad you didn't want to go out with me . . . don't know what you missed. . . . But, yeah, anyway, that's what the lawyer said, avoids probate."

"Can you put Kitty back on?"

"Sure thing. Good talking to you, Victoria. You sound good, as usual. . . . Kitty! Phone!"

"Oh, hi, Victoria. Hope that made sense?"

"Pretty much."

"I knew Dr. Joe would explain! He's such help!"

"Have you called my parents?"

"No. Not at all. You asked me not to call them, remember?"

"Yes, that's good. Don't call them."

"But what if they call here? They're bound to . . . Roberto spoke to them all the time . . . well, not all the time, but often. . . . I've been sort of uneasy about it . . . wouldn't quite know how to explain . . . I'm sure they wouldn't believe me if I told them about the document. I'm sure they'd carry on and get emotional, you know, the way those dear people do sometimes? And it makes me . . . well, anxious. I hate to say it. But it does, their emotionality. And I'm not feeling particularly strong these days. . . . This business with Roberto just not showing up for dinner really upset me."

"I'll break the news to them myself, just as soon as I get the letter and get a hold of the lawyer."

"Thank you. I knew you'd understand . . . and I thought since you had asked me not to tell them anything. . . . I'll call them later, in a few days or maybe a couple of weeks . . . just as soon as I'm up to it. . . . Dr. Joe gave me marvelous pills yesterday. Hopefully, he'll put me on it, and I can feel . . . well, I'll be able to call them, I mean."

"Kitty, I have a suggestion for you in the meantime. . . . I couldn't get through to you for two days straight, night and day. So maybe if you don't want to talk to those dear people, like you say, maybe you can just keep on doing the same thing you've been doing all along. . . ."

"Doing what thing?"

"Not answering the phone. Letting the answering machine pick up. Screening the messages."

"Whatever." Kitty at thirty below Fahrenheit.

The phone went dead. Victoria clicked repeatedly for a dial tone. Cooper had left his watch post and had stretched out on the couch with Bembé at his feet. Ideliza was taking stock of the open refrigerator, preparing to fix her son a second breakfast—*ésta es para alimentarle la cabezona. This one's to feed his big head,* she had announced in *sotto voce.*

"Was that Kitty?"

"Sure was, as she lives and breathes. The inimitable Ms. Kitty Cabot from Brahminville, Massachusetts. She neglected to ask if I

knew how Bembé was, or if he'd been found. I guess she has other
things on her mind. . . . Can you believe only a few weeks ago she
actually wanted to become his mother? I was having conniptions."

"So what's up, doc?"

"Can't believe you said that."

"Why?"

"That Dr. Joe, he kept calling my brother *the doc.*"

"Oh, you spoke with the rat?"

"Kitty put him on."

"A kitty and a rat, huh?"

"Yeah, symbiotic, no doubt."

"So, is your brother okay?"

Ideliza's neck tightened. She cracked two eggs in a bowl, listened in like an eavesdropper.

"I . . . I don't know . . . think I better call Mr. Hollister first . . .
find out about that gunshot. . . . Can't get that hollow boom out of
my head. . . . I know everything sounds like an explosion to me
since the sky fell. A balloon pops and I jump. But that shot was for
real. You think it came from Hollister's trailer?

"Awh, don't get all bent out of shape about it, Penelope. I
checked good from here, saw nothing strange. No one running or
anything. Besides, it was only one shot. Happens around these
parts. It's not New York, where you hear a shot and right away
think Mafia Don. Probably just Hollister cleaning his weapon or
playing around with the trigger. Maybe he got lucky and shot a
rabbit!"

"Glad to hear you're so sanguine about it. But there's something scary about the country to me. Anyway, I'm calling Hollister."

"Well, I was thinking that if you're serious about doing
the vineyard tour thing, we better get started pretty soon. Like
ASAP. Getting a little late if you wanna drive up all the way to
San Luis. . . . And, you know, the kid's been cooped up in this
cabin. . . . I feel bad for him. He ought to be playing outdoors,
knock off the computer for a while?"

"I agree completely. Listen, I've been catching a little cabin
fever myself. But I was about to tell you . . . we have to wait for a
FedEx package first. Then we can get moving. There's a letter from

a lawyer, about Roberto. . . . Oh, cripes, Cooper, it just dawned on me I never got around to calling Lupe. So much excitement around here. I hope we can all fit in your truck and that it's clean enough? Let Ideliza sit in the front."

"Did they find Roberto?" Princess Papaya, the fly on the wall, suddenly spoke up.

"Oh, Ideliza, I don't know. I don't know what to tell you just yet. That's why we're hanging around, for that letter . . ."

Ideliza continued to press her steely, unrelenting eyes on Victoria.

"Okay. Okay. But don't hold me to this. According to Kitty and Dr. Joe, it looks like Roberto had to go away for a while, on some government mission, a top security assignment. I understand there's a message for you and for Bembé in the letter, too. From what Dr. Joe read me, Roberto made sure to provide for you. He's leaving you and Bembé a whole lot of money, if what Dr. Joe read me is right. Roberto transferred this place to me, which I don't quite understand. But my guess is I'll have to speak to the lawyer in Los Angeles before we can sort the whole thing out. I wanted to wait to see the actual document before telling you about it. But now you know. Or at least you know as much as I do."

"But did your sister-in-law say if he was okay or not?" Cooper spoke for Ideliza, who had turned to stone.

"They seem to think he's fine."

"Well," said Cooper, "I take that in the affirmative. He's probably fine." He winked at Ideliza.

"I really don't know if that's the case or not, Cooper. I don't know if he's okay or not, all right? So please don't put words in my mouth . . . I can speak for myself, okay?"

"Robertico . . . going away without saying good-bye?" Ideliza addressed no one in particular. She let her words hang midair, grapes for the picking by anyone who cared.

"It sounds very strange to me, too, Ideliza," said Victoria. "That's why I was trying not to tell you until we could see the stupid letter for ourselves. . . ."

"But his wife, she didn't sound sad?"

Victoria shrugged, gestured with open hands: "If you mean whether I think she believed the story or not, that's hard to say.

But she didn't sound like she knew something else to be the case either. I don't think she was lying . . . unless she was lying to herself, which if you knew her you'd understand is not a very hard chore."

"Do you have a gut feeling about whatever may be going on with him, Ideliza?" asked Cooper.

"A spirit has come to me . . . Ogún, the *orisha* of gold and other things. . . . I saw him a short time ago, when Victoria was on the phone . . . he did speak to me. He said some things. He mentioned the chalice Roberto gave me, and he showed me a burning bush and a skull and a wedding ring . . ."

"Do those things mean something to you, Princess?" asked Cooper.

"I do not feel that his wife told you the truth . . . not the main truth, maybe just part of the truth . . . and it does not feel peaceful here, inside . . . something happened to Roberto, something . . ."

"Something bad?"

"I don't know." Ideliza started back for her blue bedroom.

"When Ogún visits me, it usually means I receive or find some money, even in the street . . . but I don't see how that has a connection to Roberto, or where he is. I think I better go to the room now. My *babalao* would tell me I need to do some special *trabajos*, some thinking and some listening . . . you don't mind?"

Victoria thought of Dr. Joe, of the money he'd told her Roberto had left for Ideliza, for Bembé, for herself, and her parents. That would account for Ogún. But what about the rest?

At last, a dial tone. Mr. Hollister seemed to be expecting a call, perhaps hers. She hung up, stared blankly at Cooper.

"Hollister heard nothing."

"Nothing? You're friggin' kidding? That was a Winchester, no two ways about it. Maybe he's punting 'cause they took away his permit?"

"He said he'd been working on the books all morning, placing orders, working on a plan of some sort having to do with getting a building permit for the wine tasting store. He was adamant about not hearing anything. Insisted we probably heard some truck backfire out on Route One. . . . You think we're crazy, imagining we hear shots?"

"Yeah, right. And my name is Santy Claw. . . ."

"Then he is hiding something . . . he feels a little creepy to me, you know . . . actually, more than just a little. . . . He gives me the creeps."

"Yeah. Well, I don't know him. Heard of him, though. Maybe he's telling the truth, he didn't hear nothing because he was passed out on the floor, out for the count like a bunny with big cotton balls stuck in his ears." He made ears with his hands, flopping them at Bembé who jumped up and mimicked his pantomime with his contagious smile.

"Oh, please, Cooper . . . let's get serious for a moment, all right? Do you really think Hollister shot his gun and is trying to hide the fact? This is very troubling. . . . Bembé, come here, sit next to me." She motioned and Bembé landed on her lap.

"Well, come to think of it, a guy down at the reservation did mention Bud Hollister was real fond of hooch . . . said he hates regular wine, makes his own rot gut from *grappa* . . . you know *grappa*? Just another name for grape scum, as far as I'm concerned. Burns your innards into tripe. So maybe the marshal took away his license, and he doesn't want anyone to know he's got a firearm. That makes sense, doesn't it? As much sense as anything else, I guess."

"The reservation?"

Cooper frowned, cracked his neck with a swift half turn and cleared his throat. "Yeah. Chumash. Up the road. I told you about it." He gulped the last of his coffee, bypassed her gaze.

"You didn't tell me."

"Thought I had. Told you I built my own house, remember? Matter of fact, I was hoping we could stop by today on the way to San Luis. . . . I'd like to show it to you."

"I don't understand. You live on a reservation?"

"Penelope. No, not as a member of the reservation, but on Indian land, in Buellton. Remember when I told you about what happened to me and all . . . you know, about the doctors?"

Victoria nodded.

"Well, when I was going through all that, Juan Martínez, the Chumash elder, he took me in. He and his sister Maggie Lewis nursed me to health . . . nicknamed me *tenderfoot*. Adopted me after my mom finally left . . . me. They gave me a lot of strength, both Pop and Maggie . . . taught me at least half of everything I know. . . ."

"What kinds of things?" Victoria was playing This Little Piggy Went to Market with Bembé, silently stretching his fingers one by one.

"Oh . . . let's see . . . spiritual strength, some physical skills. Taught me the ways of the land in these parts . . . how to tell a poison berry from a fruit. How to travel while remaining still . . . see things in the spirit world of the ancestors . . . how to awaken the senses and be a part of things that only the eagle and the mountain lion see. . . . They helped me get my act together, too. Get my new ID, change that F to M on the driver's license and stuff . . . not as easy to do as it sounds. And Maggie helped raise the cash to bring my grandma up from Florida to live with me. . . ."

"Oh, so your grandmother came up."

"Yeah. Stuck around till I was on my feet and people started saying *thank you, son* to me at the checkout counter without doing a double take. . . . But then she headed back to Florida. She had a gentleman caller back then."

"What about the elder, is he still alive?"

"Yeah, he's still with us, though I don't see him a whole lot. Not in the last couple of years. All the travel and stuff . . . He wants me here, on the land. None too happy about my trips, even if part of him is proud of me. Still helps me out with some work now and then. But I've been kind of avoiding getting under the tepee alone with him. 'Cause I catch hell if I don't tell him what he wants to hear . . . and I couldn't tell him that."

"I know what you mean. Exactly. This elder, is he very old?"

"Old?" Cooper chuckled, looked at her suspiciously. "Why, 'cause I told you he's an *elder*? You ribbing me, Penelope?"

"No, I'm sorry. I'm really not. I guess unconsciously the word *elder* made me think of old, but I was just wondering if he was old enough to be your father or grandfather."

"Well, yeah. Pop's been old my whole life . . . maybe all his life.

Going on ninety-six, according to the calendar. His head is still okay. Well, like a hummingbird, flies off here and there, doesn't always remember where his thoughts flew to. But folks around here still go to him to settle their problems, their fights. He helps them a lot at the casino, too. Oh, and yeah, he's the super whiz on anything to do with the Chumash tongue. A lot like you in that way. Always on the lookout for words, keeping the language alive, treating the sounds and meanings like precious artifacts. . . . Funny thing about Pop is that even if he doesn't remember what he heard ten minutes ago, he understands everything that's going on. He's here, even if he's not all there . . . know what I mean?" Cooper laughed at his own joke.

"That's amazing. Really. About this elder . . . and you on the reservation. How come you didn't tell me? I don't remember your mentioning this at all in the e-mails. Feels strange, on some level. . . . "

"I guess I didn't exactly spell it out. Not in so many words. Wasn't trying to hide. Sure I didn't e-mail you this a long time ago?

"I would have noticed . . . it's not such a small deal."

"I guess it sounds exotic to some folks, just the sound of the word Chumash. But to me, it just *is* . . . just the way life is, till somebody shows you different or gives you one of those foreign looks that has *hope you're happy in my country* written all over it. Then it's Tonto and Wounded Knee and them and us, and pretty soon the whole thing makes you feel like getting drunk or punching somebody. . . . "

"You know, Cooper, I think you just gave me the best explanation I ever heard of why people . . . why Jews don't marry out, or at least why our parents warn us not to. Who wants to be looked at from the outside, right? That's pretty brilliant, Cooper. My brother David, as young as he was, had a big thing against marrying out. I wish he could have heard you just now. So, this elder, Pop, what else did he teach you?"

"Yeah. Well, mostly he showed me all kinds of practical things. . . . I can't believe I never mentioned Pop to you in some e-mail, though. I say that 'cause people are always accusing me of quoting him."

"Maybe you did. Maybe I was so wrapped up in myself and my

so-called grief that I didn't process whatever you told me. Who
cares. It's okay. You just blew me away, that's all . . . unreal."

"Hey, Penelope, that's cheating. Don't you go calling it your *so-
called grief*. What about the lives of the other survivors whose
wives or kids or husbands blew up in the air? You gonna call their
grief their *so-called grief*? No, you ain't. So don't do it to yours,
okay? Thought we'd settled that a long time ago, when we first
started talking . . . e-mailing."

"The truth is I don't know whether I was actually trivializing
my feelings or just putting it in a different perspective. What I
mean is, I don't feel that desolate, scary, claustrophobic grief anymore . . . it just dawned on me. And, I guess it feels like waking
from some nightmare . . . real, but not as real . . . know what I
mean? So-called real."

Cooper smiled, kissed her with lips closed, held her to him,
pressing his nose between her neck and shoulders. "Should I be
preening my peacock feathers?"

Victoria pushed him away gently, aware of Ideliza in the next
room and Bembé taking it all in.

"Careful, Cooper. Told you I'm a little self-conscious. You
know, not so great at public displays . . . but, hey, yes, I'd take a
little credit if I were you. . . ." She winked at him, then gestured
to Bembé with eyes turned to the ceiling—*I'm sorry, what can I tell
you, the guy's demonstrative.*

"So, who deserves the rest of the credit? Other than me, I
mean."

"What about me, can I take some of the credit? I mean, I
didn't kill myself . . . I hung in there through thick and thin. And
maybe just the passing of time helped."

Cooper grew silent, then looked away, running his eyes
through the bare grape furrows as far out as the winery. Victoria
reached for his hand. "Hey, Cooper, don't . . . listen, of course, I
give you a lot of the credit, you idiot. Probably most of it. Give
Bembé his due, too. There, I said it. Feel better? Why did you have
to make me say it? My God, does everything have to be said?
Didn't you just hear Ideliza talk about how silly it is?"

"Heck, don't ask me. You're the writer. Thought that's what
you did."

"Did?"

"Tell, I mean. Isn't that what a writer's whole life is about? Telling?"

Victoria pointed at the sofa with her chin, inviting him to sit beside her. They sat simultaneously, holding hands, two children jumping into the wading pool.

"You have to make me think, right? Okay, I'll think. Try this. Maybe writers spend their whole lives telling about *other* people, not necessarily themselves. Sartre says that one chooses—'you either live or write,' he wrote. That make sense?"

"Sure. But what's that got to do with what we were talking about?"

"Oh, I see, okay, Mr. Male Super Ego . . . and I am sure you will not have the cheekiness to find this appellation politically incorrect, because you know whereof I speak. So, let's see. Male Super Ego wants a little more applause instead? A little credit where credit is due?"

Cooper laughed, his ears and cheeks blush-pink. "Who me? I dunno nothin' 'bout male ego . . . it's just like the president says, 'I'm a loving guy'. . . ." He shrugged, then winked at Bembé, who was riveted on the couple's banter, back and forth from face to face.

"Say, Ideliza, come over here! I told you to leave those dishes alone, will you? I want to ask you a question. Are you superstitious?" Victoria attempted to draw her into their magic circle, eager to reassure her she would not be intruding despite the constant electricity between her and Cooper.

"Is she superstitious? Holy sugarcane! Crack me up, Pene . . . Victoria. What a question, considering her religion and all, I mean."

"Cooper, for Pete's sake! How can you blurt out something so utterly prejudiced?" Victoria looked at Ideliza, still by the sink. She was reassured the intermittent, spigotting faucet had drowned Cooper's aside.

"It wasn't meant to be prejudiced. Quit saying that. I just meant that her religion has a lot of . . . oh, heck, never mind. I didn't mean anything by it. One man's superstition is another man's totem pole . . . how's that? Christ, I can think of a lot of people who would bash my beliefs, and I sure would hate it, and that ain't what . . ."

"Okay, Cooper, forget it. She couldn't hear, anyway. Let's just get our act together so we can split when FedEx finally shows up. I'll go over the papers on the way up . . . which reminds me, I should charge my cell phone."

Ideliza felt a breeze sweep in through the open door. She returned to the big room, then stepped outside, leaving Cooper and Victoria to their intimacy. She fanned herself, speeding the breeze and cooling her cinnamon skin awash with soapsuds.

"I think I better go turn the engine over just about now if we're gonna take the truck. The dang thing goes flat cold overnight. On second thought, why don't I just shoot up to my place and drive Ingrid back. It'll be much roomier. . . . Ingrid, that'll be my '87 Volvo, 240 DL. . . ."

Cooper rose and Victoria's eyes trailed. He turned back at the door, glowing with her.

"Say, Penelope, I got a question for you. Why the heck did you ask Princess Papaya if she was superstitious, anyway? Were you just trying to change the subject?"

"Actually, just the opposite. I was thinking that I didn't feel comfortable about massaging the male ego because probably underneath it all I'm a little superstitious. . . . Mind you, I think it's totally unenlightened and absurd . . . but are you ever afraid to say something or praise something? . . ."

"'Cause then it'll be taken away from me by some angry jaguar spirit, just for spite?"

"You got it. There's a Yiddish word, *kanahara*. Ever hear it? Every time somebody compliments your baby or tells you what a great family you have, instead of saying thank you, you say *kanahara*. . . ."

"Right. Hey, you evil spirits, don't look at me . . . that lucky woman, she went that-a-way . . ."

"Yeah. So, Cooper, wow, you understand."

"Think so. Did you ever hear that song 'The Gambler?' 'You never count your money when you're sittin' at the table there'll be time enough for countin' when the dealin's done . . .' It goes something like that, more or less. I like that song. Hey, guess what? I got a couple CDs in the car we can play on the way up. Willie Nelson and Kenny Rogers, Johnny Cash . . . think I even got a couple of Dixie Chicks stashed somewhere. Okay, I'm off, honeycomb."

Cooper turned on his heels, then his rubber soles came to a sudden screech. Bembé was tugging at his brain, telling him to come. Then, aware of Ideliza's protective watch at her son's side, he said "Say, come on, you, too, Princess! Wanna go for a ride? Just a couple of miles and back right quick. Do you good!"

He pushed the door all the way out and scooted Bembé under his arm and into the garden path.

"Yes, *el campo*! The *santos* have me all so *sofocá*, breathless . . . a little air is what this *negra* needs. . . . *Ay, sí,* the California flowers . . . do they have hibiscus here, and jasmine?"

She glanced at Victoria, wrapped a red silk kerchief around her head with sleight of hand, brushed down the green pant-suit she had packed for the country, and then followed Cooper in a straight line.

"Cooper!" Victoria stopped him just as his figure disappeared around the curve.

"You called?"

He came back into view, smiling and donning his cowboy hat, and walked toward her, flirting with eyes that cascaded down her face and breasts and legs.

"I was just wondering, . . ." she started, sounding some ancient *shofar* that stilled itself, reining in the invisible tether between them, so as not to miss him before he'd gone. "I was just wondering . . . about the reservation. Is that how you know so much Indian lore? About the *berdache* . . . did I get that right? Berdash?

"Yeah. That's how come. Wasn't no book learning. Did you reckon I was some kind of professor like you? Oh well, I guess it was fun while it lasted."

"That doesn't not make you a scholar, are you kidding? You know a lot about it, so in my book you are a scholar. How's that?"

"*Doesn't not,* is that so?"

"Quite so. Doesn't not." Victoria did a mock-British, half apologizing for the academic slip, half spoofing herself.

"Is that the same thing as God, he doesn't *not exist?*"

Victoria's laugh was like a dulcimer taking him by surprise. She'd managed to seduce him on the spot. "Precisely, that's it! You total spontaneous combustion genius! Proving God's existence by saying you can't prove His nonexistence. My students love it. Or did, anyway."

"Cool."

"Well, I think so. Cooper, tell me, I just want to get this straight. You are actually, officially, a *bona fide* Native American?"

"Yeah. Call me Injun. . . . Bet you can't wait to tell the folks who you're bringing to dinner?" He smiled ear to ear, tipping his hat and brushing back his copper hair, his blue eyes twinkling in the morning light.

Fourteen

Revenge is best served cold.

"IT IS EITHER A MAN'S SHADOW OR HIS BREATH that becomes his ghost after death." Earlier, she'd overhead Ideliza's Yoruba explanation of where life goes when it is life no longer. There is nothing *nether* about the netherworld. Whatever was, continues, only across a Lethe-like river of forgetfulness, in a different part of the forest—*el monte.* And if *Las Siete Potencias,* the Seven Powers, have been properly seduced during your time on earth by your dance and *tambor*—your gum-red *mamey* fruits, your soft papaya offerings, the arm-pit moldered mangos, and the vessels of dark rum and hand-rolled Partagas cigars you levied at their altar—then you're transported to an even better *campo,* one with an open pass to visit the ones you love and left back on this side of the river—even an open pass to visit the ones you left but didn't like, if your reward consists of scaring them to death for the way they treated you in life.

Victoria had been struck by the freedom and fluidity of her pantheon. There was no *there* there. That much Victoria could subscribe to. But Princess Papaya cut God too much slack—*Francisco's turn of phrase.* She didn't challenge, deny, or rush her deities, and she took her miracles in stride. Victoria would never make a vestal virgin in Princess Papaya's holy temple—she'd wreak havoc from the get-go.

Not that Victoria's objection to doctrinal religions, including her own, was informed by prejudice or cultural superiority. She simply had a congenital aversion to anything that, by its very nature, demanded her whole heart or else demanded she lie about

179

it and, if not lie, dissimulate and pledge blind allegiance to what was, in the final analysis, an unknowable god.

Yet, despite her nerve and radical objection to dishonesty when it came to matters of conviction, she could not bring herself to speak her whole heart to Cooper, voice her forebodings, or openly discuss the improbable letter she finally held in her hands, courtesy of FedEx overnight. Not quite a letter, more like a death warrant, despite its explanations and generous bequests, not only for her, but for Bembé and Ideliza and for her parents as well—although she could bet her parents would leave every penny untouched, sitting in the bank, waiting for the day Roberto returned so they could give it back.

Can you kvetch to the entire neighborhood how much your bunions hurt, whine about how meshuganah and dirt poor and wretched you are, and then expect the girl in Roseland to light up, roll over like a cat, and call you Prince Charming? But these pundits sch-pundits with university degrees in relationships say different. They throw all kinds of books by that Dr. Joyce Brothers in your face, tell you with that smug look on their face that unless you're absolutely honest and call the girl up each time you have a bowel movement and tell her exactly how you feel about everything in the world, even things you have no feelings about one way or another, she'll drop you like a hot potato. . . . You believe that? Like they say, in that case I have a bridge I can sell you, on the cheap. I'm telling you, there's a reason we have rabbis and a reason God gives you a mother. Them, you can talk to.

Sara had taught her sons and daughter well in the flip side of ways of the birds and the bees. Throughout their childhood, she waxed poetic at the drop of a hat when it came to the ways to war and peace *in and out of the bedroom*, as she liked to preface her boy-girl talks.

In turn, Victoria had rejected Sara's outdated opinions, torn into her for her pat, facile, and sexist stance on anything where gender played a part, accused her of being out of step with modern times. But now, perhaps through years of repetition and brainwashing, it seemed Victoria had, after all, taken her mother's pearls to heart. Apparently, so had Roberto. It was clear from the lawyer's letter and his sudden disappearance that neither one of his consorts had a clue as to what went on in his head. She wondered how long he had planned his escape, and why, and, of course, whether he had planned it at all. The document was not from him, but from an L.A. lawyer she'd never heard Roberto mention, stating he had full power of attorney, advising each person mentioned of Roberto's wishes regarding the disposition of his assets, affirming the moneys were strictly gifts and that Roberto himself had prepaid taxes. He neither expected nor wished to have all or any portion thereof returned to him on his return. Whoever drafted it accounted for his decision and whereabouts in as few words as possible, stating that "whereas" his duties as a physician necessitated his presence and expertise in a top security mission overseas, he expected to return to his family and to his medical practice in Manhattan within three to six months, or as soon as his affairs permitted, and that he would remain incommunicado until such time as his top security mission required it. He urged all of them not to worry, to go about their lives, and to forgive his inability to explain further.

Nothing in this living will had Roberto's scent or sense in it, except for the secretive way he'd gone about it.

Something else gnawed at her like a silent rodent: Dr. Joe's uncensored gasp over the phone when he scrolled to the bottom of the page meant for her, realizing the depth and breadth of Roberto's worldly goods. He was far richer than anyone supposed—rich enough to surprise even Dr. Joe, who evidently felt he had the goods on him. Lobo Vineyards was only now beginning to turn a profit, and as far as she knew, his only other income came from a modest portfolio their father had managed until recently and, principally, from his self-employed salary and bonuses at the Lobo-Meyer Clinic. Despite her generous mental reckoning, she could not account for a net worth in the millions—three abortions a day at $2,500 a piece, five days a week, dwindled to less than $300,000 a year, once he'd apportioned Dr. Joe's salary, shelled out estimated taxes, paid for the fancy midtown office and ancillary overhead, as well as state-of-the-art medical equipment, electronic surveillance, and security guards. Then there were the three call-girl types, those rude nurses he kept full-time, and the high-risk medical malpractice premiums, the indoor garage on Fifty-

Seventh Street, as dear as most ordinary people's apartments, at least out of town or in Queens or Staten Island. All told, an income barely sufficient to cover two mortgages at Trump Tower, a yearly Mercedes, the dues at the Parallel Health Club in the city and the Meadows Club in East Hampton, the warm-water tennis trips to Captiva in winter, the time-share ski chalet in Vail, a growing child and a mistress, not to mention a wife who shopped retail at Hermes and Ferragamo, recovered at Canyon Ranch several times a year, threw black-tie parties, and tithed generously to the Animal Rescue Fund and the International Orchid Society.

Before her visitors returned, Victoria took the opportunity to look for and charge her cell phone. She scanned surfaces, reached in her catchall bag, shook the unmade sheets—*the case of the disappearing Nokia*. She fluffed the pillows in a last-ditch effort when suddenly, the Celia Cruz CD that Bembé had slipped in her bed that morning tumbled to the floor with a plastic cuff, bounced briefly, and fell hidden behind the bedpost. She narrowed her hand to a bird's beak and reached in with closed eyes to pry the jewel case out. Her fingertips had maneuvered halfway in when she stumbled on a pointed, metal-cold object the size of a Susan B. Anthony dollar, hammered and filigreed. What she discovered when she fished it out and held it to the light triggered such disbelief that her voice grew faint. Victoria would have recognized the six-point amulet anywhere. She flipped over the Star of David and found the inscription that read "David Zacarías Lobo" and the date of David's bar mitzvah at Temple Shearith Israel.

Her first instinct was flight. She skipped down the stairs, rushed out past the garden Ideliza had pruned, past the winding road to Mr. Hollister's space, clear across to the winery building, empty of workers now that the merlot harvest had been left to age in wooden vats.

"David! Are you here, David?! Where are you? Are you here, David?" Victoria cried out for her long gone, long lost brother in the middle of that sun-seared, unforgiving valley. Suddenly, she could not distinguish the sound of her own voice. Instead, she heard the echo of muted voices trapped under the rubble of the World Trade Center, beseeching the passersby pounding on their mangled heads—rescue workers behind gas masks, ready dogs and sensors on the prowl for body parts, unaware a life hung in the balance beneath them, only a breath away. These were the phantom whimpers that had chased her for months after Francisco's defragmentation in the sky, ever since the 9-11 massacre, when thousands were immolated and now shared a common grave. For indefinite moments when she heard them call, these whimpering voices of the dead took on a greater, more corporeal reality than her own surreal, inexcusable existence as a survivor.

Victoria grasped the Star of David firmly in her hand, afraid it would slip, be swallowed by the loam. She glanced at it every few seconds, strove to reassure herself of its reality, or else dispel the mirage. She questioned her reason and even the irrefutable medal digging its six points into her skin, like thorns and nails and stigmata. She peered into the winery through the sealed doors and windows, rapped at the glass, walked the circumference of the building, and searched the myriad rows looking for ghosts amid the perfectly still, perfectly deserted fields.

Cooper was due back long ago. Where was he? Had Bembé seduced him into some uncharted exploration? Just as well. She would book herself back to New York on the next flight out of Santa Barbara, despite the cost and the inevitable connection change. It was worth it to skip the long drive to Los Angeles, which she'd found unnerving even from the back seat of the town car. Or perhaps she'd stay here until the storm passed. She'd discuss it with Cooper. On second thought, she would tell no one. She would keep her own counsel, shield her infirmity from strangers—and who could anyone count as a landsman in this forsaken place? Like Hamlet, she tried to understand how it had come to this, examining her sins, searching for the culprits who'd hurled her across the line between imagination and delusion, between memory and desire: Roberto's letter; his insensitive disappearance; his inexplicable, unlikely financial generosity; her wanton intimacy with a stranger of defective and confounded gender against all Torah precepts; the quandary of Ideliza's in-your-face grief and class struggle; the pity and beauty of Bembé; the hothouse cabin with not a single foxhole in which to hide.

She heard a car door slam and ran to the front gate. No one there. She strained her eyes, hoping the toy in the distance was

Cooper's Volvo coming down Route One. Seconds later, a sheriff's Ford cruising for speeders down the lonely road whizzed by. She would return to the house, back to the bed where David's star had miraculously sprung from the dust—or perhaps not appeared, only seemed to in some parallel existence. She would take a sleeping pill, wait for the mental reel to change. As soon as Cooper returned, she would claim a migraine, urge him to take Bembé and Ideliza for the day. And then she would lie still with her head buried in the pillow until peace dropped, until she regained her senses.

"I see you have not been reading your *tehillim*, Miss Victoria." The voice belonged unmistakably to her brother David, whose figure she discovered towering over her when she came to.

Victoria leapt to her feet, questioning the nature of this phenomenal apparition. She was overcome by momentary relief, which turned to fear and grief and joy and unspeakable confusion.

They gazed at each other for an instant that seemed to hang for minutes—two statues, each waiting for the other to blink. David looked larger and stronger than Cooper would have remembered him from that auspicious day two months earlier, when he had whisked him to freedom, delivered him by the water's edge where the Ben Gurion Rescue Brigade submarine had waited for him.

Victoria would have recognized him anywhere despite the years the locusts had eaten—his movie-star looks, his high cheeks and chiseled jaw cut like an ancient Greek sculpture. David had razored his hair and covered his head with a Yankees baseball cap. The rest of him was colored khaki green, military without the stars, stripes, or insignias. He kept one arm cocooned in a parka jacket, the other arm perched on his shoulder, hanging across his chest. His Lobo aqua eyes gazed vacantly at Victoria—deep, troubled pools betraying neither joy nor sorrow.

She needed to hold him to her, smell him, run her nails through his hair, feel his kiss on her cheek. Reassure herself of his present reality. All other explanations would keep, would come later—one by one, without rushing the years or skipping the small parts. For now, only this mattered: She'd not hallucinated his presence in this place, like Jacob wrestling with the angel and realizing *the Lord was in this place and I knew it not.*

But rather than the lingering, sentimental embrace Victoria

had rushed to give and receive, she was met by the flat impact of blinded birds crashing into a high-rise window. Stunned, rather than recoiling and turning back on her flight course, she pressed on: "Oh David! David! I can't believe it. . . . I thought I'd totally lost it the last couple of days, telling myself I'd seen your face in the glass. And then, out of the blue, your bar mitzvah star appears on my bed, and then I really thought I was toast! My God! How are you? You're okay? You look good. I mean, what can I say. You look the same. And different. All grown up! I can't get over it! So amazing . . . to see you, to have you right here, all of you, back from the dead, completely and categorically alive!"

She clung to his shoulders, forced another embrace, smiling, searching his face, chilled by his reticence.

David eased out of her grip and, as he did, the parka tumbled to the floor, revealing the first clue: Where his left arm should have been, only a slaughtered elbow stump remained. He made no effort to conceal it again, nor to explain.

Victoria closed her eyes, shook her head. "Oh my God, David . . . they did this to you . . . those animals . . ."

David shrugged, forced a faint smile. "I lived. What can I say."

She grabbed his right hand, started to lead him downstairs. "Let's go down and call Abba and Mami . . . have you talked to them yet?" So much left unsaid.

David paused. "No, wait. Vic. Don't want to . . . yet."

"You haven't been to see them yet? Why? How long since you're back? . . . My God, there is so much . . . please come, let's sit down. Tell me what happened, everything . . . or as much as you feel like, I mean . . . I just can't believe my eyes . . . it's really you, really David! Like you came back from the dead . . . I thought . . . a lot of times, over the years, I thought you were dead. . . ." She stopped midstream. It dawned on her she'd need to explain about Francisco. "Oh . . . I guess I better tell you . . . about Francisco, my husband you never met . . ."

David intercepted: "Yes, I know. I know what happened." No condolences, only the artic chill in his voice.

"How did you know? Did Mami tell you? Oh, David, I'm so incredibly ecstatic, so totally blown away to see you . . . I want to hear about you, all about you . . . how you got here, what happened to you, how come you never answered any of my letters, how you found me here . . . so much . . . I wouldn't know where to start. . . . You want something to drink? *Glezel tai?* Did you have something to eat? How did you get here, drive? I thought I'd heard a car before. . . . Oh, my God . . . I just realized, I have some people staying here . . . not worth explaining right now . . . but it just dawned on me they're walking in the door any minute, I think . . ." She rambled on, juxtaposing thoughts at random, mixing the trivial with the crucial, spinning her words like pinwheels, asking him to speak but then not yielding the floor.

"It's fine." David unclasped her hand, pushed her away gently but with unmistakable intent. "Why don't we just take a walk over by the big building, the winery. There's a place on the side of the horse farm. We can sit for a while."

"That's funny. Sounds like you know this place pretty well."

David disregarded her remark, led the way down the stairs to the back door.

"Wait, David, you sure you don't want to call Abba and Mami first?" She pointed to the kitchen phone. "Have you spoken with them? I mean, I hope you told them you're back home, in this country, right? Maybe you didn't. They didn't call me, so you didn't. Oh, David. You wouldn't believe . . . the two of them have been going out of their gourds for years . . . like dying and sitting shivah at the same time, for eighteen years. . . . Let's just at least call them for one minute and tell them we'll call longer later? I don't care if my, if my guests interrupt or come back and find us here. We're entitled to privacy. And you're my brother, back from hell. . . . I can leave them here or we can go for a walk or I can send them away on a tour or something! What difference does it make?" She started for the phone, but David's firm hand held her in place.

"No, hold on, Victoria. Wait. Let's just get out. I don't want to see anybody right now."

She acquiesced, shaking her head at him with a troubled mien that conveyed both disapproval and submission. They walked side by side, kept in stride, losing their eyes in the mountains, using the Santa Ynez as a fence between them. They circled past Mr. Hollister's trailer. The shepherd dog, who'd been surprisingly quiet of late, let out an eerie howl.

David picked up his pace and Victoria fell several feet behind him. She was finding it difficult to sort out her thoughts—*thoughts like beads coming unstrung, scattering the ground.* She prayed silently to the words of Shakespeare's sonnet. She had to gain some stillness, make room for her brother. It wasn't like David to be so ornery and taciturn—not when it came to her. But eighteen years had passed like a flood between them. A whole life. A whole marriage. A whole person. Perhaps he needed time to adjust, was more shell-shocked than he let on. *Those pigs in Cuba probably messed with his mind.* She bristled at the image of the cankered stump passing for his left arm, at the cigar-inflicted scars puncturing his able arm, spreading like smallpox across the sections of his neck and chest exposed by the light. She swallowed hard, held down the nausea welling up in spasms, gathering inexorable momentum. She would not ruin this moment or selfishly attract attention to herself—if anyone had a right to the moment, it was David. He was the one who had been tortured, robbed of an arm and . . . who knew what else . . . maybe half his mind.

David led her to the quaint picnic area she had entirely overlooked before. Smack in front of the thatched roof structure was a freshly dug barbecue pit, deep and wide enough to fit a Heffer. The farmworkers had left behind a wooden flute, a pair of greasy skewers, an empty leather holster, a cloth *relicario* of the Virgin of Guadalupe, and a string of empty Negra Modelo bottles, all lined up in a single row for target practice.

"I had no idea this was here," she said. "I just walked over a while ago, and I never even saw it."

He was standing beside her, leaning on one foot and looking away from her to the Santa Ynez Mountains.

"David?"

He turned silently.

"You put your Star of David there for me under the pillow, right?" She no longer wanted to ask that, since the answer seemed obvious, but she could not bring herself to blurt out whatever was going through her mind and risk alienating him now, before the present ice broke.

"I didn't leave it there," he answered in monotone. "I gave the star to Bembé, told him to give it to you. I wanted to let you know

I was around . . . give you some warning.'"

"Bembé? I can't believe it! You're the one who took Bembé to the airport? You practically abducted him. My God! What about the woman he mentioned, somebody named Yael?"

David nodded. His reticence spoke volumes.

"David, Roberto is missing. I'm worried. . . . It's funny, all these years I've been so worried about you, and now, out of the blue, you're here and Roberto is nowhere to be found. You know, when you disappeared, when we didn't hear back from you . . . God, David, it was so dark, so hopeless and scary . . . in a way, I disappeared, too. . . . It totally destroyed our parents. I mean, it's so bad I'm not allowed to bring you up in conversation because it's liable to unhinge Mami . . . both of them, actually, but especially Mami. And now I'm just worried sick for her, and for Abba . . . I haven't told them anything about Roberto yet. . . . And, listen, at this point, I have to say, never mind them. I'm very worried about Roberto myself. . . ."

She purposely left out any reference to Francisco's demise or her subsequent breakdown. Her husband was a stranger to David, a dead stranger at that. She wanted to draw him into the inner sanctum of family concerns, to the core of who they were and where they came from.

"Roberto? I don't understand. Didn't you get his letter already?"

Victoria bolted: "Wait a minute . . . am I going crazy here? Are you telling me you know about the letter, too? Then you must know where he is? Is he okay?"

David bit his lip, stretched his back, kept silent.

"Hey, David, listen, I'm starting to get a little shook up . . . more than a little, actually . . . and I hate it. Why can't you give me a straight answer?"

"Yeah."

"Yeah? Is that all? Yeah? So, I guess we're playing 'Twenty Questions?'" She circled around him, then stood face to face, squeezing his eyes with her stare.

"Twenty Questions?"

"Oh? You don't know? I guess that's one game you were deprived of growing up. I always thought it was boring. Still do."

David smiled. "You haven't changed a bit, Vic. You look gorgeous, too. Even more gorgeous than when I left, but that makes sense. You still had a little baby fat left. I used to tell the guys at the prisons, ten different prisons altogether, up and down the island . . . I used to brag about my gorgeous sister, tell them you were such a *shikse*. And they kept asking for your picture, but I didn't have a picture. You never sent it. In fact, never mind from pictures or even a birthday card. How about a couple of words scribbled on bathroom tissue? I could have used the tissue, especially since the bastards didn't believe in toilet paper. But can you believe everybody got letters but me? And some prisoners were lucky enough to get a visit, even from relatives in Miami. They used to fly down through Canada, grease paws with dollars just on the off chance the Fidelistas would let them see their husbands or brothers, just for a couple of minutes on the sly. Sometimes they got lucky. Eventually everyone got out but me. They signed a public declaration repenting for all the grievous acts they had committed against the revolution, and they were shipped to reeducation camps and then kicked out of the country. Or their families paid Fidel's ransom, and he sent them on their merry way. He wouldn't let all of them out, but he'd eventually spring some *shlemazle* as long as he wasn't a counterrevolutionary. I thought I should qualify. Anyway, that's the way it went. I watched a whole lot of them get out. Saw them come and saw them go."

"What do you mean? Are you serious? I wrote you constantly, and so did our parents . . . and Roberto, too, I'm sure. We kept waiting for some word from you, a letter, a quick note . . . but nothing. . . . I thought they'd killed you, David. Years ago, I mean . . ."

David shot her a hard stare.

"What? You don't believe me? Is that what that look means?"

"Where did you send the letters?"

"Are we talking about the actual street address? I . . . I don't know. Roberto took care of all that. We gave him the letters. Lots and lots of letters, several times a month. He was in charge of trying to get you back . . . even chummied up to some official at the Cuban consulate on Lexington Avenue, up in the Thirties somewhere. I guess that's how the letters went down. We did everything through Roberto to avoid confusing the issue any more than it already was. Hard enough for one person to get through to those creeps, and Roberto had that one contact. . . . Our parents and Francisco and me, we gave Roberto the $100,000 he told us Castro was demanding for your release . . . and we waited and we kept thinking any minute you'd be here, that you'd be flown to Canada and then just show up for *Shabbat* one day. . . . Every year, Abba kept a place for you at the *seder.* . . . We kept waiting, even when reason started to fly in the face of hope. . . . Frankly, I thought they'd kept the money and killed you anyway, and I mourned you secretly. I never told them. Didn't want to upset them any more. Mami kept saying she was sure they were getting ready to step up the bid before they released you. She *kvetched* that Roberto had agreed to Castro's terms too fast and made it too easy and put ideas in the heads of the rotten *ganefs*, those miserable thieves, who no doubt decided they had lowballed your price and should ask for more. She kept saying you were alive . . . all these years she kept insisting, waiting for Castro to send another ransom note, so we could get you back already. Abba and Mami saved all their money, spent a third of what they should have at their age, waiting for the time Roberto would get the news from the consulate. And Mami wrote the president and the media and every congressman, in and out of New York, Idaho, Nebraska, Kansas; it didn't matter to her, the more the merrier. . . . She even wrote Castro himself, pleading . . . gave Roberto the letter so the guy at the UN consulate would hand it to him personally. . . ."

"That snake. *Shlang.*"

"Castro?"

"Roberto."

"What do you mean?"

"He sold me down the river, Vic. Kept the ransom money you gave him . . . maybe bought this place with it, what do I know?"

"I don't believe it. Why would he do that? Roberto, it turns out, is a really wealthy man, unbeknownst to me, mind you. . . . But anyway, how can you accuse Roberto of something so unspeakably evil? He couldn't."

"Yeah. Right. Know what I'm reminded of? 'The lady doth protest too much.'"

"Are you implying I know different and somehow, for some nefarious reason, I'm trying to cover for him?"

"That's one advantage to having you for a sister. You can read between the lines. . . . Listen, all I hear from you is *he wouldn't, he wouldn't, he couldn't.* Want to say it some other way? Maybe tie a ribbon around it or something? What else?"

Victoria considered his face, his controlled body language, his self-pity and inexplicable condemnation. A man holding an ace close to his vest, stringing her along, playing cat and mouse, waiting for her to hang herself. Only she had no clue what the rules of engagement were or why they should be playing at all.

"Well, I don't think this is what you want to hear when you say *what else* that way, but you're giving me such a hard time, maybe I should start by getting something off my chest. . . ."

David paced silently in front of her, then sat back at her side, eyes turned toward the cabin. He was biting his lip, playing nervously with his hand. Occasionally, he would reach into his shirt, press on his stomach, massage it in circular motions.

"I'm sorry to bring this up now because it's so indescribably awful what happened to you, but you should also remember you chose to go to Cuba, despite the fact our parents and I begged you not to go, begged you a million times, because it was clear to anyone but a total imbecile that this was a totally harebrained idea. A boy who knew nothing about what goes on down there, to just hop on some rickety boat in shark-infested waters and sail into the sunset en route to a communist island that our parents had narrowly escaped from in the first place . . . just sailed off to a place where a hundred *milicianos* were probably waiting with their stupid rifles cocked and ready to fire . . . to do that, to risk your life to save an old man, and get this, an old man you didn't even know, a rabbi someone else at temple was related to? No, wait! Let's not stop there. Let's be brutally honest: To impress the girl who was related to the secretary at the temple who was related to the *rebbe.* Did I get that right? And for what? Bottom line, David? Somebody else got the girl. Roberto didn't get the girl, and you didn't get the girl. She married someone else, a Dr. Rosenberg who teaches hematology at Harvard, at least that's the last I heard. . . ."

David locked his jaw hard, tossed his head back to the sky, signaling she was close to overstepping the line.

"Anyway," she continued, "maybe I should stop before I really get going. I mean, I just want to ask you, did it ever occur to you what you were doing to our parents . . . and to me, too, your own little sister you said you loved so much? If I hadn't been so befuddled on account of you all these years, I would have had the luxury of getting really mad at you sooner. Furiously mad. Like I'm feeling right about now."

"You don't understand, Victoria. And I can't bother with Cliff Notes, when you don't even want the facts."

"What facts?"

"Starting with the fact that the snake set me up. Do you need to hear anything else? How much do you want me to tell you? Everything you just said, your whole beef about my having gone to rescue the *rebbe*, that was all too long ago, and a lot worse happened since. You're talking arrows and I'm talking atom bomb. But if it makes you feel better, yeah, I wouldn't do the same thing again. And, for your information, I did think about it. Had a lot of time to think about it, like half my life. I paid for acting like an imbecile, like you put it . . . and I paid for it . . . and I paid for it and, look, I'm still paying." He proffered his stump to her face until she recoiled, turned her back, and lowered her head.

"But," he continued, "that doesn't change the fact that, for starters, Roberto was a snake. Worse than a snake. He's at the top of the snake chain."

Victoria had a glimmer of what she later concluded had been the reason for David's apparitions at her window, and ultimately for the way in which he had come to visit her this day, to deliver the astonishing news of his return. She thought of the four vets back from Vietnam who had visited her high school, how it had confused her back then that, having accepted the invitation to speak, all four found it impossible to say anything original or to give details of their lives in the jungle trenches. And she remembered how Sara had often warned her never to ask about the war or make the slightest mention of Treblinka to Mrs. Margolis, the neighbor two houses down who had a Star of David tattooed on her arm.

She faced David, then forced herself to look at his stump long enough for it to register. She had been wishing she could erase this day, aware it meant that, to her mind, he'd still be dead. But she'd considered the alternative far worse: to see a man, once gentle and possessing the qualities of refined intelligence and virtue, brought low and stripped of natural power by rancor, hate, regret. She gathered her strength, stilled herself to meet her part in this joint rite of passage from which she feared no one would emerge unscathed.

"Why do you keep calling him a snake? You haven't given me any proof, just that you feel a certain way. The facts are that when you up and left, Roberto was starting med school. Why would he keep the ransom money? What would make him do such a terrible thing? Our parents had enough, and they were always very generous, as you know. Why would Roberto lie to us, put our parents and me through such a horrible thing? I know he can be weird and not so nice a lot of the time, maybe most of the time . . . and you know he's been such a *putz* with me, ever since we were small. You had to stick up for me, remember? So, I'm not even sure I like Roberto, although I probably love him, but don't ask me why. I'm the last to sign on to his fan club, though . . . I assure you. It's obvious I don't like lots of things he does and has done, believe me, despite the fact I try not to judge, because who am I to judge how Roberto should live his life or how many women he should have or . . . But keeping the money and leaving you to rot in a Cuban jail? That's over the top. Totally. I just don't understand what's gotten into you. I mean, I shouldn't say that. Actually, I think I understand. . . ."

"Oh? You do? My little sister understands . . . understands what?"

"That those fascist creeps messed you up, tortured you so badly they made you paranoid, and now you suspect your family, accuse your own brother of selling you down the river . . . and maybe you're doing it on purpose or maybe you're not exactly aware, but you're taking it out on me, really beating me up with your whole snippy attitude. You might as well call me a snake, too, not just Roberto. I tell you, this is certainly not the way I dreamed we would be talking if we ever saw each other again. . . . I mean, David, to be honest, you're scaring me. Maybe we should call a doctor, consider getting some help. Have you heard the term *post-traumatic stress disorder* yet? It's normal, after what you've gone through. . . ."

"Oh, please! A shrink? Doctor schdoctor."

"You know you're really upsetting me? I just can't believe it's my own brother spewing this *dreck*, acting so . . . As a matter of fact, you may look and sound like David, but I'm thinking you're nothing but a stand-in at the matinee!"

"That was my line!" he interrupted her. Knee jerk, before he knew he'd said it, referring to the play he and Victoria had cowritten one year for Rosh Hashanah. It was to be the beginning of their literary collaboration—Lobo and Lobo, the Rogers and Hart of serious drama.

Their eyes met quickly, kindled, then turned pages. She had become aware of the time, of how inordinately long Cooper was taking, of how searingly the sun had risen now that the marine layer had been thoroughly slurped up by the creeping roots under foot. She wished Cooper were here, now, longed to hear his voice, his reassuring homespun dialectic. Her thoughts took refuge in his glow, his unexamined constancy, the way his eyes lit when they bantered, or just because she was there and he liked her.

"David, it's getting a little too hot out here for me. . . . Can you believe they call this winter? And I'm a little worried about my guests. I should at least go in and tell them where I am. You mind? Why don't you come back to the house with me? You're probably thirsty. I'm parched."

She started back down toward the house, her figure erect and resolute, warding off any opposing thought that would prevent her from running to Cooper for cover.

"Vic! Let's stay out here for a little while. It doesn't feel private enough in there . . . that man, the groundskeeper or whatever he is . . . he's a snoop. I've seen him going around, listening in on you by the side of the house. He can't hear us from here. It's better to keep the dirty laundry out here. You agree?"

She paused, hesitated, then realized he'd given her a wedge.

"Oh, okay. But on one condition: you start answering questions, so we can get to the bottom of whatever it is that's gotten you all twisted like a pretzel?"

He chuckled. "Working the angles all the time, eh, Vic? So now I owe you? What is this—you give me the Left Bank, so now I have to give up the Temple Mount?"

She shrugged. "What did you expect? I'm a Lobo, ain't I?"

"Oh, I see. So we're talking *Ain't* now, eh? Guess it's catchy."

"What do you mean, catchy?"

"Nothing. Forget it. Talking to myself."

"Fine. So, can we talk?"

"Yes. You're right. Let's talk. Come here, come sit over by me, and keep it down a little. I think our voices carry. That man, the groundskeeper, I just saw him cut across the yard down by the house. A weirdo."

Victoria obliged and found herself next to him under a thatched roof, their backs to the house and a panoramic view of the horse farm and the mountains encircling them above.

"Well, are you going to explain?" said Victoria.

"Explain what? I thought maybe you would have something to explain. What do you want me to tell you?"

"Oh? Now I have something to explain. Well, let's say you go first, okay?"

"Okay."

"Well?"

"Well what?"

"Well this, David. *Número uno*, I keep asking myself if this is really happening. And, for instance, what's this business of taking Bembé from his house, abducting him yet, and giving him your star, and orchestrating the child's departure with his mother, actually hacking or in some way obtaining the actual ticket I had purchased for them through a travel agent, electronically . . . hello? I wish someone would explain that. . . . And can you tell me how come you didn't do the normal thing when you were able to get home? How come you didn't go directly to Mami and Abba instead, like anyone else would? Or call me, or just show up. It's too unsettling, David. . . ."

"Okay. What else?"

"What else? Can you start with that?"

"I'd like to hear what else you want me to tell you first."

"Well, this is what else. It doesn't take a brain surgeon, but if you want me to spell it out for some perverse reason. Yes, I'm beginning to think you had something to do with Roberto's disappearance. . . . Did you?" She shook, afraid of making things worse or fanning his anger, which he seemed to have brought down a few notches.

David shot up, walked away without answering, then motioned her to follow him a little further out, to stand on the promontory overlooking the horse farm, where Victoria was surprised by the figure of a small child of ten or eleven cantering a powerful Arabian around the ring.

"That child is amazing. . . . Did you see the way he handles himself on that huge horse?" She grasped at straws to bring some balance into their mutable *gestalt* and land-mined conversation. She imagined Cooper and company must be back at the house by now and organizing a search party with Bembé at the helm. She rehearsed a formal, tell-nothing introduction of David to Cooper, Ideliza, and Bembé. Then she reconsidered. She would send a smoke signal as soon as she spotted them crossing the field, would point them back to the house—*Not now, por favor, I'll explain later, thank you very much.* She had agreed to stay out here longer. She had to seize this moment with David, be present, prepare for whatever it was her brother had come to say. She turned to him with an arched eyebrow.

"David. You're driving me crazy. Are you remotely aware?"

He flapped his right hand in front of him—*What can I tell you?* His gesture called for two hands in Jewish, but it was clear. She'd caught herself reverting to certain speech patterns, family accents, subtle turns of phrase, of thought and syntax she labeled Yiddish mishmash.

"So? What's up, big bro'? Are you going to answer me already? What's this about Roberto?"

"I wish I had time so you could bring me up on all the lingo," he said, facing her, "so many new words, funny ways of saying things . . . have you noticed everything's a verb now? All nouns are verbs, practically. And with all that technology, computers, all that. But what can I say? I got off the bus eighteen years ago, with the needle probably still stuck in *groovy* . . . that's as hip as I get. Unless 'groovy' should make a comeback? Look at 'cool'. That's all I hear since I'm out. I thought I woke up in a black-and-white movie starring Lena Horn and Louis Armstrong. *Coool, man, cool.* By the way, how's my English? A little rusty? Maybe so rusty I sound like Shakespeare already? Well, my Spanish is much improved. As a matter of fact, I'm told by some people at the Brigade I speak it like a *cubano criollo* from the provinces! Even lost the accent. Kept up my Hebrew, too. Know how? Repeating and repeating and praying everything the *rebbe* back home had made me memorize. . . . Once in a while I got my hands on some books, too."

"I'm listening to you and I'm horrified, that's all I can say. Even the good parts, like your speaking Spanish and your little sarcastic joking around. Even the good sounds horrible. Like a beautiful early fall day in New York, on September eleventh at eight in the morning, when no one at the Twin Towers knew there were two planes on the way, shooting straight for their heads. . . . I'm glad to hear you kept up Hebrew, though."

"Yeah. I know. That was so horrible . . . but not strange. Nothing seems strange. Worse, improbable. You know those assassins gave us nothing to read in those cockroach prison camps unless we got it in the mail and they didn't want to keep it for themselves. Fascist communist propaganda and comic books were the only exception. The guards passed me the comics when they were done with them. It was one of their forms of punishment, restricting me to comics. But, believe it or not, eventually those comics gave me a little window to the world, a tiny little window that I could use to figure out some of the things that were going on out there. And, once in a blue moon, some prisoner would slip me a book or a magazine. When they transported me to the prison in Oriente, about one or two years into my incarceration, another prisoner, a Jew named Efraín, he took a huge chance and hid a copy of the Talmud for me in my cell. The guards kicked him mercilessly in the groin and did other stuff to him I can't even tell you about. But what can I say? After a few months in isolation, sharing a filthy cot with rats and roaches and centipedes crawling between your toes, and hauling chemical containers back and forth all day, and making do with a little rice and beans from time to time, sucking on stalks of sugarcane rotting my teeth . . . well, it took a while but eventually I stopped missing the *New York Times.* . . ."

"Oh, David. Yes, very funny about the *Times*. . . . It tears me apart to hear this. My God. I don't know that I can take it all in, not all at once. . . . I'm sorry . . . I know you went through it and I'm the one acting squeamish, like some JAP. It's not that I don't want to hear. I do, don't get me wrong. I just can't begin to fathom . . . I never considered the details before. Or I should say I tried not to think about it. I tried not to imagine what they were doing to you, how you lived, how desolate you felt . . . because I couldn't bear it. I think in some way I preferred believing you were dead— that way I knew you weren't suffering."

"Right." David had turned inward again, dark and unyielding, avoiding her touch, distancing himself, unwilling to let them off the roller-coaster ride.

"I was thinking about what you said before." She pulled on his sleeve, forced him to reengage. Intuitively, she had resolved not to give in each time his mood turned, because she felt instinctively that by avoidance they might forego this unsettling rite of passage but pay with even more exacting coinage in the end.

"I just don't get how the whole thing happened," she continued. "My letters really never got to you? And the ransom money that was wired directly from Bank of America in New York. I don't understand. Something very sinister about the whole ordeal . . . didn't they let other Americans out when their families paid the ransom?"

David sighed, clenched his jaw, squeezed his hand into a ball: "*Carajo*, you just don't want to know the truth, do you? Didn't you just hear me tell you I never heard from you once? Not from you, not from anyone else in our so-called family either."

"I'm trying to hear you, David, believe me. But, first of all, watch your mouth and don't curse at me. I don't care if that's all you heard in those miserable prisons down there. And don't keep making faces and popping your jaw, like you want to slap me and can barely hold back, all right? I want nothing more than to hear you, but I should tell you it's a lot to process."

This time, his laughter came unbridled. For the first time, his eyes lost some of the cloud, a glint of David's soul came through. "Now you sound like Mami. Exactly!"

Victoria smiled, gave him their old Annabelle the Cow long-lash wink, flooding David's eyes and capturing his imagination. Her smile fused the years together as if no time had passed since those snow-lit afternoons after school when little Vic and her older brother David reenacted book characters as they stood atop a castaway sofa in the attic of a Jersey suburb.

Victoria sat down on a rickety old wine cask serving as a garden stool. She stilled herself, afraid the impending torrent of emotions would overtake her, a torrent she had brought upon herself by willfully breaking through with all weapons at her disposal, even a weapon as low-blow *schmaltzy* as Annabelle the Cow's wink. And now that she had him, or at least now that he had begun to come around, she was unsure if either one could endure the pain of regrafting to the other, *like twins that suffer one another's wounds, except the wounds of separation, for those are mortal.* She glanced in the direction of the house and tried to discern human forms inside, but the sun had begun tilting to midday and the glass doors were refractory sunglasses. She wondered how she'd mustered the courage to speak up, even scold her older brother, a survivor of inconceivable indignity and torture. It came to her that she'd been frightened of him from the beginning, from the very moment he had appeared in her bedroom, when he half-seriously admonished her for not reading the psalms. Frightened not only of rending the joy his return would entail, but frightened of David himself, and not from anything she reasoned or because he'd used their conversation to vent his anger. *Perhaps the smell/ of fear itself/ His fear/ After long fear years/ fear/ Having fossilized/ shaped/ his crust and carapace.*

"Victoria?"

She looked up at him, standing over her. "Yes, David. I hope you're going to start talking a little nicer and explaining yourself. I have guests who are probably out of their minds because they've been waiting for me to drive to San Luis with them, and I just bailed without as much as a note. And one of those guests happens to be a child who's expecting my company, and I don't want to upset him. And I can hardly stand being out in the sun all this time. I have red hair, remember?"

"They're not there."

"What do you mean they're not there?" She came to her feet

again, prepared to go back immediately and see for herself.

"I told Cooper to take Bembé and his mother for a ride, horse-back riding or whatever he thought they all wanted to do. Told him to be back later this evening."

"You what! How dare you do such a thing! Where do you come off? What gives you the right? And not only that, but to keep me in the dark and add insult to injury . . . And I suppose Cooper just listened to you and meekly obeyed and did anything a perfect stranger told him to do?" This time, the migraine was for real. The blood was thumping audibly around her right eye and brow.

"Calm down, Vic. And keep your voice down. That guy's going to hear us."

"I don't give a damn! How dare you!"

"I thought it was best if we were alone. We needed to speak. I don't like having people around, snooping around."

"If you told him to go and he went, how come you won't come back to the house with me? In fact, why couldn't we just have been sitting there comfortably or at least more comfortably than here at a hundred degrees in the sun?"

He shrugged his shoulders, a left-handed apology. "I told you I'd seen that man snooping around. Didn't want to give him the satisfaction of listening to us."

"He can't hear us if you don't yell and we close the door and maybe go up to my bedroom and talk there. I mean, what is he, Superman who can fly over buildings and hear through walls?"

"Maybe he has the place bugged."

She snorted, blew her breath out, neighed like the neighboring horse.

"That pathetic man bugging the house to hear what I have to say? What for? Is he going to turn my conversation about chile peppers and Santa Barbara wine over to the FBI? Maybe you bugged the house, what do you say to that? . . . I hate to bring it up again, but you were in Cuba too long, and they obviously messed with your head and made you totally paranoid. And I'm sorry, but you have no right to just come in and take over my life and my guests and jerk my chain like my feelings are totally irrelevant because no one can top the way you suffered. I'm sorry. I don't think I can stand this another minute. Maybe you better call our parents and go be with them a while. I would hope you'd be nicer to them. I don't think I can stand this sadistic cat-and-mouse game of yours. I don't deserve it. Nobody does. And I don't trust you. Nothing tells me you're being truthful. Quite the opposite. I've tried to give you room, to make it easy to tell me what it is that is obviously bugging you, and look what I get!"

She started back to the house without meeting his eyes, sprinting and finally running. He followed, caught up to her halfway down, running and jogging beside her, keeping up to her frantic pace.

"I'm also a little claustrophobic!" he yelled out to overcome the wind flying into them. "I try to stay outdoors as much as possible. Since my escape, I keep having nightmares about being trapped in a house with glass doors. . . . I have these strange symptoms. Shortness of breath. My heart beats so fast I think I'm going to have a heart attack. And the minute I'm indoors my hands start to sweat . . . like I'm going to pass out . . . and I turn into a filthy pig!"

"Sounds like classic anxiety attacks," she yelled back, running, aware they were keeping pace. "You didn't have those symptoms before, when you were in jail?"

"Yeah. But different. Hard to explain. Down there it was more like being on survival mode all the time. Since I'm out, it's not survival mode. It's like honey in a sieve."

She came to a halt, regained her breath.

"I understand. Let's go in and have some tea, and maybe we can start fresh all over again. But you have to behave and, for God's sake, just call a spade a spade. No more Twenty Questions or making me guess. Just keep telling yourself it's Victoria you're talking with, not some prison guard or whatever. Is that a deal?"

He sighed, nodded sheepishly. "It's a deal."

"Good," she answered, "because I wouldn't put up with it otherwise."

Fifteen

As it turned out, despite David's proof of complicity and malfeasance, Roberto had never intended to cause his brother harm or send him straight to hell.

That winter day, some fifteen years before, when Sara and Abram received the ransom note from the Cuban government—$250,000 in cash or a cashier's check—Roberto had dutifully taken the Lexington Avenue subway to Grand Central and walked down a few blocks to the Cuban consulate, check in hand. He meant to effect the exchange as soon as possible and be entirely rid of the burden, as he was at the end of his residency at Harlem Hospital and was busy interviewing for his next move.

While waiting in the vestibule for the secretary to give him the proper form to fill out, and because the city had suddenly been blanketed by snow and there was a certain chaos that accompanies storms, delaying appointments, taking commuters off their course, Roberto struck up a casual conversation with a certain consulate official nicknamed The General. And it was this seemingly innocuous encounter that led him to taste of the tree of the knowledge of good and evil, and that sealed his fate to David's for an eighteen-year free fall from grace. And while David was undoubtedly the victim, losing life, dignity, and limb in a rotting jail, Roberto was also doing time, even while he prospered and grew in stature.

This affable official, The General, suggested Roberto keep the ransom money for himself. He offered to arrange David's safe passage through personal connections at a fraction of Castro's wholesale price—$25,000 paid in advance.

When months passed and David's release did not materialize, The General explained that the rules had changed, that he needed to grease the paws of more local officials, and promptly demanded another $25,000, also in advance. By then, David had grown suspicious, but could not bring himself to tell his parents, or Victoria, that he had mishandled the simple delivery of their hard-earned moneys and had been royally swindled by a petty communist official.

Years passed, and Roberto, burdened by his parent's suffering and unhinging, continued to pay visits to The General, imploring him to help him get his brother out, raising his voice from time to time at the consulate, hoping the man would fear exposure and keep his bargain. But the more Roberto implored, the more The General demanded money. Soon, Roberto had spent or gambled the portion of the ransom money he had kept for himself. Finally, after much haggling, Roberto and The General came to a suitable agreement: Roberto would pay him double on delivery, if the delivery would take effect in thirty days or less. Since he had no way to pay him anything by then, Roberto had reasoned that as soon as David was out of jail and back on U.S. soil, he would inform on the corrupt henchman of Marxist ideology. But before the planned exchange could take place, The General was shot dead while shopping for vegetables at a grocery store on the corner—perhaps for being on the take, though no one would say.

Weeks after the incident, which made the front page of the *Post* and the metro section of the *Times*, Roberto appealed to The General's replacement, a man they called Barbudo. And it was at this point that Roberto took the irreversible turn somewhere east or south of Eden.

Barbudo also had an offer for young Roberto, one that, as David put it, Roberto's pathological greed could not resist. And, although at first Barbudo's plans seemed modest and safe enough in scope, Roberto sowed grandiose dreams around them. He began picturing himself in limousines to Lincoln Center, in suits by Bijan and sitting on the board of the Museum of Modern Art—all this before he'd ever delivered a baby on his own or saved a patient from miscarrying.

It began with the petty theft of prescription medications, which Barbudo sold on the black market with immunity, even to Cuba, because the sick were in such dire need. Soon, his larceny escalated to medical equipment and then, as Barbudo gained confidence in him, recreational synthetic drugs.

Years passed and Roberto's sideline business grew alongside his medical practice. The volume of his extracurricular endeavors changed, grew, diminished, and grew again, according to what Barbudo termed market demands. Barbudo transferred Roberto's generous take into an offshore bank like clockwork—the same bank that had just wired Roberto's bequest to its correspondent bank in the United States.

At the conclusion of each transaction, Roberto would announce this was his last batch, unless Barbudo effected David's release immediately, for he was consumed with the idea of restoring his parent's life—and Victoria's—by finally delivering David to their doorstep, even if a few years late.

And all the while, David hung in the balance. For soon after his handshake entente with Roberto, Barbudo decided to take charge of David's fate himself, moving him from jail to jail, hiding him deep in red tape, as insurance that Roberto would do as told and, by all means, be dissuaded from ever thinking of severing their rich association.

With synthetic drug use on the rise, Roberto eventually built an impenetrable, fail-safe, state-of-the-art methamphetamine lab at Barbudo's behest, under the cover and front of the Lobo-Meyer Clinic. His part involved manufacture and quality control, aided by nurses hired by the official, with long experience in midsize operations such as this.

Barbudo managed the sale and distribution of the colored pills and driven snow cooked in large, unbreakable test tubes at the Lobo-Meyer Clinic. He came and went undetected, thanks to broad channels and loopholes afforded him by international connections and a diplomatic passport. He and his minions canvassed cities, hamlets, and college campuses for loyal customers—a fact Roberto noted with equal mix of nausea, remorse, and helplessness. It was tantamount to treason on his part, for technically it was an emissary of Castro's fascist government who was propitiating the intoxication and addiction of American children and adults in droves across the United States.

In under a year, both men grew wealthy beyond measure. One

day, in celebration of a lucrative deal at a nearby Ivy League school, Barbudo finally announced he had heard from prison authorities, and could finally arrange for the pardon, release, and safe conduct of Roberto's brother, but he warned Roberto as a friend of many years that if set free, David was sure to seek revenge because he'd undoubtedly blame Roberto for his lot and his fate.

And Roberto, now very far from Eden or his hope of sparing his parents' further suffering, took no time to respond: Never mind. You're right, it may be too late.

Victoria sat by the carport and watched David walk away in measured steps, head down, with his blue parka wrapped around his battered arm.

Sara used to call David the lost sperm of Vittorio Gassman, an Italian movie star she fancied. Victoria could see the similarities, and even more, identify in David that same curious patina actors possess innately, so that no matter how washed out or pressed they find themselves while waiting in the wings, on cue they emerge crisp, luminous, freshly starched.

A black car pulled up for him by the side of the road. David turned back and waved good-bye with his stump arm—perhaps because this way there would be no possibility of counting the days or weeks or years before he'd see her again, if at all.

The Ben Gurion Brigade had been steadfast, seen him through the first do-or-die hoop. With their help, he had uncovered the truth of Roberto's betrayal. He had turned the lies to dust, confronted the culprits as Talmudic law prescribes. Now he could get on with his rebirth—and in his case, this fact was not strictly metaphorical, but also civil, for the prison officials had deleted the embarrassing episode of his escape and, in response to a recent newspaper inquiry, had stated categorically there never was a man named David Zacarías Lobo imprisoned for sedition behind their island walls.

He would be flown to a training camp in Haifa, where they would teach him to rescue others as Cooper had done for him. The

Brigade would let him have his first mission in Cuba, although those assignments were generally reserved for freedom fighters who made their home in this hemisphere. But David explained that he had a debt to settle with his captors, and that a girl named Dolores who, like Kipling's Burma girl awaiting, waited for him. The captain would bend the rules. There was a special spot in the captain's *sabra* heart for David, as the *rebbe* David had given half his life to save had been none other than Captain Nivas' uncle.

Once his mission to Cuba was accomplished, David would return to Haifa, study at the Yeshiva, assimilate into his new country and reconstituted life, and work with the various groups that comprised the Ben Gurion Camp—Chabbad, Breslov, Gur, Slonim Chust, and Yeshivish; "olim" from the United States, South Africa, Russia, and England; Sephardic families from Latin America, Yemen, Morocco, France, Iraq, Iran, and Egypt. And he would be a soldier, ready to defend the life and blood of Israel just as his namesake, David, King of Israel, David Mellech Israel, had done long ago.

In the midst of his disquisition against those who had wronged him, David had managed to digress, to reassure Victoria that her friend Cooper, whom he had seen make love to her the first night, through the window, had had no notion that he and Victoria were related. He made a point of stating that his uncanny simultaneous presence in their lives defied coincidence and offered proof of their sealed fate, their *bashert*—which Victoria took to mean that her brother, despite his diamond-like anger, blessed their union, however it was or was not to be. In what came off as abject gratitude, he declared Cooper deserved to be a Jew— a fact she told him he would not necessarily take as a compliment, for he had his own roots, thank you very much. And he defended Cooper for keeping his secret missions from her, affirming he had followed the rules that no brave soldier of fortune must break— *keep your own counsel and don't worry about your enemies, for you know who they are. Worry about your friends.*

As to Bembé's abduction, David's intent had been, as he put it, to "smoke out" Roberto. Only the threat that harm would come to Bembé or Ideliza had made him agree to come out of his foxhole and meet David face to face—with the proviso that he could witness mother and child board the plane for California with his own eyes. It had surprised David to find this streak in a man he and his comrades thought deserved nothing short of death by slow torture and strangulation—but he explained that sometimes even hyenas have a weakness.

And although he held Roberto guilty for being the pawn, if not the architect, of his eighteen years of torture and detention, in David's eyes, Roberto was but one culprit out of four who bore the blame.

He said that from the start, he felt he could deal justly and expeditiously with Roberto. The remaining three, however, would be left to sort out their lives and stew in their sins on their own. For in the end, David had not been able to exact a proper penalty from Victoria or Abram and Sara. He confessed without hint of remorse that he had come to the winery with the express intent to play judge and executioner—bring you to justice, he labeled it. But he had failed—failed to load his .22 or even carry out the plan in his imagination. He would not tell her if he had attempted to bring on her demise before confronting her, as when he'd stalked her through the window. She asked if his intentions in taking her out back by the neighboring horse farm had been to end her life, away from Hollister's prying eyes. But again, he would not answer her, for he was at a hard point of justifiable wrath and felt she was not there to ask, but to listen.

David's reprise and argument started with this: Am I my brother's keeper? He insisted that Cain's question was rhetorical and could only be answered in the positive, or else God would not have punished him, nor would Cain have become what his very name means today to Jew and Christian. Victoria argued that whereas she did agree with him that ultimately we are our brother's keeper—although the degree and form this takes requires balance and sound judgment, since there is a difference between being a keeper and playing God—still, Cain's sin was in the fact that he killed his brother, and it was for this that he was punished.

She had spoken her mind despite her disadvantage—a sitting duck that might as well have been tied to the chair he'd made her sit on. For, once inside the cabin, David's fury had mounted with each recounting of what he called his wasted years. David reposted, his rage surging and waning and surging again. He asked Victoria repeatedly how in hell she could defend the fact that she had neglected a holy obligation by trusting Roberto to handle his ransom and release and then washing her hands and never looking back.

He preached the lesson she knew by heart—during the Holocaust, millions had known of the gas chambers and said nothing because it was too painful to handle or too dangerous. And what about the person who hears a woman's cries and does nothing because it is too painful or dangerous to look?

He laid guilt at her feet—*it was too painful to think of me rotting in jail, so you and our parents gave the keys to a brother you knew was green with envy of me and you knew wished me dead. And when the ransom failed, and when the years passed, all three of you went to sleep, looked the other way, chose to believe Roberto's lies and palliatives rather than checking for yourselves.*

Am I my brother's keeper?

She was sitting outside, on the still point when the day turns to evening, and a moon wind gathers momentum and chills the arms, which only minutes before felt so warm.

She would not hide behind well-crafted rationales to find legitimate excuses for what she had come to understand had been, at the very least, her unconscious, negligent participation in David's undoing. Wherever she went, it would cast a shadow over her, by night or sunlight, in laughter, in mourning, and even when she'd think she'd forgotten herself for an instant.

Soon, Cooper would turn the corner, stop, and at the gate roar in with his happy caravan, unaware that years had passed for her in the course of a single day. She would take them all for dinner to the Hitching Post that night, a restaurant David had recommended she try. Come morning, she would give Ideliza the good news of her fortune, take care of the logistics for her and for Bembé. As to Roberto's fate, David had never answered her straight. Perhaps the shot heard across the bow was but a ricochet, a prescient flare of her brother's fate. She would not speculate, but neither would she hide from truth again nor be doomed to the coward's *kismet*.

She would stay on a while, and she would listen closely for a sign in the days ahead, and she would strive to stay awake even in sleep, and she would be glad to wake up to Cooper's eyes, for as long as it felt right.

H...A...P Victoria was cat-curled on terra-cotta tiles, interlacing her fingers on the kitchen floor that faced the new garden, where red poppies tilted to the hum of the wind and demarcated the entrance to the round house Cooper had built a few months earlier.

She was going over the alphabet letters with her right hand held up for Bembé, drowning in his aqua eyes, caressing his fingers to her lips from time to time so that he could feel the vibrations of her sounds and somehow transport them into that secret chamber of his brain, where words turned into electric images. She was insisting he articulate each word, one sound at a time. Bembé wrestled and stumbled on the sounds. The whole alphabet came tumbling down like a pyramid of wood blocks smashed against the floor. Then, a few minutes later, one and then two letters rang out, as crystalline and high-pitched as the bell way down the road by the wrought-iron gate of the Lobo Winery. Then, at last, he managed to separate each word and verbalize the sound. H-A-P-P-Y B-I-R-T-H-D-A-Y...

That would be his present to Ideliza on this day, on her birthday. The words that Victoria had been teaching him for days—those and many others—since she had taken the full rein of Bembé's education with intense dedication and intent, making that her priority and life mission for as long as it took—at least for right now.

"Happy birthday, Mamá!" Bembé finally rolled the words with confidence, then smiled with delight at Victoria's explosive applause, tilting his balloon head backwards, scratching the nape of his neck left and right with his nappy curls.

At last, he was ready for the evening party, for the cake with the wood statuette of Santa Barbara/Changó that Cooper had carved for Ideliza. They would release white, helium-filled balloons like doves toward the heavens at twilight. Victoria had a surprise for Ideliza when she returned that day from her rounds at the Franciscan Manor, a nursing home in Lompoc, where she'd secured a job as companion to the elderly. Victoria would announce that the Lobo Winery compound would be the head-quarters for Ideliza's spiritual practice, now that New York City was behind her and she was calling central California home.

The mailman's ring interrupted the lesson. Bembé shot out toward the gate, sneakers untied, in full equine gait. Victoria stood up, startled but satisfied they'd at least completed the most impor-tant lesson of the day. Somehow, he seemed to be awaiting some word from Roberto, although there'd been no word or sign of him since David's visit on that dark and decisive day. She watched Bembé's extraordinary speed through the glass door. From her vantage point, she could see not only Bembé's leaps and the mail-man's pantomime as he proffered a colorful stack of packages and letters, but the phantom outlines of three of the five round hous-ing structures Cooper had managed to build in less than six months time.

Ideliza and Bembé's home was the closest, less than a five-minute walk. And although mother, child, Cooper, and Victoria had fallen into the habit of having almost every evening meal together in the big house, Cooper had built a full new kitchen for Ideliza's commodious three-bedroom domicile, with an indoor and outside barbecue and even a dishwasher, which so far Ideliza had disdained because she preferred to wash and dry dishes by hand. She claimed she had to hear the pots squeak between her thumbs to ensure their absolute pulchritude. Further back, toward the rows of merlot grapes just beginning to burst under sunlight, stood two other houses. The smaller one was Mr. Hollis-ter's, whom Victoria had put in full charge of the wine-making business. She'd also made him a limited partner in the venture. Curiously, that gesture, which she considered only fair, had made the old, embittered man swear off his whiskey and join a local AA group that met on Friday nights at the old Purisima Mission. A few yards down from Hollister's new house, she could see the cut-ting-edge accommodations for the grape pickers, the sharecrop-pers who now, thanks to Cooper's reorganization, had become shareholders, too. Come harvesttime, one-tenth of the returns would go to each *bracero*, and thus the Lobo Vineyards would become the first co-op winery in all of central California, from the San Joaquin Valley all the way down to Santa Barbara.

This curious Marxist or Christian system had come about rather spontaneously, almost unplanned and under cover of darkness. At dawn, in bed after a night of lovemaking that left them both undone, Victoria had casually asked Cooper what he would do if it fell on him to run the Lobo Vineyards she'd inherited.

"That's a no-brainer," Cooper had piped up, holding Victoria's naked frame against his, kissing her lips as he spoke, which was generally his preference. "I'd make every worker on this land a partner. I'd make sure everyone whose sweat contributes to making Lobo wine good is rewarded for it. Why should you pay those poor people a miserly wage, exploit them, and then scoot them out of here like cat litter? Doesn't that stick in your craw? It's a no-brainer . . . the sort of thing César Chávez prayed about. . . . Know what I mean, Penelope?"

He still called her Penelope, but despite that, she'd grown accustomed to taking his words seriously.

And that was how it began. Each worker was a partner and got his share. And Mr. Hollister, who'd lost his land to Roberto, was at the top of the list. From that emerged the idea of the indigenous, Caribbean-style round houses for each one and an African *batey*, or sacred African/Caribbean town center, around which all the houses would be built, a microcosm of the way Cooper thought human coexistence should be. It was a village Ideliza had known in her heart and now could see before her like a miracle.

"Look Victoria, there's a letter from Roberto!"

Bembé could not yet say it in so many words, but his muffled cries, his animation, and an envelope postmarked from Haifa made Cooper, Ideliza, and Victoria aware that something was afoot. The letter had arrived earlier that afternoon, hours before the cake and ices and Bembé's debut wishing his mother happy birthday both in English and Spanish.

"When did this come?" Victoria asked, taking the letter from Bembé.

"It looks like it's from Israel," said Cooper, reaching over Victoria's shoulder.

"*Ay Dios mío,*" cried Ideliza. "You think it really could be Robertico? You think he's . . . you think he's fine?"

Victoria tore open the envelope. It was night and because of Ideliza's birthday dinner, nothing but candles lighted the room. She placed the paper under a flame.

"It's . . . God, I can't believe it," said Victoria staring into the legal-size newspaper clipping that had emerged from the envelope.

"What is it? Is it Roberto's?" Ideliza asked anxiously, feeling Bembé's tug at her skirt.

Cooper picked up the paper, then held it closely to the light.

"It's about David . . . a wedding announcement in the Haifa paper . . . David and Dolores. . . ."

Ideliza sighed, then whispered, "So it's not from Roberto."

Victoria looked at her. She'd never dared tell her what she thought David had done to him. She'd simply told her Roberto had gone away, fleeing the authorities for undeserved claims against him for his practices at the Lobo-Meyer Clinic. But now was her chance. Sooner or later, Ideliza deserved to know. . . .

"Say, wait a minute!" announced Cooper, interrupting the speech Victoria had barely prepared. "See this writing on the bottom . . . it's in Spanish. . . . Can you make this out, Victoria?"

Victoria grabbed the paper, held it close to the light, and strained her eyes: "*Don't show this to Roberto if you see him.*"

The words, in David's handwriting, were scribbled on the edge of the paper. It was a message, a cryptic message letting her know that perhaps, in the end, he was not able to exact the punishment against the brother he'd loathed more than Joseph had decried his brethren.

Victoria sighed. She smiled to herself, then looked Ideliza in the eye: "It's not from Roberto, Ideliza, but it's not bad news either."

"What do you mean?" Cooper asked the question, but Ideliza's eyes were the true interlocutors.

"I mean, no, it's not about Roberto . . . but from what I can make out, I wouldn't be surprised if Roberto is around somehow. . . ."

"Really?" asked Cooper in disbelief.

"I've had a feeling! Changó told me!" asserted Ideliza.

Victoria looked at Bembé and pulled him up in her arms.

"You're getting so big, Bembé. . . . Pretty soon I won't be able to do this anymore. . . ."